VITAL

THE NEW PROTECTORATE STORIES: VOLUME FOUR

ABIGAIL KELLY

AUTHOR'S NOTE

Vital is a standalone novella within the wider *New Protectorate Series* and can be read as such. However, it does contain some spoilers for other books in the series. A full reading list and character directory can be found at abigailkkelly.com. Content warnings can also be found there, as well as in backmatter of this book, alongside a glossary.

~Abigail

For those who find beauty in strength
and strength in beauty

CHAPTER ONE

AN EXCERPT FROM THE ARTICLE "EXPLORING LYSSA: The Story of Josephine Wyeth," written by Elise Sasini and featured in The San Francisco Light May 17th, 2048—

Vanessa Beornson is a woman not to be missed.

Even if you tried, you would be hard-pressed to ignore someone who holds herself with so much self-assurance. When Vanessa strides into the glossy dining room of the Palace Hotel, every eye turns toward her like the slow drag of heavy metal to a magnet. Even those who resist inevitably change their course.

She's striking not only because she stands at a full six feet in height, and not because she has icy blonde hair shorn into a trendy cut over confident shoulders.

It is the way she looks at you that arrests attention: chin up, lips pursed, and eyes fixed on yours with unflinching bravado. Those eyes are something else all on their own. One is a blue so pale, it borders on white. The other is a deep green with a starburst of yellow around the pupil.

When she comes over to our table, I stand up to shake her hand. Her grip is firm, her skin soft, and when she cracks a smile, I notice that her nose is dusted with dark freckles. Up close, she appears disarmingly youthful.

I introduce myself, and in doing so, get the feeling that she is examining me as closely as I am examining her. We settle into our seats and, after ordering our drinks, I thank her for taking the time to meet with me.

Vanessa waves my gratitude away with one manicured hand. "Don't worry about it. I always make time to talk about my parents."

It's understandable, considering their fame and the recent surge of interest in their story, but still, I argue, she must be enormously busy. Newly appointed to Head Curator of the Fairmont Museum of Art, San Francisco's premier institution, Vanessa instantly made a name for herself by announcing the summer's newest exhibit: *Exploring Lyssa*.

She waves her hand again. "Busy-shmisy. This sort of thing is half the job, and even if it wasn't, getting the word out about Were issues is more important than my schedule. Paperwork can wait."

(Editor's note: The term Were derives from an archaic German word for "man" and was originally written as "wer". Traditionally, it is a term that has not been capitalized, and many names for the Were community have been used all over the world, causing no small amount of confusion. Examples include wyr, wyrm, werwulf, and so on. Ms. Beornson requested that we capitalize Were, to solidify the identity of those discussed in the article, though her preferred term is the less commonly used "lyssian".)

It isn't a stretch to understand why those issues are personal for Vanessa. Not only is she a Were herself — the first to hold any position at the FMA, let alone Head Curator — but the exhibit she's come to discuss with me is all about her mother, Josephine Wyeth.

Interviews are always unique. One approach does not apply to all people. However, I do normally try to ease into things, no matter my subject's temperament. Usually there's smalltalk. Sips of coffee. Maybe some light discussion about my work, their family, the weather, why the city hasn't filled that pothole yet. No one likes an interrogation. An interview should be a directed conversation, one in which the subject should feel a level of trust that lends itself to vulnerability and the truths it exposes.

With Vanessa Beornson, however, I immediately sense that frankness is key.

She's steely-eyed and harbors no apparent need for the easy comfort of smalltalk. When the words stop flowing, she is content to sit in silence, those striking eyes fixed on my face.

She is not a woman who suffers fools, nor flatterers. I like her immediately.

Instead of easing into the hard subjects, I only wait for our drinks to hit the table before I ask, "So, are those issues the reason you decided on the *Lyssa* exhibit as your first?"

"Oh, absolutely," she answers. The look she gives me is all eyebrows. "Everyone told me not to do it, you know. There's a real stink around *kicked puppy* projects, and people think it's a bad look to make my first big exhibit something so personal, but I say fuck that. This is a story that belongs to everyone. This is my chance to tell it. If it's the only one I'm *ever* allowed to tell, then okay. No regrets."

"Was this prompted by the news that Angelique Batacan filed for representation in Congress?"

"It has certainly proven to be good timing," she answers, shrugging. "But no. I would have done it anyway. I've had the plans for this exhibit for twenty years. They didn't want it in the Orclind because they don't like facing their own ugly history. The EVP doesn't seem to have that problem. The fact that the Merced pack made history the same week we announced it was— I mean, I'm not religious, but you could make an argument for fate there."

"And how does your family feel about the exhibit?"

Vanessa takes a moment to sip from her martini. "My brother's pissed. He doesn't like being in the spotlight, you know, but I do think he understands why I feel like it has to be done. And so what if we're in the spotlight, anyway?" She rolls her eyes. "He's a mountain man. The only person who might recognize him out in the wild is a lost hiker or two. He'll live."

"And your parents? What did it take to convince them to put their story in front of the public eye like this? Up until recently, no one even knew your mother's name."

"My dad's super protective of her, so he's not— he's not exactly *pleased* about it, but he's also proud of her. He wants her to get the recognition and empathy she deserves. My mom's spent her entire life more or less in hiding," she answers. Her expression is suddenly fierce. "She shouldn't have to anymore. She should be able to put her name on her paintings and feel proud of who she is, *what* she is."

"And what is that?" I prompt.

Vanessa leans forward to tap one manicured nail on the table. "The very first Were."

Chapter Two

An excerpt from the diaries of Josephine Wyeth generously provided by the Wyeth-Beornson family to the Fairmont Museum of Art:
   October 10th, 1867-

Washington was burned to the ground in a sea of blue flame yesterday.

   We're moving again.

CHAPTER THREE

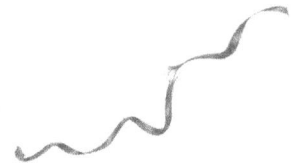

NOVEMBER 1870 - MEADOW CREEK HOMESTEAD

WHILE SHE HAD ALWAYS BEEN A PRISONER, JOSEPHINE had once been able to imagine herself away from fear. She could watch people on the street and imagine they knew her. She could paint the figure of the ice man as he pushed his cart up the sidewalk. She could open her bedroom window the three allowed inches and listen to people talking, to the women thrashing their laundry in the alley and the cats scrapping at night.

Now, there was only the green waste of the prairie all around her, foreign and loathsome.

Before they moved, her only exposure to greenery was through the glass of their parlor window, which overlooked the garden she had never been allowed to explore.

Josephine had grown up in cities. Her earliest memories were of the crowded, narrow streets of Boston. Then there was their towering, absurdly narrow house in Baltimore with its maze of rooms. And then, for most of her life, she lived in Washington.

That city was a smoking ruin now. What was left of it was overrun with vampires, who had swooped in to claim ownership of the rubble as soon as the shadows of dragon wings cleared the horizon. Their home escaped dragon fire by inches, and by sunrise the next morning, her father's mysterious benefactors came to extract them. Into a wagon she went, her wrists shackled and every one of her precious belongings packed into a trunk at her feet.

The shackles went on whenever they were forced to allow her outside. Her father had never forgotten her first and only escape attempt. He never forgot anything.

It was some small solace to know that her mother hated their new home almost as much as Josephine did. There were no parties on the Meadow Creek homestead. There were no Coven events, no galas nor ceremonies for her to bask in. Even as the war made luxuries scarce and events somber affairs, she hadn't seemed to notice.

Evangeline Wyeth didn't notice much of anything — including her daughter.

She had eyes for her husband, the glory of her Coven's name, and whatever it was she sipped from her dainty silver flask every day. If ever they accidentally landed on Josephine, the situation was rectified immediately, so as to end the discomfort of perceiving her existence as quickly as possible.

Josephine had long ago decided it was a blessing that her mother believed she was beneath her notice. Her life, such as it was, would be made a thousand times worse if she had to endure both of her parents' scrutiny.

As it stood, she could only just survive her father's.

In the city, it was easier to find refuge from his notice. He was always busy in his lab, and he had less use for her when he had a fleet of assistants to help him. The only times he needed her were when he intended to use her. When she wasn't recovering from the pain of his work, she was free to paint or read in solitude.

That ended the day they moved into Meadow Creek.

It was her father's boon and her great misfortune that the

homestead came with a traditional orcish barn made of sturdy stone and timber. While her father's lab was set up inside the half-buried stone home that made up the main structure of the homestead, he ventured out to the barn when subjects were delivered by those same glamoured beings who provided everything else he needed.

Prior to their move, she did not think that she could loathe a place more than her father's lab. After two years of regular visits to the barn, she now understood what it meant to hate and fear a place so profoundly, just the sight of it through a window made her sick.

Her respites between visits had grown shorter as her father's success rate increased. Once it'd been a trial endured every handful of months; then it became something to suffer through every two months, then one, then three weeks. She'd begun to fear the moment when her periods of rest shrank to days, hours.

The barn had only been empty for a week when Josephine's bedroom door was thrown open.

She flinched under the cover of her blankets. Moving sluggishly, every joint aching, she dared to peek over the edge of her quilt.

Harrod, the only one of her father's assistants to make it out of the devastation of the battle of Washington, stared at her from beneath his brows. Like her father, he always wore neatly pressed suits of heavy wool and crisp cotton — no matter the hour or the season, Harrod always looked as if a seamstress might stick a pin in his side at any moment.

"You're needed in the barn," he announced, enunciating with the tip of his tongue and sharp edges of his teeth to cover the thickness of his country accent. "Up, Miss Wyeth."

You're needed in the barn.

She heard those words in her nightmares. Even in sleep, she couldn't escape them. Drowsy and sluggish from her monthly exertions, Josephine still felt them land like fists against the flat of her sternum — *thump, thump, thump.* There was hardly space to breathe between each blow.

For a moment, she drifted on a wave of disbelief. It had only been a week since the last subject was taken by the benefactors. They never made another delivery so soon.

Except Harrod was too straightlaced to bother with mind games. If he said she was needed in the barn, then it was the truth, as horrible as it was.

The wave of disbelief crashed. In its place rose a choking sort of resignation tinged with a terror so visceral, it made her teeth rattle.

All the while, Harrod stood there, straight-backed and cold, the toes of his shoes just over the edge of the door jamb — the farthest he had ever come into her space.

Though she was horrified by the prospect of returning to the barn, the fact that he expected her to get up at dawn the day after a full moon did not surprise her. Harrod was cut from the very same cruel cloth as her father. Her pain didn't matter to him any more than it mattered to the esteemed Doctor Wyeth. She was a *thing*, not a person.

What did surprise her, however, was his disregard for polite boundaries.

While Harrod had never treated her with anything other than cool detachment, he had paid as close attention to social boundaries as he did the parameters of an experiment. He did not linger in rooms alone with her. He did not touch her when unclothed examinations were deemed necessary. He used her proper title and opened doors for her when needed. On the surface, he treated her as he might treat any young woman of his acquaintance.

At least, he *used* to.

A great many unhappy changes had begun to metastasize since their arrival in the homestead, and one of those was the gradual deterioration of Harrod's respect for the invisible lines Josephine counted on to keep herself safe.

When she found her voice, it was rough with discomfort and

lack of sleep. "Excuse me, Doctor Pierce. I would greatly appreciate it if you would not enter my room before knocking. I haven't dressed—"

"It is nothing I haven't seen," he coolly replied, dark eyes flicking to where her chemise had fallen off of one shoulder during her fitful night.

Josephine felt the monster that dwelled in her snap at its tight leash. It did not like the way Harrod looked at her, nor how he lingered in her doorway. It disliked his scent, the very energy he carried, and it most especially did not like the way he stepped into her private space as if he had all the right to.

She did not always understand what the *thing* in her tried to tell her, but this message was simple enough: *danger.*

Swallowing around the lump of cold fear in her throat, she did her best to assume the neutral expression that pleased the men in her life best. Hopefully he wouldn't notice the sheen of cold sweat on her face, nor the way she nearly vibrated with overlapping tremors. "Ah, yes, that is true. Forgive me. If you would give me a moment, I can put a dress on and follow—"

"A minute, Miss Wyeth," he told her. "Any longer and I will assume you need assistance. Doctor Wyeth won't be kept waiting."

She *did* need assistance, but she would never ask for it. "A minute, then. I'll be ready."

Josephine didn't breathe until the heavy, sigil reinforced lock on her bedroom door latched. Normally she detested the sound almost as much as she hated the slashing clawmarks on the wood around it, but at that moment, any reprieve from Harrod's cold gaze was welcome.

It was a battle to get out of bed.

The air in her room was always too cold for her, and on the mornings after a full moon, it felt particularly biting. Every joint ached. Her skin was so sensitive that the moisture in the air and the terrible scrape of her chemise was agony. Her fingertips were clumsy as she struggled to pull on her stockings, tie her bloomers, and adjust the fit of her corset.

At least she was not dressing up for one of the few social engagements her mother felt pressured into bringing her to before her father's great success. Those required layers of ruffled fabric, padding, a crinoline, and cumbersome sleeves. Josephine could hardly manage her linen blouse, long wool skirt, and shawl.

There was hardly the time, nor the necessity, to look *nice*, but still, she hobbled over to her wash basin to quickly scrub her face and slick back her long hair. The cold water brought some color to her pallid skin, at least.

By the time Harrod opened her door once more, Josephine was breathing hard but moderately presentable. Her hair was loose, but she could braid it as they walked. She wouldn't have bothered, but a single stray hair in her father's lab would send him into a rage. Even knowing their destination was the barn, the habits of a lifetime were not to be disregarded.

Grabbing an old ribbon from a coil on her nightstand, Josephine carefully averted her eyes from Harrod's pinched expression. His lips were pursed, but his eyes, cold and flat, roved over her figure in a way that raised her hackles. The beast snarled in the back of her mind. Despite her father's great hope, she did not think it was particularly inclined toward violence. But backed into a corner, threatened by this man who had begun to look at her differently, Josephine feared it might finally slip its leash.

Harrod made an impatient sound in the back of his throat. Josephine jumped, her nerves shot, and hurried to shove her feet in her unlaced boots.

"I'm ready." She hugged her shawl around her shoulders. It would take work to keep from tripping on her laces, but she didn't dare make him wait a moment longer. The gods knew how he would take his revenge on her if the esteemed Doctor Wyeth upbraided him for tardiness.

"Away, then," he commanded, gesturing sharply toward the door.

She kept her head down as he led her down the dark, partially subterranean hallway and into the main living space of the homestead. Their modern furnishings looked ridiculous in the circular orcish home, with its stone walls and rugged beams, but no one asked her if she would prefer lacquered curios and fainting couches to comfortable orcish lounges and thick cushions.

Not that she had ever experienced those luxuries herself, of course, but she'd spent most of her life reading about the world she would never be allowed to see. Books on architecture were of particular interest, as they tended to come with illustrations she could study and replicate in the safety of her room.

That was how she knew that their home was of traditional northern orcish design, though she still had no clue where exactly it was located or who it truly belonged to.

Occasionally, she dared to ask a question, but she did not make a habit of it. Her father was not predisposed to explaining himself to anyone, let alone her, so it was much better use of her limited energy to glean her answers through other means.

Josephine tugged her shawl up to cover her chilled nose as Harrod led her up the steps and out the door. The wind was biting, and it defied her attempts to gather her hair into a braid as they hurried across the yard to the hulking, sunken structure of the barn.

Giving up, she simply bound the length with the ribbon at the base of her head and tucked the tail beneath her shawl. Hopefully her father wouldn't notice.

Perhaps he wouldn't care if he did. They were going to the barn, after all. Not his lab, that sacred space where he gleefully ruined lives again and again. The barn was kept in rigidly sanitized condition, but a stray hair did not risk years of work in there.

Her stomach turned over as they neared the large double doors. They were painted a cheerful red, and the turf roof of the structure was speckled with bright wildflowers. The stone walls that disappeared into the ground were dusted with velvety moss.

Were it serving its intended purpose, it would have been homey. It might have even been beautiful.

As it stood, Meadow Creek's barn did not house cows nor workhorses. There were no sheep in those stalls, nor pigs, nor goats.

After the completion of the lab, the renovation of the barn was her father's top priority. Plumbing was added, the stone stalls were enclosed to make several small rooms, and thick iron rings were thrust into the gritty mortar between stones.

And of course, there were the metal doors.

Despite the frigid weather, sweat gathered under the collar of her blouse. She never knew what fresh horror might lie in wait for her beyond those metal doors. Who would she meet next? How would they react when they comprehended the crime committed against them? What would happen to them if her father's experiment proved unsuccessful?

Don't think about it.

Of course, she could repeat the phrase a thousand times. She often did just that. It never worked. Very little could soothe the terror and acrid nausea that assailed her as Harrod pushed one of the doors open and ushered her inside.

And nothing, *nothing* could assuage the guilt.

A ramp led down to the packed earth floor. She imagined that once the dust had been stirred by hooves and heavy boots, but now there were only the impressions of cultured men's footwear, large boot prints, and the telltale drag marks winding a path to the largest cell in the back.

Josephine's steps faltered. *I can't do this again,* she thought, suddenly frantic. Fear was a wild thing in her breast — a galloping, rearing sort of animal desperate for escape from the horror that awaited her.

Again and again, it awaited. There was no reprieve, and the more she considered that, the worse her panic became.

Her life was an endless tunnel of darkness. It did not matter how fast she ran, how loud she screamed. There was no light to strive toward. The harder she struggled, the closer the walls moved, like a great contracting muscle, around her.

At the smallest sign of hesitation, Harrod wrapped his long, pale fingers around her upper arm and marched her the rest of the way. She stumbled on her laces, her knees knocking, but he didn't stop to help her.

Onward they went, deeper into the shadows. The tunnel contracted again, closing in until she could barely breathe through its constriction.

She could hear the faint clink of glass and metal instruments in the unnatural quiet of the barn. There was still the faintest tang of animal in the air, but it was buried beneath layers of terror, bile, and blood.

There was some small solace in the fact that the blood, at least, was mostly her own.

Her vision went blurry as her muscles locked. It didn't matter that she knew fighting was useless. Even if she was fierce, there would have been no use.

Fighting had never gotten her anything but pain. If she scratched, she was strapped down. If she screamed, she was gagged. If she kicked, she was shackled.

It never made any difference. The experiments always happened with their cold efficiency. Blood was taken. Tissue excised. Her reactions to stimuli noted. She was powerless, no matter what the beast in her breast howled.

So why did her body still *fight?*

"Keep moving," Harrod snapped. His fingers tightened around her arm at the same time that he gave her a quelling look. "Don't be bothersome. How many times have we done this, Miss Wyeth? If you just do as you're told, it will be painless."

"It's *never* painless," she dared to answer.

Speaking through his teeth, he said, "That is because you never do as you're told."

He was right. Josephine was rarely as obedient as they wished.

Not in this. Fighting was useless, but *resistance* — that was never beyond her, no matter how much misery it caused.

A teeth-rattling roar tore through the air.

Josephine began to shake in earnest. *Please, gods, don't let it be a shifter.*

But the gods didn't listen to her. They never did.

Chapter Four

When Harrod dragged her to the farthest cell, where the hulking metal door with its single slot for meals stood open, she knew that once again her prayers had been ignored.

Her father stood in the doorway. He was half turned toward her, his shoulders slightly hunched as he scribbled something in a notebook. The hand holding the notebook was also loosely clutching a pair of calipers.

Measurements, then.

The thought was fleeting. It only lasted as long as it took her to glance over her father's shoulder, into the gloom of the cell, to see wild golden eyes staring back at her. A growl, so deep and dark it rumbled the marrow of her bones, echoed off of the stone walls.

A predator.

Fear increased its weight on her lungs.

Josephine's shoulders curled as her breath shortened. The beast balked at entering the dark, confined space of the cell with a predator. Instincts screamed as his scent reached her — musky, wild, and tinged with the horrible antiseptic solvent her father had all his subjects scrubbed with when they came into his tender care.

She couldn't make out much in the dusty shadows of his cell.

There was just enough light from the tiny, barred window far above his head to discern the savage cast of his features: a crooked nose, lips pulled over distended fangs, several days' worth of beard growth, a heavy brow dropped low over those glowing eyes.

Shifter. Oh gods, let it not be a shifter. Not again!

An incoherent sound of alarm — a shameful animal's whimper — escaped her throat before she could stop it.

The shifter's eyes opened wide enough for her to make out a ring of white all around his golden irises.

Instinct compelled her to look down, but she found that she couldn't. For the span of a heartbeat, she met his eye boldly. There was no sound. There was no cell, no Harrod, nor her father. There was only that hard face, the rich scent of him, and the syrupy heat that pooled in her belly when she watched his lips part with a rough exhalation.

And then she blinked.

There was a beat of silence before he threw himself against his bonds, canines extended, and roared again.

Josephine's mind shut down. It didn't matter that she knew he was restrained, chained to the wall like all those who came before him. After the third time she was attacked and nearly killed, her father and Harrod had made sure they restrained the subjects — if not out of some great love for her, than to protect their greatest asset.

She knew there were sigil-lined chains and shackles holding him against the wall. She knew that he could not shift when he was cuffed. She knew that no matter how he tried, he could not hurt her.

It didn't matter.

Yield or die. That was what the beast frantically whispered to her. *Bare your throat and hope he shows mercy.*

Another whimper escaped. Was it not bad enough that she was forced to harm another being so irreparably? Now she had to endure the beast's mindless terror, its absolute certainty that the being in the cell would rip her to shreds at the slightest provocation. A high whine slipped from her at the terrible mental image.

"Enough of all that," her father commanded. He closed his journal with a snap and gestured toward the bound man with it. "Making noise won't get you anywhere. If I can hear you from my lab, I'll be forced to gag you." His dark head turned to fix Josephine with a dismissive look. "And you, too. You know how I feel about your noises, Josephine."

No tears. No screaming. No arguments.

It was Wyeth way, for as long as she had been alive. Even before she was changed, when she was simply a stain on their family's reputation, her father never tolerated excess noise.

Now that she was a prisoner and his greatest accomplishment, he had even less patience for it.

Words rose up to clog her throat. She desperately wanted to beg him not to do this. It was always this way, but now there was a hysterical edge to her desire to plead with him.

Josephine's eyes flicked back over his shoulder. The shifter was watching her, wild-eyed. When she moved even an inch, his gaze tracked her.

"Papa," she began, words tumbling one over the other, heedless of the danger inherent in argument, "are you certain it's safe? What if he gets loose?"

She felt the painful bite of Harrod's fingers as he and her father shared a look of profoundly male exasperation.

"I've explained this to you," her father answered, distaste in every word. "No one can break those chains. I promised there wouldn't be anymore attacks, didn't I?" He stepped aside and motioned for Harrod to push her through the doorway. "Besides, it's not like it wouldn't do you some good. Perhaps if you were attacked again, you might actually show some progress."

Harrod released her arm with a small shove. She pitched forward, laces tangling, and landed hard onto the scrubbed tile floor, specially installed for the ease of sanitation. Her shawl sagged until it slipped off her shoulders entirely.

Cold sweat broke out all over her body. She scrambled to get her sore limbs to work, trying to stand, but they wouldn't cooperate. Her muscles locked in a rigid position, frozen by the beast's fear.

Her tongue felt heavy in her mouth when she tried one last time, "Papa, please—"

Continuing as if she hadn't spoken at all, he briskly informed her, "We are following all of the established protocols. Three days' exposure. Three days' contact. If he's not showing signs of infection by then, we proceed to the bite." His expression hardened. "Don't disappoint me this time, Josephine."

There were tears in her voice when she begged, *"Papa,* please don't leave me with him."

The door swung shut. A mere moment before it latched, she heard her father say, "Start the clock, Harrod."

And then there was only silence.

Josephine's eyes took a moment to adjust to the gloom. Her vision was so much better during the full moon, but with every hour that passed, she lost more of the power her father so coveted. In the dark, frozen in a crouch on the floor, she was nothing more than an arrant — a being with no magic, no claws, nothing with which to defend herself.

The beast dwelled within her, but its only use was in telling her what she already knew: that she shouldn't move, nor even breathe, lest the predator before her deem her worthy of its notice.

For the span of many frantic heartbeats, there was no sound in the cell besides her own overloud panting. She could almost pretend she was alone, except for the scent of him, the *feeling* of his gaze on her.

A low rumble, too low to be truly audible, made the hair on the back of her neck stand up.

Muscles unlocking with a burst of frenetic energy, Josephine gasped and threw herself backward. Scrambling on her hands, she crawled until her shoulders hit the cold metal door. Bile raced up her throat.

The shifter was *huge.*

He was not merely tall. She'd seen a great many tall people in her life. Her father was one such person, and she had long ago come to the conclusion that she was actually rather small in comparison to most people.

Even so, the shifter was a mountain made flesh. It appeared that every bone was wrapped in coils of thick muscle — even the tiny ones of his fingers. His face was a harsh assemblage of crooked angles, and his hair was a shoulder-length snarl of what she could only assume was blond waves.

He was bruised, his shirtless torso crisscrossed with slashes and old wounds hastily stitched. He was exactly as terrifying to look at as she suspected he would be.

Josephine made to clutch at her shawl, desperate for something to hide behind, but her fingers grasped only the linen of her blouse. Her eyes darted to the middle of the room, where it lay in a heap nearer to him than to her.

It might as well have fallen into Tempest's great abyss, for all she was able to reach it.

Its small comfort gone, she wrapped her arms around herself and curled into the door. Her ribbon had fallen out, too. That was at least a boon. It allowed her to shake out her hair and hide behind its dark length as she buried her face in her knees.

Instinct compelled her to make herself as small and nonthreatening as possible. Perhaps if she did, he would not look at her. He would forget she existed. It wouldn't save him from the plans her father and his overseers made for him, but it was what the beast wanted.

Be small. Be meek. Yield. Surrender keeps you safe. Submission keeps you alive.

Never, in all the years that she had endured time in the barn had she ever been as afraid of a subject as she was of this man. Whatever he was, the beast knew he could end her life with ease. Just a *look* was enough to make her submit and bare her throat. Gods knew what would happen if he was free.

That strange, rhythmic rumbling slowly rose in volume. It competed with the rushing of blood in her ears before it eclipsed it entirely. It was a nice sound — baritone, almost thudding in its rhythm — though she had not the faintest idea why she liked it.

The beast recognized that it was not a sound of aggression, though it was bewildered as to what exactly it meant, or why it was almost... comforting.

Josephine dared to sneak a glance through the curtain of her hair.

The shifter was sitting rigidly against the stone wall, his shackled hands fisted in his lap. Gone was the animal who raged against his bonds. One knee was drawn up to his chest; his head tilted back. It was a deceptively casual pose. The stiffness of his spine ruined the illusion, as did the chain that ran between his ankles and the one hooked to his metal collar.

Of course, then there were also his eyes.

Pure gold, they glowed like sinister coins in the shadows. They hadn't strayed from her. She got the unsettling impression that he hadn't even blinked since she looked last.

He continued to make the strange sound. The more she listened, the more calming she found it. Intellectually, she knew there was no reason to do so, but she was as capable of stopping it as she was able to fight any other automatic reflex.

Josephine felt the fluttering beat of her heart begin to slow. The tension in her fingers and the fine muscles of her neck began to release.

Good sound, the beast sighed, half in wonder and half in relief. *Safe sound.*

Without meaning to, Josephine found an answering noise bubbling up the back of her throat. It was a sound she had never made before in all her life: an almost inaudible purr.

The shifter's rumbling stuttered, as if with surprise, before it stopped completely. Much to her relief, her purr cut off the instant his did.

Into the sudden silence, he rasped, "Well, I'll be damned."

CHAPTER FIVE

AN EXCERPT FROM THE ARTICLE EXPLORING LYSSA: THE Story of Josephine Wyeth, written by Elise Sasini and featured in The San Francisco Light, May 17th, 2048—
The term Were is a source of much controversy. The first recorded mention of those afflicted with an archaic version of the LYS-93 virus is in *The Epic of Gilgamesh*, when the titular hero refuses to sleep with a woman because her previous lovers were turned into wolves. There are many mentions of proto-Weres throughout history, and there has been renewed interest in the subject in recent years.

For much of history, the virus has been viewed as "man's darkest nightmare." Prayer tablets written on behalf of an afflicted person — clay or lead slabs inscribed with sigils and pleas to the gods — have been found dating as far back as 5,000 BCE. Madness, rage, insatiable hunger, and agonizing muscle spasms are but a small slice of the symptoms sufferers experience before their bodies begin to shut down. Sufferers have long been associated with wolves, ostensibly because their transformation echoes the lupine.

Up until 1860, it was considered a death sentence with a side of torture. And then came Doctor Joseph Wyeth and his daughter Josephine.

Vanessa, her youngest child, owes her entire existence to the virus that so many fear.

"What happened to my mom was horrific," she tells me. Vanessa speaks with her hands, and when she says the word *horrific*, her right hand slices through the air with the swift menace of an axe strike. "It shouldn't have happened. What my grandfather did— the lives he ruined? Countless. It will never be okay, but we have to adapt to the world he made."

Vanessa takes a breath and leans back in her chair. "And to me — you know, it feels a bit like taking something back from him when I think about how grateful I am to be a Were. He wanted to cause pain, but without him, my parents would never have met. My mom probably would have died in the war. My dad, too. Lives have been ruined by him, but they've also been... I don't know. I think we have to take our triumphs when they come."

We're both quiet for a while as we digest that fundamental truth: that power can be found in joy, even in the face of profound pain. Perhaps even *more* than in the context of comfort and safety.

When the air begins to feel less heavy and Vanessa's shoulders have relaxed again, I ask, "Is that why you chose to gear the exhibit toward your parents' story and not Doctor Wyeth's?"

"Yes," she answers immediately. "Yes, one hundred percent. Why should he be the focus? He's the villain. He deserves infamy, but not a spotlight. You know what deserves a spotlight? Perseverance. Hope. Beauty. Love."

"Of course, it helps that your mother is a world-famous artist," I tease.

Vanessa laughs. She's the kind of woman who tips back her head and roars with mirth, and doesn't care one whit about the looks she gets from other patrons of the restaurant. "Yes! It definitely helped sell the exhibit to the board. They wanted to call it

The Unmasking of JW Beornson, but I fought tooth and claw to get *Exploring Lyssa.*"

"Why?"

"Because I didn't want it to be about this big reveal, you know? I wanted people to walk into the exhibit and think, *Oh, I already know her!* Everyone has seen her paintings. They're hanging in museums all over the world. She worked on some of the most famous ad campaigns of the last century. A whole visual language is attributed to her work. There's no *unmasking.* It's an expansion — maybe even a reintroduction, like when you see a friend again after a decade."

It's rare that one meets someone as fiercely proud of their parents as Vanessa is. When she speaks, it's with a rapidfire staccato, each word fired off at top speed for maximum impact. When she takes out her phone to show me a picture of herself standing proudly in front of a striking portrait done by her mother now hung in the Louvre, she nearly glows with joy.

"You're terribly proud of her," I say, unable to hold back my smile. "Does she know?"

Vanessa tucks her phone away and motions for the server again. After ordering enough appetizers to feed the entire editorial staff at *The Light,* she replies, "Oh, she knows. You think I'm bad? You haven't even met my father."

CHAPTER SIX

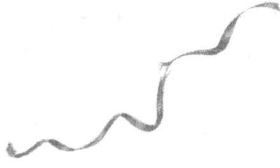

AN EXCERPT FROM THE DIARIES OF JOSEPHINE WYETH generously provided by the Wyeth-Beornson family to the Fairmont Museum of Art:
    September 2nd, 1868-

I am well aware of the fact that Papa only indulges in my art because it gives him something to hold over me. I do not care.

I let him think that regular deliveries of precious walnut oil and pigment, rolls of canvas and solvents, are the road to which he might gain my compliance. It is a benefit to me to let him think so. If I act accordingly, the paints and ink and brushes flow into my hands, but I am keenly aware of the fact that my compliance is not truly necessary. He will do as he sees fit regardless. It is merely convenience he seeks, and that which I grant him in exchange of every drop of oil.

Just the same, I would make art whether he allowed it or not.

One does not need pigments from Europe to make a painting, nor conté crayons to sketch a landscape. I have mixed my own paint from onion skins. I have thickened ash with wax to make crayons. I have shredded and soaked old newspapers to make paper.

And when my hands don't work as well after a full moon, I forgo tools entirely. If I must, I will dip my aching fingers into coal dust and smear it on the stone floor of my room. Art is the one thing he cannot take from me, even if he believes otherwise. Perhaps especially because he believes otherwise.

When I am strapped to the table, I escape by examining the instruments, the tilt of my father's head, the folds of Harrod's coat. How would I render that? Mastering perspective is tricky business, and so there is a release from discomfort when I try to solve the puzzle of a beaker or a scale in my mind's eye.

There is truly only one situation in which I cannot use art to soften my circumstances.

When I'm in the barn, there is no escape. It is a new height of cruelty, this scheme my father has finally been allowed to enact. At last, I am able to speak with those outside of his poisonous influence — and in so doing, I damn them.

CHAPTER SEVEN

It had been at least five years since he last came within sniffing distance of one, but Otto's animal would know a submissive anywhere.

What neither he nor the animal could figure out, however, was what she *was*.

This was a mystery piled on top of a heap of the great many things he didn't know. For instance, he had no idea how he'd ended up in a stonewalled cell, how he'd gone from an old, blood-spattered uniform to nothing but thin cotton trousers, or what was going to happen to him now. He didn't know what they'd drugged him with, or if his grogginess was a result of the hit an orc had delivered on the battlefield just before everything went dark.

He didn't know what the lean, aged witch in the wool suit planned to do with him. He had no idea if he was a prisoner of war or something worse.

All he knew was that he could not shift and that the little woman curled up against the metal door of his cell was... something. Something tantalizing. Something that made his animal sit up on his back legs and *growl*.

His kind didn't exactly have alphas, since they rarely formed true packs, but that didn't mean he wasn't just as dominant as any alpha wolf might be. Otto was dominant through and through — and any dominant shifter worth their salt could pick out a true submissive from a mile away.

They were rare, and when they did pop up, packs tended to swaddle them. If you weren't trusted, you'd be lucky to even get a glimpse of a pack's submissives. They were soft. They held the power of the pack. They were to be protected at all times by those who had the stomach for fighting, for dominance.

To encounter one of those rare creatures *here*, of all places, made him balk.

The younger witch, lean and flinty-eyed, had practically tossed her into the cell. When she stumbled, landing hard on her palms with a pained sound, he'd strained so hard against his collar that the dull metal began to slice into his throat. Even sluggish, injured, and confused, it was pure instinct to come to her defense.

She called the older man *papa*, but what kind of father treated his cub like that? And why didn't she smell witchy? There was magic in her, certainly — a tang like metal left to bake in the sun, like fresh blood — but it wasn't the same as his.

Shifter, then, he'd thought, but that couldn't be right, either.

It drove him crazy that he couldn't scent the animal in her. It was *there,* but it was indefinable. Everything and nothing.

He didn't *do* indefinable. You either were something or you weren't. It was the animal in him that needed certainty, but the man wanted it, too. He'd had vanishingly little to be sure of since the Packlands had been pulled into the war, and for reasons that escaped his foggy mind, it was vitally important that he be certain about Josephine.

When she didn't say a word, but rather huddled somehow closer to the door, Otto let out a huff through his nose. Everything in her posture screamed at him to back off. Somewhere in the back of his waterlogged mind, he remembered that submissives tended to get that way around unknown predators, particularly when they weren't being cared for properly.

Going by her thin cheeks and tears, Otto thought it was safe to assume Josephine was not getting that care.

"Josephine," he tried again, working hard to keep his raw voice gentle. "I'm not going to hurt you. I'd just like to know what's going on. I don't know where I am or who you are. Could you explain it to me, *lille mus?*"

For a while, there was only the sound of her ragged breathing. Otto had to reach deep for the good humor and ease his people were known for as he waited for her to answer. The years of violence he endured since he got roped into the war had all but stamped that part of him out.

Losing his temper with her wasn't an option, though. She was scared enough as it was.

At last, her soft voice made it past the folds of her blouse and fall of hair she hid behind. "I can't tell you where you are because I don't know. I'm not told those things. I believe we are in the midwest, on a homestead called Meadow Creek." She took in a shuddering breath. "And— and I'm Josephine. But you know that."

Meadow Creek? The name sounded vaguely familiar, but he couldn't place it. As soon as it began to stick in his unstable memory, it slipped away again.

He was becoming more certain by the minute that he'd been drugged. His thoughts were too sluggish, and his throat itched with an unnatural thirst. Focusing was almost impossible.

Except for when it came to her.

He had no problem thinking when he looked at his little mouse, probably because his animal was fixated on her in a way he'd never experienced before. If it could have, it would have burst out of his skin to run its nose along her hair, her neck, sifting through the layers of her scent to figure out exactly what she was.

His kind did love a puzzle, after all.

Clearing his parched throat, he said, "Josephine is a pretty name. I'm—"

"It's best if you don't tell me."

He blinked. "Why?"

She peeked at him through the curtain of her hair. It was difficult to make out her expression, but he thought she might look *anguished.*

"Because," she answered, voice thick, "it always makes it worse."

Otto felt his pulse jump in his throat. The animal that was his other half wanted to rear up on his hind legs and *roar* at the sight of so much fear in her eyes, so much pain. He fought the compulsion to jerk against his chains again. Doing so would only scare her more, but being still, watching her hurt when she was so close was unnatural.

Go to her, instinct bellowed. *Fix it!*

Sweat broke out across his chest and neck as he wrestled with those useless urges. "What is this place, *lille mus?*"

She sniffled. Then, in a raw but practiced voice, she explained, "You're here to be infected with a sickness. You'll be locked in with me for three days. If you're not sick by then, Papa will move onto another three days of— of contact. And if you're still not sick, then..." Josephine cut herself off. Her shoulders hunched again. "It never works. He always ends up having to use me in the end. I'm sorry."

Otto shook his head in a vain attempt to clear his thoughts. He could barely follow what she was telling him, but he wasn't entirely sure it was the drugs that made it difficult.

"What kind of sickness?" he pressed. "And why? Why are you here with me?" He eyed her more closely. Lifting his face a little, he sniffed the air again, hunting for any trace of sourness in her scent. "You don't smell sick."

"I am," she answered. "It's not something you can catch from the air, or even my touch. Papa knows that, but he's a scientist. He needs to test everything a thousand times."

A sharp pang of worry struck him. Tone hardening, he asked, "What sickness is it?"

Her voice was muffled by the folds of her sleeves when she

said, "It's new. Papa said he found it in a rabid vampire. It took ten men to kill him. He thought it was strange that he didn't show signs of dying, so he experimented." She turned her head *just-so*, allowing him to get a glimpse of her pert nose and furrowed brow. Gods, she was a delicate little thing. When he touched her, would she shatter?

And he *would* touch her. The animal needed—

Otto shook his head, trying to focus his wandering thoughts. *You're a prisoner, fool. Figure that out first.*

Misreading the gesture as impatience, Josephine flinched and rushed to finish, "He thought he could make people stronger if he infected them."

"With *what?*"

One eye peered at him. Even in the gloom of the cell, he could tell that it was as blue as a winter sky. In a voice barely above a whisper, she answered, "Lyssa."

"Lyssa," he echoed, uncomprehending.

"Yes." Her voice was so soft, it required a predator's hearing to pick up that single word.

It took a moment for his foggy mind to place the word.

He'd heard it whispered in the same hushed tones people used when speaking about rabies, or childbed fever. It was a killer — random, cruel, and terrifying to witness.

A young man in his village had been bitten by a lyssa-infected vampire when Otto was still too young to understand what that meant. All he remembered was the stark look on the faces of the elders who gathered in his father's house, and the guttural, animal howling of the young man chained in the shed next door.

Otto and his family were not at risk of catching the disease, but others in the village, mostly arrants, were. Something needed to be done to keep everyone safe. Besides, it was not merciful to let lyssa take its true course. Executing the infected was the only kind option.

His father, being the closest thing to an alpha they had, took responsibility. He still remembered the haunted look in his eyes when he returned from the shed and quietly washed his hands in the basin by the stove. The water was pink when he was done.

Senses strung taut and heart beginning to throb with acute panic, Otto raised his head and sniffed again. His *lille mus* did not smell sick. She didn't have the telltale signs, either. There was no elongation of her limbs, no foaming snarl, no jagged claws. He'd only glimpsed the young man through a small hole in the side of the shed before his execution, but Otto would never forget the monstrous symptoms he witnessed.

She could speak coherently and move as a healthy person might. She did not have extended fangs, nor the insatiable need to bite anyone and everything. There was no wildness in her.

Lyssa was known for turning its victims into raving, violent monsters — their bodies transformed into beasts bent on infecting others before they expired in a haze of foam-speckled blood and madness. It came on fast and burned hot. He'd never even heard of someone surviving more than a week with it.

If his Josephine had it, she would not only be showing the signs, she would almost certainly already be dead. *She must be mistaken, then.*

Relief washed through him. Slumping against the cold stone wall of the cell, he tried to offer her a comforting smile. "*Lille mus,* it's all right."

That glimpse of her sky blue eye disappeared again as she returned to burying her face in her knees. "It's not."

"I can't get lyssa," he explained. Otto's fingers curled on the tile floor, moving instinctively to comfort her even when she wasn't near enough to touch. Though he fully believed she was mistaken, it wouldn't hurt to reassure her. "It only takes vampires and arrants. I'm a shifter."

Perhaps it was stupid of him to puff up a bit when he said the last sentence, but he didn't care. He was a shifter — a damn impressive one. It would suit him just fine if she noticed that. "You are safe with me, *lille mus.*"

He watched her shoulders rise and then fall slowly as she took a deep breath. "They always say that."

His brows dropped down into a deep furrow. "That you are safe with them?"

"No. That they won't catch it." Her slight frame trembled. Otto's gaze flicked to the shawl coiled on the floor.

"You're cold," he said, a deep note of disapproval in his voice. "Come get your shawl and put it on again."

There was a brief pause, then, in a pained whisper, "I can't."

His temper was beginning to fray as the animal paced back and forth in his mind, huffing and growling with displeasure. Thoughts were scattered, slipping from his grasp almost as soon as he found them, but he knew she should not be uncomfortable. It grated against him. "Why not? You're shivering, *lille mus.*"

"It's too close to you."

He tried not to be offended by that. Submissives tended to be extremely cautious, and in this context *anyone* would be wary of coming too close to a chained shifter. He understood that.

Except the animal was nonetheless wounded by her hesitation. It didn't want to hurt her. It wanted to run its dark, square nose over the soft skin of her throat, to curl around her to keep her warm, to—

Oh.

Otto blinked. His breath shortened as a wave of prickly heat washed over his bruised body. His heart accelerated until he could no longer feel the individual beats.

Drugged or not, beaten or not — Otto knew exactly what his animal was telling him. He'd have to be *dead* to misunderstand that single, all-important message.

Mine.

Chapter Eight

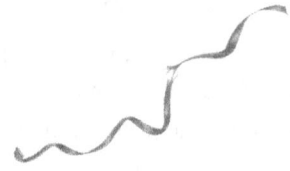

His voice was considerably rougher when he said, "I promise I won't hurt you, Josephine."

Never, he vowed, looking at her with open wonder. *I'll never hurt you, min lille mus.*

"They say that, too," she replied, soft and sad.

"Who?"

"The others my father has experimented on." Her shivers intensified. "Other shifters — a cat, a wolf, even a deer. Arrants, too. A witch. They tried an elf once, but he... it didn't take with him, no matter how hard they tried. And he did not like being restrained."

Josephine slowly turned her head to address him, but her gaze remained down, as if she couldn't bear to look at him. Long lashes obscured her eyes when she said, "Sometimes they think that if they threaten or hurt me, Papa will be forced to let them go." Her eyes darted up to meet his for the span of a single heartbeat when she added, "It never works."

Otto recalled the way she begged as she was thrown into the cell, how wild she became when she saw him chained there, and a rolling wave of bile threatened to scale the walls of his throat.

His little mouse was not just mistreated by her father, but had been hurt. Badly. Perhaps more than once.

"I understand, *lille mus.*" He tried to swallow the bitter taste scalding the back of his tongue. He had to tread so, so carefully with her. Any wrong move and he could terrify her.

"Here is how we will do things, you and me, yes? I won't move without telling you what I plan to do, and I promise that when *you* move, I will hold perfectly still. No surprises. Would this work for you?"

That seemed to surprise her. Josephine was quiet for a moment before she asked, "Where would you move to? You're chained to the wall."

It wasn't funny, but Otto's instinctive reaction to most things was humor, so he smiled at her when he answered, "Only a little."

That was a massive understatement, of course. When he woke up in the cell, the first thing he did was try to shift — only to feel the sharp edge of the collar around his throat. Instinct took over and halted the transformation before he could accidentally behead himself.

The same principle applied to his hands and feet, which were also shackled. While he had plenty of room to get up, lay down, and even use the ridiculous, fancy toilet tucked into the corner of the room and obscured by a partial wall, he was restrained enough to make shifting impossible. Obviously, the good doctor had done this before.

"I only want to bring your shawl closer to you," he explained, softening his voice. "You stay there and I will move it for you so you don't have to come near me."

Josephine shot him another pained look. "You're going to regret being so nice to me."

So nice? As if caring that she is shivering in this awful damp is the act of a saint! Otto worked hard to keep the outrage off of his face. *When we escape, I'll show her what it means to be truly cared for.*

"I will not regret it," he answered. "Now, *lille mus,* I am going to move slowly toward your shawl. I will pick it up and then toss it as close to you as I can. If I scare you, tell me to stop and I will."

When she gave him a small nod, Otto beamed at her. A deep rumble emerged from his chest — a rhythmic, thrumming purr that was distinct to his kind. He watched her tense, then noticeably relax again after a few seconds.

Not a shifter, but she reacts to my purr, he thought, moving away from the wall with painful slowness. Part of that was his bruises, which seemed to cover his entire body, and part of it was caution. *Not a vampire. Not a witch. Not an orc. A submissive, and something animal, too.*

His chains rattled, making an awful racket in the cell, but Josephine didn't seem to mind the noise as much now that she knew what he was up to. She remained tense in her huddled position by the door, her eyes barely visible through her hair as she tracked his movements.

Otto shuffled forward on his knees to grasp the shawl. It was butter soft in his callused hands. A sudden, raw wave of possessiveness froze him in place.

So soft, the animal part of him sighed. *Smells so good.*

His head swam.

How long had it been since he touched something soft? Smelled something delicious and earthy and sweet as her scent? Not since he made the stupid mistake of thinking there might be something for him in the Packlands. There was talk about shifters having their own territory — a real, unified shifter's territory — and it was enough to pull his roaming toward the blighted land.

The war is in a lull, he'd been told. *There's room for shifters there. You can stay out of the fighting if you stick to the wild.*

Fat lot of good that did him. He'd made it as far as Duluth before he got sucked into the fighting. The gods only knew what the war was about anymore. What began as a territory dispute between the Elvish Protectorate and the Orclind had set fire to the entire continent. One by one, even the holdouts had been dragged in — the shifters, the splintered Draakonriik, and even the factions of the south.

Perhaps once there had been a political reason for the fighting, but he'd never known it. For decades the war had been blood for blood, flame for flame, as petty warlords rolled the dice with the lives of those poor folk just trying to defend their loved ones.

The trap closed around Otto the moment he pledged his loyalty to the men fighting for the dream of the Alliance. He couldn't abandon them now, not after they'd fought together for so long.

So he stayed, sacrificing softness, the chance at a mate, a den, for a dream that had long since lost its shine.

The shawl in his hands was not particularly nice. It was not silk or trimmed with velvet. It was a plain dark blue, with a satiny fringe that had begun to fray, and was probably sold in a shop alongside many others.

But it was *soft*. It smelled like the pretty woman locked in with him. When he held it, he felt a great throbbing in his chest that was one part longing and another exhaustion.

Fighting the urge to bring the fabric to his nose, Otto forced himself to ball it up and toss it with both hands in her direction. It landed in a pile beside her. Only when it landed did he notice the pink ribbon that had hidden beneath it.

While she was distracted, he snatched it up and hid it in his fist — a treasure he intended to keep. It was soft and worn in his palm, just like the shawl. "There," he said, shuffling backward again. "Put it on now, *lille mus.*"

A small, pale hand snapped out to grab it. Her expression, or what he could make of it, was shy as she wrapped it around her shoulders. "Thank you."

"You're welcome."

"Can...can I get you some water?"

His raw throat gave a reflexive quiver at the thought. Still, he answered, "This isn't an exchange. I only want you comfortable."

She looked at him, bolder now, from behind a fold of her shawl. "Why?"

He didn't think she would be open to the real answer yet, so instead he answered, "Seems to me you're just as much a prisoner as I am. It's not my habit to be cruel to victims."

"I'm going to end up hurting you regardless." Her tone was stark, as if his fate was a foregone conclusion.

"I told you, I'm not in any danger," he replied. "And neither are you. You and I— we are going to figure out how to get out of here."

Josephine didn't respond. Instead, she braced one palm on the door and slowly began to pull herself up. A burst of panic tightened his muscles. His fingers clenched around the ribbon. "What are you doing? Are you leaving?"

Don't leave. An acute discomfort bordering on pain rippled over him at the thought of losing sight of her. *Gods, don't leave me.*

"No," she whispered, beginning to limp along the wall. "I can't leave until the time's up."

The relief he felt was dizzying — and momentary. Otto watched her move with obvious pain to a shadowy corner of the cell. "Are you hurt? Tell me, *lille mus.*"

"It's only aches," she answered. "They go away."

A high ringing noise filled his ears as a rage unlike any he'd felt before scorched a path through the lingering fog. His voice dropped into the signature shifter double timbre when he demanded, "Have you been beaten?"

Josephine froze by what looked like the vague shape of a basin. Her head snapped in his direction, giving him his first unrestricted view of her face.

Otto's mind blanked. *Gods help me, she's beautiful.*

Her hair was long and dark, with a slight wave that reminded him of a rippling brook. It framed an oval face with high cheekbones, button nose, and small, rosebud shaped mouth. She looked like an artist's muse, or one of those ladies who met her friends for tea in fancy parlors he would never be allowed into. *If they even still exist.* Hard to imagine they did when one spent decades on a battlefield.

But her most striking feature was her otherworldly eyes.

They were large and tilted slightly downward in the corners, giving her a doe-eyed look that made her seem all the more vulnerable. He adored them instantly, but not because they gave her the look of painful innocence. It was because one was a pale, pale color he could only assume was blue and the other was a brown so dark, it looked almost black. They were utterly singular.

"No," she answered, oblivious to the whiplash of worry and admiration he was experiencing. "I always feel sore after the last night of the full moon. It's the lyssa."

Just as quickly as she turned to look at him, she gave him her back. Hunching her shoulders, she fiddled with something until there was a metallic creaking sound and the rush of water.

His throat convulsed at the sound. He was so thirsty, his mind skated away from what she told him as soon as she turned around with a small wooden cup held carefully in both hands.

Josephine's voice shook when she said, "I'm going to— I am going to put the cup near your foot. Please don't move until I am out of reach." Her voice dropped. *"Please."*

"I won't," he assured her, ragged. "I promise I won't, sweet *lille mus.*"

She stared at the floor for several beats, her eyes wide and white around the edges, before she began to inch her away over to him. Each step seemed to cost her, and with the shortening of the distance between them, her breaths quickened.

Otto was so painfully tense, he heard his teeth squeak against one another. He watched her kneel to set the cup down. The contents splashed against the rim with the force of her shaking.

So brave. He ran the pad of his thumb over the stolen ribbon. Even in his state, he could appreciate how much it must have cost her to come so near to him.

"I will *never* hurt you," he vowed as she hurried back to her side of the cell. When she wasn't looking, he quickly stuffed the ribbon beneath the rough metal of his left cuff.

That done, Otto rose up onto his knees to reach for the cup, but he kept his gaze on her even when his fingers closed around the wood. "Do you understand me, Josephine? *Never.*"

Her back hit the metal door. Sliding back to the ground, she replied, "They say that sometimes, too."

"Not like me," he shot back, lips touching the rim of the cup.

No one could make the promises to her that he would. No one would ever be as safe from him as she would be. No one would matter more, or be as important to him, as her.

He felt her gaze on him as he gulped the cool water down, soothing his parched throat. Gods, he hadn't tasted water that crisp in an age.

"What are you?"

Licking his lips to get every last drop of water he could, he answered, "I told you I'm a shifter."

"But what kind?"

Otto withheld a pleased rumble. It was good that his little mouse was curious about him. Curiosity was the first step to trust, and it was critical that she begin to trust him. He couldn't grasp much with his mind full of holes as it was, but he knew that with absolute certainty. "I thought you didn't want to know anything about me?"

Josephine tightened her shawl around her narrow shoulders. "It's not about wanting. It just— it's easier."

"For who?"

"Everyone." Her chin dipped. "Me, especially."

He rolled the cup between his palms. The links of his shackles tinkled with every slight movement. "Why?"

"Because they always leave," she answered, suddenly tired, "and they always hate me when they do."

Otto set the cup down with deliberate slowness. "Well," he began, "I won't pretend to know what is going on here, but I know two things for certain, *lille mus.*"

"What?"

He relaxed against the wall and offered her a slow, drowsy grin. "I will never be able to hate you." Heat crawled up his spine and bloomed over every nerve when he added, voice pitched to a sensual growl, "And when I leave this place, I'm taking you with me."

CHAPTER NINE

AN EXCERPT FROM THE ARTICLE "EXPLORING LYSSA: The Story of Josephine Wyeth," written by Elise Sasini and featured in The San Francisco Light, May 17th, 2048—

I ask Vanessa to tell me a little bit about her father. I've barely gotten the words out before she tilts her head back and laughs again.

"What is there to know?" She is still grinning when she says, "He's exactly how you would expect him to be: laid back, intensely curious, loves to laugh. He keeps a great den and will rip your arms off with a smile if you upset Mama. He'd be the first person to tell you he's a simple guy."

"You say that like he hasn't lived an incredibly interesting life. Isn't part of the exhibit all about the intersection of the virus and the war your father fought in?"

"It's funny that you assume I equate *simple* with *uninteresting*," she's quick to point out. "Why is that, exactly? A minimalist painting is simple, but we have a whole wing in the FMA dedicated to them. I once caught a woman weeping in front of Ayolo's *Blank Canvas* — a five by ten foot white painted board. When I asked her what she found so moving about it, she said, *'It's the brush strokes. When you get up close, you can see them all.*

They're so small and so close together. It must have taken him years to paint this.' Not so uninteresting."

Chastened, I hold up my hands in surrender. "You're right. There's no reason to equate the two."

Vanessa goes for a tiny meat pie arranged neatly on a platter, nestled amongst sliced cheese, honeycomb, and meat-wrapped melon. "My Dad's a bit like *Blank Canvas*. He's simple at first glance, but if you step closer, you see all the brush strokes that make him so unique. If you talked to him today, you would probably never guess that he set out from his village at seventeen and spent sixty years in the wilds of the Northern Territories, entirely on his own, until he migrated south to join the Packlands."

The village she speaks of is now the capital of Kalaallit Nunaat, Nuuk. I cannot imagine what fortitude it might have taken for a boy of that age, in a time before electricity, hiking boots, or helicopter rescues, to wind his way down from the edge of the world. Then again, Otto Beornson is considerably more adapted to such a journey than myself.

"Unless you saw his scars, you probably wouldn't guess that he fought for forty years, holding the line between the Orclind under Lee Seymour's command." She pauses to take a bite of her pie. When she speaks again, there's a wistfulness in her voice that I recognize. "But you know— when my mom walks into a room, if you watch his eyes, it's like, *wow*. There's so much more going on there. You can sense it in him."

"Brush strokes," I venture.

"Brush strokes," she echoes, wiping her fingers on a cloth napkin. "So many brush strokes."

Chapter Ten

An excerpt from the diaries of Josephine Wyeth generously provided by the Wyeth-Beornson family to the Fairmont Museum of Art:
November 12th, 1870-

My father's lyssa protocols are as follows:

<u>Stage one — Exposure</u>

The subject must be exposed to me in a small, closed room for three hours, six hours the following day, and twelve hours the day after.

<u>Stage two — Contact</u>

The subject will be given food I've touched and blankets I've slept with. If he shows no sign of infection, I will be put back in the cell to maintain what Papa calls "close quarters contact." If he still shows no signs of sickness, then the next day is dedicated to "full contact."

I hate this stage the most. I am used to regular humiliation, but I do not think I will ever be able to accept stripping down with a stranger who hates or will come to hate me. They see everything, and when hours and hours of contact fail to produce the results my father seeks, as it inevitably will, they will think of me — fleshy and white and scarred and monstrous — with revulsion for the rest of their days.

<u>Stage three — Exchange</u>

[One sentence has been crossed out many times, making it illegible.]

Today is the second day of stage one with the shifter. He hasn't tried to kill me yet. I suspect this will change when he accepts what is happening to him, and for reasons I cannot explain, this inevitability upsets me more than it ever has before.

CHAPTER ELEVEN

As she expected, the shifter showed no signs of having lyssa the next morning. She knew this because Harrod fetched her again, but it was hardly a surprise. A subject had never shown signs of infection before stage three.

Harrod would not catch her unawares this time. Josephine made certain that she was up and dressed just before dawn broke over the pale blue mountains far in the distance.

Although her stomach remained in a riot of unease, she felt a niggling compulsion to dress neatly, to wash her hair, comb it thoroughly, and braid it tight against her scalp. Her clothes felt strange when she donned them, so she fumbled through dressing herself three times before she settled on a dark skirt and ruffled blouse.

For reasons she couldn't articulate even to herself, it was of the utmost importance that not a hair or thread be out of place when she entered the shifter's cell.

I will never be able to hate you. And when I leave this place, I'm taking you with me.

They were pretty words, and ones she heard in some form or another several times over the years. Josephine knew better than to believe them.

And yet, the heat in her blood had not died down, nor did the fluttering in her belly when she thought of the shifter's hard features, the fervent way he said the words.

They swirled in circles in her mind as she smoothed her hair back behind her ears. She was not allowed to use pins, as they might be taken and used as weapons by her father's subjects, so she made do with a few ribbons woven through her braid and around her head.

It was just as well that she took such care in her appearance, since Harrod disregarded her request for a knock once more.

He gave her a cool look from her doorway. "Ready, then?"

Josephine dropped her eyes to the floor, where hundreds of shallow claw marks lay etched in the polished stone. Pulling her shawl up against her throat, she answered, "Yes. Will I be allowed breakfast before we go to the barn?"

He made an impatient sound and stepped over the threshold. "You'll be fed in the cell. Come along."

Her eyes widened in alarm. He was not supposed to enter her room. *No* one entered her room. "Sir," she began, voice pitched high.

Harrod was a lean, hollow-featured man. When he moved, it was with swift efficiency. While she had never seen a rattlesnake in person, she had read that they struck suddenly, fangs bared, and seemed to appear as if from the ether when one least expected it.

Her father's assistant moved like that when he wrapped his fingers around her arm, in the exact same spot he held her the day before. She could feel his fingertips digging into the bruises. He found them unerringly, the way drivers find grooves left by cart wheels in a muddy street.

The cold, astringent scent of antiseptic made her nose itch. It seemed to permeate his clothing, or perhaps emanate from his pores. Below it was a muskiness that made the beast quiver and growl with unease.

Looking down his long, narrow nose at her, he said, "It pleases me when you wear your hair up, Miss Wyeth."

She kept her eyes on the button just below his collar. Her pulse hammered in the base of her throat. "I... Thank you."

"You'll style it like this more often."

No, I won't. The defiant impulse was a hot lashing in her mind. She had no desire to please Harrod, and would not set the dangerous precedent of doing so simply to appease him.

Though he had great capacity for cruelty and many opportunities to cause her harm, Josephine knew there were limits to the ways in which he could make her life worse. While she may be only a *thing* to her father, she was the most precious thing he owned. He would never allow Harrod to permanently damage her.

But there are many ways one might be damaged impermanently, she thought, stomach sinking.

Though she had been locked away for ten years, Josephine was not entirely ignorant of the ways a cruel man might think to punish a woman he perceived as his lesser. Her father's subjects had threatened her with all kinds of terrible things, usually in explicit detail, when they finally realized what awaited them.

Instead of answering him as she wished, Josephine sweetened her voice and replied, "My father dislikes it when my hair gets in the way of his work."

As she hoped, the mention of her father appeared to do the trick.

Harrod straightened his spine until it looked fit to snap. His keen, almost avaricious expression slid away. It was replaced by the cold detachment she was used to. "You are correct. We shouldn't keep him waiting."

It was a curious thing to feel relief as he escorted her out of the house and across the yard to the barn. She was afraid, of course, but a different sort of anticipation prickled under her skin when he thrust open the door and marched her inside.

Things are truly dire if I'm beginning to see this cursed place as a refuge.

Her father stood by the cell door, his ever-present notebook in hand. His dark hair, streaked with gray and shoulder-length, was mussed. The high, starched collar that had — according to her mother — gone out of fashion a decade ago was slightly creased and yellowed where it rubbed against the underside of his chin.

When he looked up at her, there were dark circles under his eyes.

"Josephine," he greeted her, nodding toward the metal door. "Six hours today. Since you were good yesterday, I've left you a cushion."

By *good*, he meant that she had not screamed and banged on the cell door as she used to. He didn't care what she did in the cell, so long as she followed the protocols and remained quiet.

Out of habit, she stared at his shoes when she whispered, "Thank you, Papa."

"You are welcome." He closed his book with a snap. "Now, let me look at you."

Josephine closed her eyes and held herself rigidly still as her father's cold, dry hands probed her jaw, the soft flesh under her chin, and then prompted her to open her mouth.

"Hm. Everything looks normal, except your gland is slightly inflamed. Touch it with your tongue. Does that cause discomfort?"

She did as instructed. The roof of her mouth was a bit sore, but when she pressed her tongue against it, there was no pain. Rather, it felt like some small pressure was being relieved.

"It doesn't hurt," she told him, licking her lips.

Her father dug around in his pocket for a moment before he pulled out a worn, collapsible measuring stick. Commanding her to open her mouth once more, he held it up to each of her small, retracted fangs and made another thoughtful sound.

Her father and Harrod shared a look. "Interesting. Harrod, I want you to measure her fangs when her time is up. They are slightly elongated, which is abnormal for after a full moon."

"Of course, sir," Harrod answered immediately. Her stomach

clenched with a new anxiety at the thought of him sticking his hands anywhere near her face.

"Good, good." Her father waved a hand at the door. He seemed more harried than usual, which was alarming. "Get her in there. You and I have work to do. I've received a pressing letter that you will want to read. We have much to do, Harrod. Too much."

With the tip of his finger, Harrod traced the familiar shape of a sigil on the metal above the heavy locking mechanism. A small, hot burst of magic filled the air with an iron, blood-like tang before he slid the bolt to one side with a heavy *thunk*.

Josephine held her breath, her stomach tumbling over and over, as he pulled the door open.

There he is, the beast sighed, pleased and afraid in equal measure.

A wave of hot pinpricks rushed over her skin when she made out the shape of him against the wall. His great bulk looked relaxed as he casually crossed his ankles and folded his shackled hands in his lap.

And just like the day before, those golden eyes glowed in the dark. They were fixed squarely on her.

Since she wasn't fighting him this time, Harrod didn't toss her in. He simply gave her arm a warning squeeze before he turned on his heel to leave the cell. The door closed and locked with a clang.

She managed only a single quick look at his intense expression before the anxiety of being in a predator's presence began to edge out her bubbling anticipation. Her muscles seized, preventing her from moving back against the door.

She was stuck there, sweaty fists balled in her shawl and trembling so hard her knees shook.

His scent was stronger than the day before. It seemed to permeate the whole cell with something rich but sharp, indefinable like the scent of a candlewick newly blown.

It screamed *danger,* but the more she breathed, the more she began to notice the ache in the roof of her mouth intensifying.

His chains rattled as he got more comfortable. She could not look him in the eye, but she could watch his scarred chest, broad and covered in a sprinkling of pale hair, move as he leaned forward. *"Lille mus,"* he finally rasped, "how are you?"

Josephine let out a shaky breath. "I'm not the one chained to a wall, so I must be fine."

"You aren't chained, no, but I see the way that man handles you. I heard how they speak to you out there." A deep, dangerous growl made his voice almost unintelligible when he added, "Good behavior for a single *cushion?* You're a prisoner here just as much as I am. Those men treat you like a dog."

No, she wanted to argue. *They don't.*

Her mother had a dog once. A small, fluffy thing that bounced in and out of her earliest memories, back before they knew she was worthless. Her mother loved that dog. It wore pretty ribbons around its neck and ate from a crystal dish. It slept at the foot of her mother's bed, and when it passed suddenly, Josephine remembered how her mother wept and demanded Chérie be cremated so she could keep her ashes on her nightstand.

Chérie had never once worn so much as a leash. Josephine could not go out in public without shackles on.

But she could not tell that to the shifter, who already looked at her too closely. She knew from past experience that pity would only make things worse in the end.

Still, she found herself asking, "Are *you* well?"

She wasn't sure how she knew, but she was certain he was smiling when he answered, "Well, see, last night was the first night in nearly forty years where I did not worry I'd wake up in dragonfire, or to an orc standing over my bed with a rifle, or to the sound of a man pissing too close to my bed roll. My stomach was full and I was not rained on in the night. I had a roof, a bathroom, and the hope that a beautiful woman would speak to me in the morning. All things being equal, not so bad."

Of course it struck her that he called her beautiful, but

Josephine was immediately distracted from the thought by the casual way he spoke of his time in the war.

Unable to stop herself, she breathed, *"Forty years?"*

"Yes. Not as long as some, but once you get sucked into defending your territory and keeping your friends alive, there's not much that'll get you out save the end of the war or death."

"That's awful."

"War is, yes." He shifted, suddenly restless, and asked, "How far is the front from here?"

Josephine shook her head. "I don't know. We moved here two years ago after the dragons razed Washington. I wasn't told where we were going. All I know is that we are in the midwest and that the homestead is named Meadow Creek."

The shifter lifted his hands to run his fingers through his tangled hair. The links between his shackled wrists clinked together.

She couldn't look at his face, but his shoulders were tense when he muttered, "I was drugged, but I couldn't have been out that long. Ten hours, maybe. This place can't be too far from the Black Hills, then."

He let out a miserable sigh. "Unless they used an m-gate, in which case we could be anywhere."

She could only offer a helpless shrug in response. "I'm sorry. I'd tell you if I knew."

"Why don't you know? Is it intentional on their part, or is it another thing that's better not to know?" He didn't say it in an accusatory way, but Josephine still felt a flush of shame.

"They don't tell me because they know I talk to the subjects," she replied, more than a touch defensive. "Papa would never risk me telling one of you where we are because you might find your way back, or tell someone else once you're released."

"Released? Why would I be released?"

"Because they want you to fight. Once you're infected, my understanding is that you can replace a whole battalion of soldiers. Maybe more."

"Infected with *lyssa*," he said, tone dripping with skepticism.

Josephine felt weary down to her very bones when she answered, *"Yes."*

"And who exactly would I be fighting for?"

Again, she could only offer a shrug. "I've tried to find out who my father's benefactor is, but I haven't any idea. The men they send are always glamoured. I can tell that some of them are orcs, some are human, some are dragons. All types of beings come."

"We *must* be in the Orclind," he pressed. "I was fighting orcs along the border, in the Black Hills. If they didn't use an m-gate, that means we are very close to the front. The Alliance is making incursions on orc land every day, Josephine. I don't think it's safe for you here."

For the first time since the door closed, Josephine found herself briefly meeting his wild gold gaze. "Safe?" she replied, bewildered. "I've never been safe in my life."

The shifter sucked in a breath. Then, in a quiet voice, "You're breaking my heart, *lille mus.*"

Feeling suddenly too exposed, as if she could feel the shifter's gaze *inside,* Josephine cleared her throat and changed the subject. "Have you had water today?"

The shifter was quiet for a moment, perhaps deciding whether or not he would allow her diversion, before he answered, "No. If you could refill my cup, I would be grateful. Whatever drug they gave me seems to have finally faded, but my throat hasn't recovered."

Guilt was a lead weight in her belly. Her life was miserable, but at least she had free access to food and drink. *Now.* It had been at least seven years since her father deprived her of those essentials to see how she would react.

Steeling herself, she asked, "Might I ask— if you could please move your cup closer to me?"

"Of course, *lille mus.*" There was the rattling of chains again. She watched those heavy, callused hands and thick arms move as he grabbed his wooden cup and placed it as far from him as the chains allowed. "There. Is that far enough?"

She swallowed. "Yes." *Perhaps.*

It was a fierce battle, attempting to get her limbs to move her closer to him. Her steps were halting, her breathing ragged, but she kept reminding herself that he had not shown any aggression the day before, and that, for reasons beyond her, the beast her father created seemed to enjoy his company on some fundamental level.

The roof of her mouth pulsed with a strange sort of pressure as she forced her knees to bend. She knelt by his left foot and extended a shaking hand toward the cup.

"Josephine."

The sound of her name, spoken in such a deep, gravelly baritone, made her spine lock. Her blood swirled in her ears as her eyes drifted up his stomach, over his chest, to settle on the dip between the bars of his clavicle.

"*Lille mus,*" he murmured, "would you look at me?"

The fingers of her outstretched hand trembled. "I cannot."

"Why?"

"It's... it's too hard."

He made that comforting rumble again before he gently asked, "What are your instincts telling you?"

Sweat dewed on her temples, sticking the fine hair there to her skin. Josephine fumbled to curl her fingers around the cup, but found that she could not make herself rise. Stuck there at his feet, she found herself answering, "That you could kill me. That if I make one wrong move, you'll have my throat."

Instead of telling her how ridiculous that was, seeing as he was chained to the wall and she knelt just out of reach, he said, "Do you understand why you feel that way?"

"Because you're a predator."

"That is true, but not all of it, I think." The tangled hair around his shoulders moved as he tilted his head to one side. "What are you?"

Chapter Twelve

Josephine closed her eyes. There was a name for what she was, but it was ill-fitting. "I don't know. My father infected me with lyssa and it made me— I am different than I was before. Changed."

The shifter made a thoughtful sound in the back of his throat. "You aren't a shifter, then?"

"No."

"What were you before this change?"

Her whisper was so quiet, it was barely audible even in the insulated space of the cell. "Arrant."

She expected some reaction, perhaps even derision, but the shifter only made that soft sound again. "And these instincts you feel, the ones that tell you I'm a threat, did you have them before?"

"No, I didn't."

Certainly she had intuition, as all creatures do, but there was no beast in the back of her mind with its own will, its own senses. It could not truly speak, but it often felt separate from her, like it was trying to tell her things through impulses.

Only on full moon nights did it have true autonomy.

That was why her bedroom had a lock on the outside.

Josephine knew better than to try and escape. But the beast? The beast never stopped trying.

"So you don't understand any of your instincts, then," he surmised, sounding troubled. "You don't know *why* you're so afraid of me. Why you can't look me in the eye."

Pride smarting, Josephine finally summoned the will to stiffly rise, cup in hand. She moved her gaze away from him as she scurried over to the tiny sink in the corner. "You're a predator. Predators are dangerous. I know that much from experience, sir."

"Ah, I didn't mean to insult you, *lille mus*," he replied. "I only meant that you don't understand hierarchy."

"What does that mean? Of course I understand hierarchy. It's a power structure. I know quite a bit about that. It's muscle versus weakness." Josephine filled the cup as much as she could without spilling any water. Holding it in both hands, she crept back over to the shifter and cautiously deposited it by his feet.

He waited until she made her way over to the square cushion by the wall to answer, "Yes and no. Shifters have a hierarchy. Where you fall in that hierarchy determines your role in the pack, and that is decided based on your natural tendency toward dominance or submission. Most people are a blend, but there are those who exist at opposite ends of the spectrum. The most dominant usually become alphas or security for their packs. The least dominant tend to take the day to day tasks, like money management, caring for cubs, and making sure dens are being looked after. They essentially run the pack."

He huffed a breath through his nose, as if he thought something was at all funny in their situation. "You might believe that the submissives in a pack don't have power, but you're wrong. They have *all* the power. Us dominants are just— what would you say? *Muscle.*"

Josephine sank onto her cushion and curled her legs to one side. Wrapping her shawl tightly around her shoulders, she said, "I'm not a shifter."

"I know." He shrugged. "But you *are* a submissive. One at the very farthest end of the spectrum, I think." In a softer voice, he added, "That's rare. Very rare."

She folded her hands in her lap and made a study of them. Instead of replying to him, she pressed her tongue flat against the roof of her mouth, soothing that curious ache.

When the sound of his chains rattling against one another filled the cell, she dared to peek at him through the fringe of her lashes. Her breath caught.

Whatever he was, the shifter was *magnificent*.

He was not pretty, nor elegant. His face was quite brutish, his hair unkempt, and his scars many, but when she watched him move, Josephine was stricken by his grace, the power of his limbs.

Her fingers twitched in her lap. *I could draw a man like that for hours.*

That would never be possible, of course. Her father hadn't allowed her to take a sketchbook or drawing implements into the cell since she foolishly allowed one arrant man to use a pencil, which he promptly turned on her. She still had a small, silver scar on her throat from where he'd pressed it in, demanding her father release him.

She thought of that man whenever she brushed her fingers over the scar. It reminded her to always be on her guard.

The shifter took a noisy gulp of his water before he wiped his mouth on his bare shoulder. Though she dared not look past the height of his brawny chest, she was absolutely certain he hadn't taken his eyes off of her.

"Tell me, *lille mus*," he rumbled, settling back down against the wall, "have you eaten anything?"

"We'll receive breakfast shortly."

There was a curious note of pleasure in his voice when he replied, "So we'll eat together, then."

For lack of a better response, she nodded and began to fiddle with the fringe of her shawl. It was impossible to resist looking at him for long. Inevitably, her eyes were drawn back to the fascinating cross-hatch of scars, the sprinkle of blond chest hair, the compelling topography of his arms. It was an arresting sight, but the more she looked, the more she noticed his nakedness and the chill in the air.

Fingers combing through the frayed fringe, she summoned the bravery to ask, "Are you cold? I can give you my shawl."

"Ah, sweet *lille mus*, only if you intend to share it with me."

Josephine felt a wave of heat roll up from her toes all the way up to her face. As far as lewd suggestions went, it was not even close to the worst thing a man had suggested to her in the cells, but it managed to make her nerves flutter more than any had before. "No, thank you."

"Worth a try."

"Why?"

"Because you might have said yes," he said, the words drifting on a wistful sigh, "and then I might have been able to discover if your hair is as soft as it looks."

If her face got any hotter, she worried that she would begin to glow in the dark.

Josephine self-consciously raised a hand to touch a wispy lock of hair by her ear. "What is that thing you keep calling me? *Lily moos.*"

"*Lille mus,*" he corrected her. "It means *little mouse.*"

The butterflies in her stomach died.

Little mouse. Of course he would see her as a mouse. Wasn't that what her father thought, too? That she was just some weak creature, born to lay pinned to a board and flayed open for the sake of his ambitions? Was she not meek, and small, and afraid of the predator who played with her?

Josephine straightened her spine against the wall. It was the second time he stung her pride. The beast bristled, and though she did not have claws in this form, she found her fingers curling in her skirt as if she did.

He must respect me, the beast growled from the depths of her mind. *I will not accept less!*

"I am *not* a mouse," she told him, bravery buoyed by trembling, guttural outrage. "You have no idea what I am, sir. None at *all.*"

No matter what anyone thought, Josephine knew she was not born to be stepped on, nor to be eaten by someone bigger than her. Circumstances had molded her into the shape best fit for survival, but that did not mean she was worth any less than the man on the other side of the cell.

There was a beat of silence. Josephine held very still, her throat closing tight, and waited for the inevitable negative reaction her outburst would have.

When the shifter spoke again, she was shocked by the baritone register his voice had taken on. It was almost an animal's growl, deep and sensual; the voice of a man who knew he could touch her without so much as lifting a finger.

"You're right," he purred. "You are not a mouse. I'll call you *kone* instead."

She sounded the word in her mind. *Koh-ney.* A soft *k* rolled into a lilting *neh* sound. It was not the prettiest word, but when he said it like that, it was as if he was drawing his fingers over her skin, touching her like he *owned* her.

Heat pooled low in her belly at the same time that the roof of her mouth gave another deep, uncomfortable throb. She stared hard at her clenched fists. "And what does that mean?"

Instead of answering her, he asked, "Will you still not let me tell you my name, *kone?*"

She wanted to ask him where his accent came from. She desperately wanted to know his name. She wanted to ask him where he hailed from, what his favorite book was, if he had siblings. She wanted to know *everything,* but she couldn't.

Knowing too much about him would only hurt her in the end. When he was shipped back to the front, changed irreparably because of her, she did not want to have sewn his name into her heart, as she'd once done with others.

It will be worse with him, she thought, dread bubbling under the foreign heat in her blood. *When he leaves, it will hurt more.*

But why? He had been kind to her, but others had as well. He was no different than anyone else.

Except he was. For reasons that mystified her, Josephine felt a tether between them, pulling tighter with every minute they sat together.

Why was her breath so short? It wasn't fear that pinched her lungs, but Josephine had no name for the feeling that gripped her when he spoke to her in the rolling, accented timbre.

Dangerous. Everything about him is dangerous.

"No." She fought the urge to shake her head, knowing on some level that it would not clear it of the strange fog clouding her thoughts. "No, I don't want to know."

"Then I will tell you when you ask me for my name."

"I won't."

"How much time do we have today?"

Josephine blinked, taken off guard by the segue. "Six hours. Tomorrow I will be here for twelve."

"Then by the end of the day tomorrow, you will say my name." He said it with such confidence, such ease, that she was momentarily taken aback.

"I— no, I *won't.*"

"Why not?"

Angry and sorrowful at once, Josephine pressed the tips of her fingers into her forehead to block the sight of him. "Because you will *hate* me when you leave. I do not want to remember the name of one of the few men who has ever been kind to me when I know a week from now you will wish you'd gutted me."

What levity had been in the air evaporated. *"Never,* Josephine!"

She felt the words like the crack of a belt across her back. Josephine flinched, her bravery gone, and turned away from him, instinctively presenting her side and the curve of her shoulder rather than her vulnerable front.

The beast held very still inside of her, frozen with a confusing mixture of apprehension, hurt, and outrage. That part of her couldn't understand why he would speak to her that way, but the rational mind, the woman, was not surprised.

The shifter was not her friend. Either he would figure that out now or later, it was all the same. It was for the best that he had given her a reminder to not get comfortable. Still, it hurt.

Across the cell, she heard him suck in a sharp breath. The chains made their awful music, closer this time, as if he was attempting to crawl toward her, when he rasped, "I'm sorry, *kone*. It's been too long since I was around submissives. I forgot that raising my voice would— I should not have done it. It won't happen again, I promise."

When she didn't answer, but instead curled closer to the wall, he made a pained sound in the back of his throat. That single note plucked at something inside of her, though she was at a loss as to what exactly it was.

"I was upset because I don't understand what's happening," he explained. "And when you talk like I will hurt you, it hurts *me*. I don't know why you think this, *kone*. Please explain it to me."

Josephine breathed deeply, girding herself, before she answered, "We are in stage one, when my father tests to see if exposure to my air will infect you. After tomorrow, we will be in stage two, where he will see if contact will infect you. When that doesn't work, we will go into stage three."

There was a hesitant sort of interest in his voice when he asked, "What's stage three?"

Her stomach turned, at odds with the urgent, almost pleasurable way the gland in the roof of her mouth pulsed. That pressure built until she felt soreness in the roots of her small fangs.

It seemed that for the first time, *one* part of her was eager for stage three. That eagerness both shocked and disgusted her.

"Stage three," she said, voice thick, "is the bite."

There was a long pause. When he finally spoke, his voice was markedly huskier than before. "You will bite me, *kone?*"

"No." The word burst from her, vehement and full of pain. "I refuse. I always refuse."

"Then why—"

"Papa demands it, but I won't. I don't care what he does to me. I won't do it, especially not to a shifter." She began to breathe faster, her heartbeat worked into a frenzy at the prospect of what was to come. "I can't. I know what happens because I overheard Harrod talking about it. I won't do it. I don't care that it means I get the needle. I don't *care.*"

Out of the corner of her eye, she caught the shifter rising onto his knees. He strained upward, head lifted, and demanded, "What needle? What happens to you if you don't bite me?"

"Don't you care about what will happen to you if I *do?*"

"No," he snapped, hard and low. "Tell me, Josephine."

She tightened her arms around her shoulders and squeezed her eyes shut. "If I don't bite a subject, Papa takes a needle and sticks it into the roof of my mouth to extract my venom. Then he puts it into the subject. The first time, I thought maybe it would not work the same, but I was wrong. It still works."

She could practically hear the shifter's thoughts whirling around in his mind, trying to process all that she told him. At last, he asked, "Does that hurt you?"

She lifted a shoulder. Josephine did not intend to tell him that every time it felt like a knife was sliding through her soft palate and into her brain. Like the drawing of the syringe's plunger felt like a nail being slowly pulled from her finger. She got the sense that he would not like hearing that, and since she had every intention of refusing her father again, it did not seem right to trouble him with the knowledge.

Except he didn't appear to need her confirmation. The shifter strained against his bonds so hard, she could hear the chain links squeaking against one another. "*Kone,* you will not refuse him this time. Bite me."

She was so shocked by his command that she lifted her head to give him a brief, horrified look. "Are you *mad?*"

"No," he answered, expression cut into such a fierce visage, she could not look away from it. "No, I am not mad. I am *afraid* for you. Your father tortures you, *kone*. I cannot let it continue. Not one minute more. You will bite me. Trust me, it is no hardship."

"You shouldn't be afraid for me," she argued, heartsick. "You should be afraid for yourself!"

"I told you, I cannot get—"

"You can! I've seen it again and again!" Josephine's voice dropped to a hoarse whisper. "Do you know what happens when a shifter gets my venom?"

"What?"

A hot tear splashed down her cheek. "They lose their animal."

CHAPTER THIRTEEN

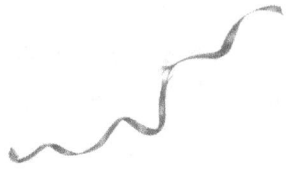

An excerpt from the article "Exploring Lyssa: The Story of Josephine Wyeth," written by Elise Sasini and featured in The San Francisco Light, May 17th, 2048—

I am not entirely sure how it happens, but by the end of the evening, I've somehow been wrangled into accompanying Vanessa up to the Coven Collective in two days. It feels less like an invitation and more like I've only just been informed of plans already decided on.

"Come up to the Gulch with me," she demands, cheeks pink with her second martini and those remarkable eyes sparkling. "I have to go up anyway to finalize some stuff with my mom, so it'll be perfect. You can sit her down for an interview."

Of course, I'm thrilled by the invitation, forceful as it is, but I can't help but ask, "Doesn't your mother historically turn down interviews?"

Vanessa waves her hand again. "Yeah, but I'll be there. It's different."

I keep expecting Vanessa to sheepishly rescind the offer. It never happens, but somehow that is enough. A handful of spare text messages come through. One contains flight information. The other ominously advises me to "pack boots and bug spray."

Two days later, we board the m-jet to Seattle. Vanessa spends the entire flight with a champagne flute in one hand and her tablet in the other. When I ask her what she's reading, she tilts her screen to give me a look.

It's an announcement from the Sovereign's Office. I'm surprised I missed it, given I am usually first to know about these things, and then I remember that I'd spent most of the day packing and spending time with my mate, who was huffy about my short trip. Out of respect for him, I'd shut off my devices until it was time to leave for the airport.

I skim the first paragraph of the announcement and feel my eyebrows inch closer to my hairline.

"Three million dollars?" I ask, rereading the sentence twice more.

"Three million to *start*," Vanessa replies, sounding more thoughtful than overwhelmed. Pulling the tablet back over to her lap, she gives me a quick run-down of the announcement in her brisk, no-nonsense way. "Looks like the sovereign's consort has picked her charitable cause. She's donating a bunch of money to Were outreach and health services. The director of Solbourne General is taking the lead, looks like."

It's a huge deal, considering the Were community has only been officially recognized as such recently. For many years, an infected person was simply thrown out of their community out of fear and a lack of resources for managing the changes. Having funds available for care and the public support of the highest ranking people in the territory could be revolutionary.

"You don't seem surprised," I venture. *Or particularly pleased.*

"I'm not." Vanessa's thumb moves over to the screen. When I peek at it, I see that she has scrolled to the bottom of the statement. There, beneath the straightforward promises and clear plan of action, is a signature.

Margot Goode, Healer & Sovereign's Consort

Casting me a sly glance, Vanessa says, "Did you know that our squeaky clean SC used to run an Underground clinic off of Carolina Street? Right next to the brewery."

I'd heard rumors aplenty about the sovereign's shocking marriage to a witch, but not that. "Really? I had no idea."

"Mostly she treated Weres," she explains, a certain fondness in her tone. "I never went to her, but I heard through the grapevine that she never asked for payment or tried to report numbers to the health board. Just healed what and who she could. I even heard that Angelique counts her as an honorary member of her pack."

I wonder just how far up my eyebrows can go. "And now she's using her position to help more people."

"Looks like."

I note her thoughtful expression as the plane begins its descent into the cottony clouds obscuring Seattle's skyline. "You don't seem too happy."

"I am," she assures me. Then she shakes her head with a small sigh. Glossy blonde hair swings, and I see several people's heads turn to watch her. Even on a cramped plane, Vanessa shines. "I'm just worried that she hasn't accounted for how stubborn Weres are. It's hard to win our trust. You start sending in committees and healers and paperwork... I don't know that it'll be as easy to help as she thinks."

"How would you suggest she do it, then?"

Vanessa considers the question for several moments. At last, she says, "You have to win the animal, and you can only do that one on one."

CHAPTER FOURTEEN

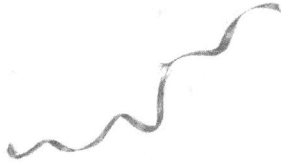

AN EXCERPT FROM THE DIARIES OF JOSEPHINE WYETH generously provided by the Wyeth-Beornson family to the Fairmont Museum of Art:
April 4th, 1860-

My father's ambition, as far as I can discern, has always been to create a more perfect being. Sometimes I wonder if he would have had the same goal if I were not so dreadfully imperfect.

Both my parents are witches. My mother comes from a distinguished, if relatively minor, Coven. My father is famed for his intellect and his sigilwork. It was merely the whims of the gods that gave their only surviving child not a flicker of magic.

He used to tell me that the experiments were to see if he could somehow fix what's broken in me. Every serum, injection, or slice was endurable when I believed they might result in retrieving that lost part of me.

Nothing succeeded, of course.

I thought he'd given up, but this morning over breakfast he told me he'd found something new in a vampire. He said that it is a quite remarkable venom, and that he'd distilled it in the preserved brain matter of a deceased shifter. He said that he firmly believed this is the cure for my ailment, my perverse lack of ability that so shames him and my mother.

As much as I wish to have hope, I do not trust him. I do not trust anyone. A man who wanted the best for me would not shackle me, nor put bars on the windows. I know that he is cruel and that he cares for me as much as he cares for his lab animals.

Perhaps less. At least they have proven useful over the years.

Chapter Fifteen

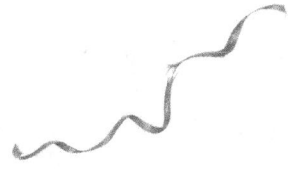

In general, Otto liked to think of himself as a man who moved with the flow of life rather than against it. He preferred to laugh rather than fight. He did not see any point in wasting the limited breaths he had on Burden's Earth worrying over things he couldn't change.

His brothers and sisters had always called him affable, a pleaser. Of course, like any dominant shifter, he was prone to fits of temper, but they passed as quickly as they came on. It was the shifter way to resolve hard feelings with a punch or two before moving on like the dispute never happened.

Animals were frank. They saw the world in the facts immediately discernible to them and acted according to prior experience. Shifters, though vastly more complicated than animals, tended to have a similar mindset.

They were stubborn, decisive, and lived for the moment. When they made a choice based on what they could sense, on *instinct*, they were damn near immovable from that choice.

Common wisdom held that it was the animal part of a shifter that decided on a mate. It was the animal's need that sparked the mating fever. It was the animal in control when the fuse of those instincts lit.

As someone rarely provoked to any strong feeling by his animal, Otto had always thought that was a bit of bunk — right up until he saw Josephine.

Even through the haze of drugs, the animal knew she was different. It ached to be near her. It roared at the injustice of being kept from her. It *wanted* her.

The man was a bit slower to catch up, but he got there soon enough.

A part of him thought he might have dreamed his previous encounter with the winsome creature. If it wasn't for the stolen ribbon he caressed in her absence, he might have believed it.

After at least a full day in the cell, his mind was much clearer. His memory was a bit foggy, full of patchy recollections of being washed with cold water and being measured all over, but he was certain she'd said she would be back.

The pressing need to see her compelled him to sit up just as dawn broke. He stroked the ribbon, calluses catching on the satin, and wondered if he would react to her the same way as the day before. Was his drug-addled mind correct about who she was? He wouldn't be sure until she returned to him.

And then he heard her voice on the other side of the metal door.

It took everything in him not to strain and snap against his chains when he listened to her hushed voice, the way the men spoke of her like she was little more than a dog. Only the memory of how she cowered kept him back against the wall.

It had been so long since he'd encountered even a mated submissive that he had to rifle through the dust of memory to find the skills to handle her. Even before he made the foolish mistake of joining the war, he'd been in the woods an awfully long time.

His kind were solitary by nature except for when they mated and had cubs. The most socializing he did before the war involved sending letters and occasionally stepping foot in a saloon or market. What he knew came from the other shifters in the village he grew up in. One of his closest boyhood companions was a soft-spoken submissive wolf shifter, but it had taken the better part of a bright northern summer to win Jacob's trust, and even that was only accomplished with the patient coaching of the elders.

Those old skills in handling submissives were already rusty long before he stepped foot on Alliance soil. At least he still knew enough to hold very still when she shuffled into the cell, her arm clasped by the odious witch who looked at her too closely, with *want* in his eyes.

Neither the man nor the animal liked the way the witch dug his fingers into her arm. They *especially* disliked the way he kept his gaze on her slight form, eyes lingering on her back as he closed the door.

However, as soon as the bolt slid into place, Otto's sole focus became the little enigma.

Be gentle, instinct urged. *Be soft. Earn her trust.*

What was gentle? What was soft? He'd been on the front lines for forty years. Before that, he lived in an isolated den in the Northern Territories. His last experience with softness was the day he left his mother's embrace to set out for the wild, as all of his kind did.

Even under ideal circumstances, he imagined he would have struggled — and their circumstances were far from ideal.

They lose their animal.

The hair stood up on the back of his neck whenever he remembered her heartbroken whisper. Otto remained unconvinced that lyssa was at play here, but now that he was lucid, he knew *something* was going on.

Of course, being at the front as long as he had, Otto had heard rumors that the Orclind was employing some sort of new weapon. They were being pinched on two sides — with the Elvish Protectorate closing in from the west and the Alliance from the east — and growing increasingly desperate. Tall tales of monsters on the battlefield, *werewolves,* had begun to proliferate amongst their numbers, threatening to damage already flimsy morale.

Lee Seymour, the young elk shifter in command of the northern half of the Alliance packs, had tasked Otto's battalion with investigating the rumors, seeing as they were closest to the border.

Now that he was thinking straight, he was dismayed to realize how well Josephine's story matched up with those rumors.

However, that didn't mean it was lyssa. Whatever it was she claimed to be infected with, it couldn't possibly be that nightmare disease.

And nothing, as far as he knew, could kill the animal in a shifter.

Just the thought made his stomach twist with nausea. To not be able to shift was a nightmare. Even being chained was unnatural. A shifter needed to move freely from one form to the other, lest their minds begin to fray and their instincts spin out of control. If not, they tended to grow increasingly lost to the animal's desperation, making them volatile and dangerous.

He thought of all of this as Josephine quietly retrieved a tray from the slot in the door. She hadn't spoken to him since her whispered admission, and what little progress he made with her seemed to have evaporated as she skated well around him, as if there was an invisible barrier erected three feet from the tips of his bare toes.

Otto tried very hard to summon the man he used to be. The one with seemingly infinite patience, who would have thought nothing of taking his time winning his sweet submissive mate, no matter how long it took.

That man died a handful of months after his first battle. Now he was harder, with sharp edges previously unknown. Now he knew what profane cruelty the world had to offer. When he stared at the downturned, somber face of his little *kone,* he saw every one of them.

They did not have *time* to do the traditional courtship dance. Urgency pressed down on him from all sides. Josephine was obviously mistreated, the gods knew what her father had in store for him, and he grew increasingly worried that they were much, much closer to the front than it seemed. They needed to escape.

He needed her to trust him *now.*

The only relief he felt in watching her carefully stoop to set a bowl of porridge by his foot was that she appeared to be moving better than the day before.

When he said as much, Josephine hunched her shoulders and hurried back over to her cushion. "The aches go away," she answered, sitting down and lifting her own bowl into her lap. Her fingers looked frail and white against the wood, but elegant, too. A musician's fingers, maybe.

He wanted to pursue the topic, to press for any and all information that might be useful, but he was wary of upsetting her more. Her trust had to come first, or else all the information in the world would be useless.

Because no matter what happened, he intended to escape this strange, unsettling place. Josephine did not believe him, but he knew with absolute certainty that she would be coming with him. That endeavor would be markedly easier if she didn't fight him the whole way.

So instead of asking why she ached, what it had to do with lyssa, what that meant for *him,* Otto slowly reached for his bowl and pulled it into his lap as well, intentionally mimicking her pose.

"You have very pretty hands," he told her. "Do you play an instrument?"

He watched her eyes move over the tile between them, as if she might find an answer to his question there. "No. I played piano when I was little, but I forgot a long time ago."

"Your parents didn't keep up with your lessons?"

Her wooden spoon dragged slowly across the inner surface of her bowl. "They didn't think it was worth the money after they discovered I was arrant. There was no point in improving me."

He'd already decided on hating the man he'd heard her call

papa, Doctor Wyeth, but he was still surprised by the surge of protective fury that swelled in him when Josephine spoke.

Being arrant, a person without the ability to use magic, was no more shameful than being left handed. It was simply another difference, neither good nor bad. The way Josephine said it made it sound as if the word *arrant* was blasphemy. A defect to be reviled. A *flaw*.

Not only was it inherently wrong, but it was also incorrect. His kind had incredibly keen noses and the scent of magic was unmistakable. His *kone* was no arrant.

"What is it you like to do, then?" he asked, swallowing down the rage with some difficulty. "I see passion in your eyes, sweet *kone*. You must have a pastime of some sort or another."

She spooned another mouthful of porridge past her lips, eyes down. Carefully following her actions, Otto did the same. When she ate, he did. When she shifted her legs, he followed suit.

Not only did it make the animal rumble with approval, as sharing food was an essential part of courtship, he knew that mimicking behavior helped submissives feel more comfortable.

After a long silence, she admitted, "I draw and paint."

Of course you do. Otto could see it clearly. His sensitive mate, with her soft eyes and pretty hands, would make a wonderful artist. He could easily imagine her with a long, spindly paintbrush in hand, dabbing paint on a canvas as she squinted at a vista.

We will have a beautiful den, he silently promised her as he chewed and swallowed the tasteless, gritty porridge. *I'll hang your paintings in every room, and when there's no more space, I will build another room for you to decorate.*

"I can't wait to see your paintings," he said, trying desperately to show her how pleased he was with her small show of trust. "You will show me all your drawings, too. I want to look at everything."

He could tell she wanted to point out that he would never get the chance, but Josephine held her tongue. Instead, she shook her head and pointed out, "You don't even know if I'm good."

"It wouldn't matter to me if you weren't."

For a split second, he could have sworn she almost looked up at him, perhaps to roll her eyes, or give him an otherwise exasperated look. He felt quite suddenly that he would do anything, anything in the world, to be on the receiving end of her sass.

The surest sign that a submissive trusted you was when they developed an attitude. That brattiness was downright tempting to a dominant shifter on the hunt for a mate.

Josephine's tone was just shy of tart when she said, "A painting must be *good* to be worth looking at, sir."

"I think you're wrong. I will like it because it was made with those pretty hands and those lovely eyes and that quick mind. Is that not enough reason to like a thing, *kone?*"

"I... I don't know." Josephine's voice died away. Even in the shadows, he could make out the flush in her pale cheeks.

Heartbeat quickening, Otto deepened his voice into a soothing purr and continued, "And this thing you keep saying, calling me *sir*. I don't like it so much. Won't you choose something else for me, if you still refuse to learn my name?"

"*Sir* is respectful," she argued, a touch breathless. "My only other option is *shifter*, which seems worse."

"I would like it more if you were not so respectful. Maybe then you would believe me when I say you're safe with me."

"And how would *that* help?"

"Because," he explained, firm but soft so as not to startle her, "you can claw at me all you want, *kone*. I will never lift a hand to you. I will never scold you. If it will help move things along, I invite you to try."

Even with her face tilted slightly toward the floor, he could see her eyes widen with alarm. "You want me to *scratch* you?"

"I already told you to bite me, didn't I?" he asked, amused. He'd meant it, too. The animal wanted her bite more than anything. The man wanted it too, if only to save her from whatever torture her father inflicted on her when she refused to give it.

That's a lie. I also want it because I want to know what her bite feels like when I make her mine.

Aghast, she replied, "I could never hurt another person, especially someone chained to a wall."

Sweet, gentle mate. Otto ached to be near her. It was like ants under his skin, this feeling of urgency. He felt every inch that separated them, and with each second that ticked by, he was more compelled to shield her, to cup her in his hands so no more harm could come to that soft heart.

"*Kone,*" he rasped, clutching his bowl to keep himself from attempting to crawl across the floor, chains be damned, "I promise you could never hurt me. Do your worst."

Her brows, dark and angular over her striking eyes, drew together. He liked that she'd bound her hair into a complicated series of braids and red ribbons. It allowed him to see her face clearly, even when she wouldn't look him in the eye, and it reminded him of his stolen token, tucked safely under his left wrist cuff. "I don't want to try."

"Perhaps you want to touch me in other ways," he offered, half-joking. "I've heard I'm quite strokable in either form."

"I can barely stand by your foot, yet you think I might be able to stroke you without fear?"

Godswilling.

Otto cleared his throat, trying to dispel the image of her long-fingered hand curling around his stiff cock. He would bet anything in the world that her skin was soft as silk. Softer even than the ribbon rubbing against the skin of his wrist.

Shifting to hopefully disguise the growing erection in the loose folds of his strange trousers, he managed to speak with only minimal huskiness. "Submissives respond well to touch. All pack beings do, but submissives especially. If you can trust me enough to hold still while you explore, it will build a foundation between us. Someday soon you will even be able to look me in the eye, *kone.*"

"Why would I want that? You are only going to be here for a

few more days." There was no mistaking the pain in her voice when she said that, as if she couldn't bear to watch him go.

Perhaps she felt that way about all her father's subjects. It didn't seem farfetched to imagine this strange experiment was her only socialization. It would make sense for her to become attached to the only people she was exposed to — and why she would consequently put such hard limits on getting to know them. Still, Otto chose to believe it was because she felt their connection and did not want *him* to go.

Following instinct, he chose not to remind her that he promised to take her with him. Instead, he cajoled, "Then there is no harm in it, is there? Don't you want to see if you can? Test my theory about what you are. If touch doesn't help, then maybe you aren't a submissive after all."

Sass me, he silently urged her. *Take my challenge. Act on your instincts, kone.*

CHAPTER SIXTEEN

JOSEPHINE SET HER BOWL ONTO THE TILE WITH A hollow *thunk*. Appearing both conflicted and vexed, she twisted her hands into her shawl and muttered, "This sounds like a trick. The moment I come close you'll strangle me or worse."

"I will turn my back to you," he offered, pulse thudding in his throat and, regrettably, his cock.

This wasn't about sex. Obviously she was miles away from being anywhere *near* ready for that, but the fever was unforgiving. He felt only its first licks of flame and already he worried about his control.

Desperate to get some contact, anything at all, he continued, "I'll place my hands on the wall and be on my knees. Come now, sweet Josephine. Don't you want to prove me wrong? You're no *lille mus.*"

Several seconds passed before she said, almost as if baffled by the words herself, "I'm not supposed to touch you until stage two."

Sensing victory, Otto set aside his own half-eaten meal. "And do you always listen to your father?"

"No." She thrust her chin out. Bubbles of pure pleasure popped in his veins at the sight. Josephine was a submissive to her bones, but that did not mean she was a doormat. His mate had pride. He was willing to bet she had claws, too, when necessary.

Speaking softly, he pressed, "Then it is all the more reason to try, yes?"

"I..." Her expression moved through a series of different feelings, spanning the spectrum of confusion to yearning to fear and everything in between. She reached up to rub the side of her neck. "I shouldn't. I've been tricked before."

Otto forced himself to breathe slowly. *Someday she will tell me. Trust first.*

"This is no trick."

"How do I know? You could say anything. People do that."

It was a strange thing to sense so much innocence in her yet see a look of such jaded sorrow on her expressive face. "Do you want my honesty, *kone?*"

She made a soft, anxious sound his animal recognized on a fundamental level. "Yes."

Since they were speaking animal to animal — or whatever Josephine's other half was — Otto sucked in a deep breath before letting the other side of him surge up to the surface of his mind, close enough to see but not transform.

They mingled, man and animal, when he growled, "I need your trust. I need you to need *me.* Most of all, I need you to touch me. I feel like I might die without your hands on my skin, *kone* — and believe me, I know what being close to death feels like."

It was easy to pick up on the way her breathing quickened. To his sharpened senses, it was as loud as a gunshot.

"I am— I will not be used that way," she told him, voice trembling. "I'm not—"

"I want nothing more than you wish to give me," he assured her, knowing full well that his erection was nigh unmissable now. "A hand on my shoulder, a touch to my hair — even those small gifts would please me, *kone.* And I think they will give you something too, if you allow it. Build this bridge with me, sweet Josephine. Let us see where it leads."

When she said nothing, Otto pressed forward. It was a cruel touch to what he suspected was an old wound, but if it moved things along, it had to be done. "Tell me, how long have you been a doctor's plaything? Have you ever known what it's like to be touched gently — to stroke another?"

He didn't need her to answer. It was written all over her tormented expression, in the stark loneliness of her eyes. Josephine had never known the comfort of affectionate touch.

Otto snapped powerful jaws around the fury that threatened to burst from him. His mate had been starved and abused. The gods only knew what horrors she had suffered, and he suspected her only contact with the outside world had been in this very cell.

Gods know what kind of men have been pulled off the front line, he thought, paling. *They could have locked her in with any kind of half-mad, battle-hardened being.*

He knew she'd been attacked in the past, but now he wondered what else could have happened to her. He'd been fighting for forty years. He knew how war changed men, how desperate and twisted they could become. He knew they were often ravenous for companionship, and when locked in a tiny room alone with a soft, submissive creature like Josephine...

Suddenly, he didn't resent the chains nearly as much as before.

Otto swallowed hard. Had he made a mistake in pushing her? There was no reason for her to trust him, and there was *every* reason for her to be suspect of his insistence. "Josephine," he began, voice thick with regret, "I apologize if I've—"

"Could you— turn?"

For a moment, he could only stare. Then, in a rush, he said, "Yes, of course. Yes."

It wasn't an elegant maneuver, with his hobbled ankles and the long chain attached to the back of his collar, but he managed to get on his knees and brace his cuffed hands against the rough stone wall. It was cool under the heated skin of his palms.

Otto held his breath.

There was a pause, then the soft sound of a shuddering inhalation and the rustle of fabric.

Brave girl, he thought, chest tightening. *My fearless little mate. You've no idea how I'll treasure you.*

Her steps were slow, the hardened leather soles of her boots loud in the tense quiet. Each scuff of her heel seemed to echo off of the stone walls. Her breathing was a rough scrape against his sensitive ears, each puff a testament to how terrified she was.

And yet she crept closer.

Otto felt himself begin to shake all over. Every muscle shuddered with the need to move, to shift, to do *anything*. Restlessness made his fingers twitch involuntarily against the stone, but he was too terrified of scaring her off to do so much as shuffle his knees on the tile.

At last, he began to feel her body heat radiating along his bare spine. All the fine hairs on his body stood on end as the soft cloud of her scent enfolded him — rich and smooth and earthy, like the oil he'd rub into wood for a fine, velvety polish.

He swore he could feel her reach out to him, but her touch didn't come.

Speaking so softly he worried she might not be able to hear him, he said, "Touch me, *kone.*"

"You have... scars." There was a peculiar note in her voice that he couldn't place. It was almost *awestruck.*

"I do," he answered, pressing his palms flat against the stone to quell the urge to reach for her. "There aren't so many healers anymore, and I've been fighting for a very long time." Otto did his best not to think of those wretched souls who'd been conscripted into the war. It was *wrong* to hurt a healer, but they were always the first targets on the battlefield. A living healer could keep a battalion going for years, after all.

Sometimes he wondered if there were any left in the world. His battered body certainly hadn't seen one in at least fifteen years. Maybe more.

He hesitated, then, "Do you find them ugly?"

He'd never considered it before, as he had never bothered with any aspect of his appearance, but Otto was suddenly afraid that his mate would not find pleasure in his body.

The war had warped him in many ways, but he'd never been particularly beautiful. Josephine, on the other hand, was beauty incarnate. What if she did not crave him the way he craved her? *A nightmare.*

"No," she whispered. "I also have scars."

"If you'd let me, I'd kiss every one of them." He didn't intend to say that aloud, but he didn't regret it, either. It was a promise he fully intended on keeping.

He heard Josephine suck in a breath. "Why? You don't know me at all. I'm just a woman to you."

"Not *just* anything. Never *just*. I—" Otto gasped. The cool tips of her fingers kissed the muscle of his shoulder, over what he knew was a mottled scar left by an explosive. The damn thing had nearly taken his arm.

He didn't think of that when she touched him, though. His head swam with sensation from just that featherlight touch and then, like the strike of a match to dry kindling, an inferno ignited.

Magic popped in his blood, desperate for an outlet, as his fingertips shifted into claws and his canines extended. *Bite,* the animal roared. *Bite her!*

Visions of whirling around, wrapping his arms around her, and rucking up her skirt to thrust his cock into her hot, wet cunt nearly unwound every fine thread of his control. Sweat beaded on his forehead as he wrestled with instincts blunted into a hammer over the course of forty years.

Once, he might have been able to feel the burn of the fever without such vicious urgency, but after fighting for so long, his animal was half feral. It did not abide restraint, nor hesitation.

It saw their mate was near and would not risk losing her. It wanted him to rear around and sink his teeth into the soft flesh of her throat without regard for how it might affect her, because it firmly believed that claiming her was the surest way to protect her. *No one* would touch his mate. One look at his shifted form and only those with a deathwish would even try it.

But Otto refused to claim her without her consent. He'd known her for a day and already he understood that Josephine had never been allowed to choose when to give, *what* to give. In this, it was imperative that she steer things.

Submissives must have the power, he'd once heard an elder say to a young wolf shifter caught harassing a submissive. *They can't fight back. They can't say no without fear. If you take advantage of that, you're worth less than scum. You let them come to you or you walk away.*

So he endured her fluttering touches. He bent his neck and tried to breathe when she pressed the pad of a finger against the divot of a vertebrae or the curve of a muscle. He didn't rush her. He scarcely twitched.

Josephine's breathing was choppy. "Your skin is— Are you feverish? You're so hot."

Feverish? Yes. *Sick?* No. He was merely struck dumb by the mating rush, that legendary heating of the blood that marked a shifter as having found their mate. It would not abate until he'd sunk his fangs into her throat and bonded with her.

"Shifters have hotter blood than most," he managed to answer, not quite lying.

"Oh."

This time, when she pressed the tips of her fingers against the muscle bracketing his spine, she didn't immediately lift them again. They pressed hesitantly before they slid down a few inches in a slow, teasing drag.

Otto couldn't help it — he arched his spine, eyes closing, and let loose a deep, appreciative purr. His kind made a unique, rhythmic thrumming sound that was quite loud in the little cell, but he couldn't find the will to quell it.

"Goodness!" Then, with open wonder, she said, "I can feel that coming from your chest."

"Do you like the sound? Stroke me more and I'll keep purring for you, *kone,*" he rasped.

"I do like it." Josephine spoke as if she could not understand *why* that was so, but she didn't hesitate to run her fingers down his spine again, firmer this time.

It was a chaste touch, the exploration of a woman who'd never even known gentleness, let alone the carnality of sex, but to Otto, it might as well have been a full body massage.

"Your hands feel like paradise," he breathed. "Like silk, just as I thought."

Another hand joined the first, and then her palms were flattening against his skin. He could feel her trembling, but he could also sense the way her fingers spread, how they pressed more insistently into his skin. "Do you still fear me, *kone?* Or is it better now?"

She hesitated, but eventually answered, "I think it is hard to fear a man who arches his back like a cat when one rubs him."

A cat! The greatest of insults.

Oh, he wanted to turn around and nip her ear for that. Since they were not at that stage yet, Otto settled for a deeply disgruntled *harrumph* and quietly savored the tiny bite of sass. "I am no cat."

Soft hands smoothed up and down his spine, over his shoulders, and down to the waistband of his trousers with growing confidence. It felt like she was mapping him, *learning* him. When those curious fingers slid over the slopes of his hip bones, edging perilously close to his front, Otto felt his stomach tighten. His balls drew up tight against his body and a damp spot appeared on the thin material covering his thigh.

Great gods, it feels like she's stroking my cock.

If she kept it up, he was absolutely certain his overwrought nerves would see him spilling his seed in his damn trousers like a boy again.

"Will you tell me what you are, then?"

His reply came through clenched teeth. "Do you still not want my name?"

Her fingertips tickled the feathery edges of his knotted hair, almost as if she was tempted to touch it but did not know if she had permission. Otto huffed and tilted his head back, giving her free rein over the unruly mass.

"No name," she answered, sounding somewhat distracted as those quick, gentle fingers began to comb through his hair, untangling the snarls. She had no way of knowing that it was a purely submissive behavior. They were notorious for their love of grooming.

"Then no, you don't get to know what I am yet." He swallowed back a groan of pleasure as her blunt little nails began to scrape lightly at his scalp. "My *kone,* you have no idea how this soothes me."

Her breath hitched. "I... I find it soothing, too."

A grin creased his cheeks. "Tell me what your instincts say now."

"That you are still dangerous. That you are a predator." There was a lengthy pause. Her fingers never stopped moving, though, as she gathered her courage. "But also that touching you is... right. That you trust *me.* It's overwhelming."

"Do you want to stop?"

Those restless fingers curled into his hair and held fast, making his scalp tingle and his cock jerk. Otto's hips twitched, desperate to move. *Gods save me.*

"No," she answered, voice slightly strangled. "No, I do not want to."

His words came out slightly choked when he replied, "Whatever else you are, *kone,* you are without a doubt a submissive."

"Does that mean I'm weak?" She sounded troubled, as if being soft in a world as cruel as theirs was not an act of profound bravery, but one of shame.

"Weak?" If wasn't worried he'd startle her, Otto would have

reared his head around to give her the look that word deserved. "What weakness? You felt the animal's fear of death and you came to me anyway. What great bravery that took, *kone*, I cannot imagine."

He thought he heard the faintest sniffle. "I don't feel very brave."

"I should think that if you did, you would not need to be so brave in the first place."

A shuddering breath escaped her. "Will you explain to me what it means to be submissive — even though I'm not a shifter?"

Otto would have given anything to be free to clutch her to him then. "It means," he began, voice rough with feeling, "you are cherished. That you bring joy and warmth to those who are lucky to meet you. That you are soft, and provide a home to those of us who are not. It means you have needs that are different from mine, yes, but that's not a flaw. It means that it is my job to see you taken care of."

There was the rustle of skirts. Her hands disappeared, but before he could panic — or begin to beg — Otto was stunned to feel a silken cheek between his shoulder blades. Gradually, in the smallest increments, Josephine leaned her body into his, her arms tucked against his back and her form huddled against him.

She wasn't clutching him, but rather curled up against him, limbs held tight between their bodies. It was as if she hoped to melt into his back if she pressed close enough.

"This feels like care," she whispered. Otto felt some great shift inside of him, followed by the shock of a fissure opening up in the foundation of his being — a monumental movement of his sense of self, his heart, his priorities. *Everything.*

"Can I stay here a while?"

Otto slowly lowered his hands into his lap and leaned backward a few inches, giving her a more comfortable spot to lay her weight. "As long as you need, *kone.*"

"Thank you." There was a world of hurt in that simple phrase.

Thank you? Otto squeezed his eyes shut and counted backward from one hundred. He had to bite his tongue to stop himself from telling her there was no reason to thank him.

The fact that this was so remarkable to her was disturbing. Had she never known a hug? A gentle combing of her hair? Was her whole life an endless parade of violence and threats?

Rage boiled almost as hot as the fever. If he hadn't been chained, Otto was certain he would have shifted and hunted down the wretched man she called a father already. *I'll do it,* he promised both himself and the animal. *I'll rip his fucking throat out.*

And then he'd take his mate somewhere far away, deep into the wilderness, where no one could ever touch her again.

At last, when he had his temper more under control, he began, "*Kone,* how you've been treated is *not* how things— *Kone?*"

It took him a moment to realize that his mate had drifted off to sleep.

CHAPTER SEVENTEEN

An excerpt from the diaries of Josephine Wyeth,
generously provided by the Wyeth-Beornson family to the Fairmont
Museum of Art:
   November 13th, 1870-

I have spent a day with a shifter. I don't know his name. He is
blond and powerfully made. I am terrified of his nearness, let
alone his attention.

   But he let me touch him today and now I am aflame.

CHAPTER EIGHTEEN

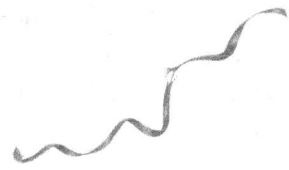

JOSEPHINE WALKED THROUGH A HAZE, HER MIND adrift.

She didn't hear her father's mutterings over dinner, nor her mother's high-pitched censure. She didn't feel the weight of her clothes on her skin. She didn't taste the food their long-time cook made with the unpalatable ingredients supplied by her father's benefactors. She didn't even notice the way Harrod's eyes tracked her from across the table.

All she smelled was the shifter's wild, musky scent. All she felt was his skin under her hands. All she heard was his baritone, whispering sweet things to her.

Josephine usually left the cells drained and heartsick, but after six hours with the shifter, she was full of restless energy such that when she was excused to her room, the bolt locked tight, she couldn't get ready for bed.

He consumed her thoughts, and with every one of them, her stomach fluttered. The roof of her mouth ached fiercely, too. When she ran her tongue over the gland there, it felt inflamed in a way that was entirely new.

It was alarming, to be sure, but Josephine was too overwrought to give the development proper attention. She could not stop thinking about how she dozed against his back, listening to the steady sounds of his heart, his breathing, his delicious purr. She recalled how, when she woke some time later, he did not complain about her heaviness, but rather seemed immensely proud that she'd trusted him enough to sleep.

Josephine didn't explain to him that she'd slept fitfully since her father began his experiments on her, nor that his body heat had acted as a drug to her senses, lulling her into a place of pure bliss. She didn't need to. Even without seeing his face, she could tell that he knew.

And he hadn't asked her to stop. When lunch came — the usual grim fare of hardtack, mash, beans, and canned peas — she worked up the courage to sit beside him, their legs touching, though she didn't dare meet his gaze.

He gave me his peas, she thought, heart racing and aching all at once. He noticed that she ate them first, as they were her favorites, and had silently scooped his portion onto her plate.

When they were done, he gave her his back again. They'd spent the rest of the day speaking quietly, with Josephine telling him all she knew as she rubbed her cheek against the hot, tanned skin of his shoulder, her hands roaming with ever-more greediness.

While she traced sloping muscle and gnarled scars, she explained what her father had done to her, how he'd tampered with the lyssa-infected vampire venom to make her, how it did not do as he expected it would after she woke up from three days of feverish delirium and agony. She even confessed to how she lost her mind each month, when the beast took over her body to rage and howl. He listened quietly, asking questions only when absolutely necessary, as he arched into her hands.

The truths spilled from her easily, like rotten blood from an old wound. When she touched him, breathed him, listened to his crooning voice, the poison of her misery simply... slipped away from her.

It was not only the tactile pleasure that made her beast keen with delight, but the way her hands seemed to *learn* him. The more she touched him, the more she felt her comprehension of his form grow.

Previously, she'd only known the human form through anatomical drawings and the nightmarish days of contact in the cells. She'd never had the chance to observe the form in person without duress.

But after six hours in the cell with the shifter, mapping his body with her hands, she felt her artist's mind had expanded.

Attempting to channel all her restless energy and block out the way the beast howled to return to the barn, Josephine got onto her knees to haul her trunk out from below her bed. In it were all her worldly possessions, which mostly consisted of art supplies and her journal.

After writing a frantic, truncated summary of the day in her diary, she stored it again and retrieved her sketchpad and charcoal.

She picked the softest willow sticks, precious in their rarity now that they weren't being made in the territories. It was thinner than a pencil and three times as delicate. Holding it with a practiced grip, she began to commit all she'd learned to paper.

Beautiful, she thought, smudging a smoky line with her thumb to create a shadow beneath the curve of his left shoulder. *So beautiful.*

When her stick snapped under the force of her enthusiasm, Josephine laid the pad on the floor and used the bits with increasingly frenetic swipes — long drags of her arm over the page, short, sharp strikes, accompanied by the rush of taking her palm to that sketched form to smear it all into ghostly ash. Fishing out a tiny lump of what was once a proud conté crayon, she went over the smoky images again, carving out form and movement with elegant, spare lines.

By the time her lamp burned out, her floor was covered in drawings of the shifter. She loved and loathed them all. They lacked his vitality, his *life*. How could she hope to capture it when she had only studied him for a day? The flaws in her drawings bothered her artist's eye even as the woman, the *beast* stared at them with growing hunger.

Frustrated, exhilarated, as well as exhausted, Josephine at last surrendered to sleep when there was no longer any light by which she might work. Her hands were blackened; a corner of her skirt was similarly stained, as she'd used it to wipe away tone, creating the illusion of light on his magnificent form.

Gathering her drawings with clumsy fingers, she hastily stuffed them into her trunk before she made her way over to her wash basin, where she scrubbed her hands with abrasive lye soap.

Even it would not cleanse her completely. Charcoal had a way of getting everywhere and staying there. Its grit was so fine that she often didn't feel it rubbing against her fingers as she smudged and smeared. Only when she could no longer discern her fingerprints on her most used fingers did she realize how even the silky-soft powder had tooth to it.

Donning her nightgown, Josephine reluctantly crawled into bed and pulled her blankets up to her chin. Was her bed colder than the night before? Perhaps it was the temperature changing, but she couldn't help but feel it was more than that.

She'd known the shifter's warmth for so little time, but already it felt unnatural to be without it.

Curling up on her side to conserve warmth, she looked out her window to see a sliver of the barn's turf roof.

Is he cold? Josephine's heart lurched. *Papa doesn't give them blankets anymore. It must be so cold in there for him, chained as he is to that awful wall.*

It was a thought she'd had before, particularly in the harsh winter months, but never with such urgency. The idea of the shifter being uncomfortable, even harmed by the cold, made her heart begin to race unpleasantly.

Wrong, the beast whispered in the back of her mind. *Should be with him. Should care for him.*

Certainly he would be warmer if they were together. What paltry body heat she could offer had to do something. Though she could hardly believe it, Josephine actually wished she could go to the barn.

If I could, then I would free him rather than offer my body heat.

Her heart lurched again. It was an awful feeling, as if the organ was so repulsed by the idea of him leaving her that it wished to exit her chest entirely. To follow him wherever he went.

It was useless to dream. It was even worse to connect, to crave the company of a subject. Josephine had learned those lessons early on.

And yet she found herself breaking all the rules as she stared longingly out the window. She imagined herself striding across the yard, into the barn, and opening the bolted door. She pictured herself unshackling him.

She closed her eyes as she felt her imaginary shifter hoist her into his arms and spirit her away from Meadow Creek, to some fine house with large gardens and children all around.

Her breath shortened as she considered what it might be like to feel *him* touch *her.* His hands would be rough on her tender skin, but he would be gentle. He'd proven that already. He would learn her as she'd learned him. He might even kiss her.

A deep, curious throbbing took up residence between her thighs. Josephine squeezed them together, instinctively trying to ease the unfamiliar ache as her core clenched.

What would it be like to not fear him? Would she love it when he embraced her? Would she feel a thrill when he pressed his weight down on her? Sex had always been leveraged as a threat against her, but with the shifter, she dared to imagine what it could be *without* fear.

No one had ever touched her that way. Would he?

Pain, sharp and immediate, speared the roof of her mouth. Josephine gasped, fingers flying to her lips, and helplessly pressed the tip of her tongue against her venom gland. It was the same one vampires were born with or grew after being infected. Normally, it stored venom that was renowned for its ability to numb flesh and create a euphoric feeling in the bitten.

Hers did no such thing. As far as she was aware, its only use was in infecting people with lyssa. It had never bothered her before — at least when her father wasn't sticking a needle into it — but now it couldn't be ignored.

It felt hot and swollen. When she pressed on it, there was some relief, but only for a moment before the source of the pain shifted down to the roots of her retracted fangs.

The throbbing between her legs seemed to increase the pain in her mouth until they were intimately intertwined. Urgency, the craving for touch, the relentless need to go to him all stole the breath from her lungs.

In the cold darkness of her bedroom, Josephine thought, *Oh gods, I want to bite him.*

～

It was with a sick feeling in her gut that she followed Harrod into the barn the next day. All the joy of the previous day had soured like turned milk. She barely slept, could hardly even stomach a sip of water.

She was both horrified by her body's reaction to him and desperate to see the shifter again. The urge to touch him grew stronger by the hour, just as her fear and repulsion did.

She could think of nothing beyond the need to bite him. The fevered imaginings of sinking her fangs into the hot, golden flesh of his throat kept her up all night, her damp thighs rubbing restlessly against one another.

For all that her father demanded she bite his subjects, Josephine had never felt the impulse to do so. She'd overheard her father say that their other subjects, once infected, often felt the desire to bite anyone when provoked to a rage, but she had never experienced anything of the sort.

Even in her monthly frenzies, she never felt compelled to bite.

She clawed. She howled. She fought until the skin of her hands tore, but she didn't ever *bite*.

So why, when she stepped into the dark cell again, did she reflexively clench her teeth at the sight of the shifter standing tall and proud? Why did her core give a terrible, deep throb when his scent hit her nose? Why did she feel a fire in her blood, building hotter by the second, when the sound of his sharp intake of breath reached her?

She couldn't bear to look him in the eye, but her fangs ached when she watched his shoulders flex, his hair shift over his scarred skin.

Hot shame flashed through her. On its heels came a foreign feeling, equally warm, but fizzy, electric. It was like excitement but more urgent. Restless.

When the door shut, the shifter murmured, "You have no idea what agony it is to watch you leave, *kone*, nor what bliss it is when you return to me." She heard him swallow. His voice dropped so low, she wondered if it vibrated the stones around them. "Will you not greet me? I've missed your touch."

Josephine didn't answer right away. Instead, she hurried over to the sink, where she filled up his cup. It was all she could do to buy herself some time, and the need to look after him competed with the other restless feelings that seemed to pull her in all directions at once.

Keeping her eyes on the ground, she carefully walked back over to him before she stopped abruptly. When he sat on the tile, it seemed natural to put the cup by his feet. Standing, however, it made her survival instincts bristle. Those feelings grated against the urgency to touch him, bite him, guide his hand between her thighs—

Josephine gave herself a hard internal shake. Should she bend down to do it, she would be in a vulnerable position, the back of her neck exposed, her center of gravity lowered. But if she *handed* him the cup, she would be putting herself directly in front of him, near enough to grab. Both options made the hair on the back of her neck stand on end.

Steeling her courage and buoyed by the beast's desire to be closer to him, consequences be damned, she inched her way into his space. "Here," she croaked, raising the cup.

Hands, hot and rough, gently closed over her own. Her breath escaped her lungs in a great *whoosh*.

"Sweet Josephine," he whispered, not taking the cup but using it to slowly, with the utmost care, reel her closer. "How are you today? You look tired. Did you not sleep well? Are you ill? What is this on your hands — coal dust?"

"It's charcoal," she found herself whispering, blushing hard at the memory of her frenzy, how desperately she sought to commit his form to memory and paper. "I drew last night and it— it doesn't wash off easily."

Strong fingers slid over hers, warming her as he inspected them. "Ah, I see. Was it your drawings that kept you from sleep?"

They were close enough that she could feel his body heat radiating between them. Josephine felt herself flush to the roots of her hair as her core clenched. "I... No, they didn't. I just couldn't sleep."

"Why? Were you frightened?" His deep voice rumbled even lower, sounding aggrieved at the very possibility. "You would not be if I were with you. I would keep nightmares away."

"Not nightmares," she croaked. *No, I was thinking of sinking my fangs into your throat as you thrust your cock into me.*

A different sort of nightmare than what he imagined, certainly.

"What, then? When you left me yesterday, you were soft and sweet with me. What changed?"

There was not enough courage in the world for her to explain her explicit, violent fantasies, but she felt compelled to tell him some version of the truth anyway. Her tongue tangled the words into helpless knots, but she forced them out. "I worry that— after yesterday, when we... when I touched you, it made me feel different."

His fingers flexed around hers on the cup. "In what way?"

"When we touch, I believe it makes me compelled to *bite* you," she admitted, horror plain.

A beat passed. He said nothing. He didn't even tense. If anything, he leaned *closer*.

She expected him to balk, but of course he didn't. This was the same man who demanded she bite him only moments after their meeting. His lack of reaction was further proof that he still did not believe her. He didn't believe that she carried lyssa, nor that his infection would kill his ability to shift — his very soul.

Tears were hot and heavy behind her eyes. *I can't bear that.*

If he were infected, the guilt would eat her alive. He would be broken. He would *hate* her. Then what would she have? The tortured memories of the warmth of his skin, the way he spoke to her, soft and understanding?

She carried with her so many horrors. She'd witnessed the depths of desperation and the depravity of her father's ambition. She thought she knew pain in all its guises.

Now, standing before her shifter, with his kindness and his warm hands, she feared that she did not know pain at all.

Worst of all was the shame. She was ashamed of how fiercely she wished to bite him, knowing what she did. She was ashamed of her senseless, overwhelming arousal. She was ashamed that even at that moment, when she considered all the pain to come, she *still* ached to nip his throat.

All these terrible thoughts accosted her, one after the other, in the space between one breath and the other. Josephine blinked. A tear, fat and crystalline, splashed down her cheek.

"Ah," he breathed. It was a pained sound, the kind one might make when a bruise is pressed.

Those warm hands left hers. Immediately, her baser side slid into acute panic at the loss, but the worry was quelled when rough palms cupped her jaw. His hands were so large that they practically encompassed the entirety of both sides of her head, and the chain linking his cuffs clinked as it rested against her décolletage.

Josephine froze. In that instant, she was aware not simply of his nearness, but of the ease with which he might simply wring her head from her neck.

Instinct screamed. Her muscles locked.

He made a soft shushing sort of sound and then, with deliberate slowness, leaned down from his great height to press his lips against the tear track. His beard, unkempt and a little prickly, tickled the soft flesh of her cheek and jaw.

A purr filled the cool air of the cell. The shifter's hands, so strong and work-worn, trembled.

A weighty stillness settled over her. It was a sort of internal quiet she had not experienced since the day her father injected her with the distilled venom of the dead vampire. There was no conflict between her rational mind and that of the beast. For once, they were in perfect accord.

Then, without warning, she felt herself cleaved in two — broken open by some monumental force to expose a part of herself she had never suspected existed.

From that place a single thought arose, drifting soft and sweet as a sigh: *I'm safe.*

CHAPTER NINETEEN

THE CUP TUMBLED FROM HER NERVELESS FINGERS.
Cool water splashed on the tile between them as it rolled away.
Josephine's knees buckled.

The shifter's reflexes were much faster than her own. In a
blink, his chained wrists were looped over her head to wrap his
arms around her back, pulling her into his scarred chest.

Josephine dug her fingers into the dense muscle of his back.
She pressed her nose into the dip between his collar bones, heedless of the rough metal collar that scraped against her forehead,
and breathed so deeply that her lungs could not contain all the air.

The excess escaped her in a shuddering, heaving exhale — not
quite a sob but close. Without conscious thought, that exhale
blended seamlessly into a frantic, high-pitched purr.

The shifter rested his chin on top of her head. His voice
rumbled through her when he asked, "Do you know what it
means when a shifter feels called to bite another?"

Josephine shook her head.

"It means that they have met their mate." His arms tightened
around her, but she felt no fear, no worry that he would press and
press until her fragile spine snapped. She felt only the shelter of
his embrace and the warmth of his skin. "It means that they wish

to bind their souls together, to form a pack, to breed and know the joy of watching cubs grow together. The bite — it is a blessed thing, my *kone.*"

"I am not a shifter," she cried, plaintive and heartbroken. "I am a werewolf, and if I bite you, I would steal your soul. It is a *cursed* thing for me."

"Ah yes, you have told me this," he replied, his tone even. Infuriatingly reasonable. "You believe this is true, and I trust you, so I must accept that it is even though a lifetime of experience has taught me otherwise. I must also accept that you are something I have never seen before, and that your needs, your urges might be different from my own."

A heavy hand cupped the nape of her neck. It was so large that he could press the pad of his thumb under the corner of her jaw even from that position. Lifting his head, he did so, urging her to look up.

It was habit to keep her eyes on his collar. When he continued to press, gently insisting, Josephine was startled to realize she *could* move her gaze up over the bearded chin, the full mouth, the crooked nose, the broad plains of his cheekbones, the winding scar that bisected a brow and cheek, to stare directly into eyes alive with the shifter glow.

"Oh." Her breath hitched. "You have freckles."

"And you have the prettiest eyes I've ever seen," he replied, expression pinched as if in pain.

A tangle of pride, pleasure, and shame twisted her up inside. "They're proof that I'm right. My eyes were both hazel before. After I was infected, they changed. They always change. It's the sign that lyssa is— that there is no hope." She tried to swallow, but it was like a lump of iron had wedged itself in her throat. "In a shifter, it means their animal has died."

The skin around the shifter's eyes and mouth pulled taut. "If it is as you say, then so be it, *kone.*"

"You are mad," she breathed, at once heartsick and aglow with warmth. "That is your *soul.* I would never allow—"

"If I must surrender it to have your bite, then I will." The shifter's eyes gleamed with a feverish light. "Do you know why, *kone?*"

Josephine licked her lips. His eyes tracked the movement with rapt focus. "Because— because you do not want me to take the needle again?"

"Yes," he answered, "but not only that." The shifter lowered his head and, using the hand on her nape, tilted hers to one side. Her blouse was a hand-me-down from her mother, so the collar was quite loose. He nudged it aside with the tip of his nose.

Josephine held her breath as he pressed his mouth, slightly parted, against the juncture of her neck and shoulder. She expected to feel the mind-wiping terror she normally experienced whenever someone came too near to her vulnerable throat, but it didn't come.

Instead, her insides went molten.

A soft exhalation escaped her. It was a sound of wonder and need.

His lips moved over her skin, dragging slowly back and forth, as his breath puffed in great, hot gusts. Something warm and wet darted out — his tongue, she realized with a tiny, nearly inaudible whimper.

"I want to wear your bite proudly," he grated. "I want you to dig your wee fangs in deep and draw blood from me, *kone.* I want you to savage me. I want you to mark me so all who see it will know I am yours."

"M-Mine?"

"As you are mine." Teeth, sharp but careful, scraped her tender flesh, sending a frisson of pleasure down her spine. Josephine was so shocked by it, she dug her nails into his skin, desperate to hold on.

A groan rumbled from deep within his chest. "You say that your bite will kill my animal. If this is true, then it will die with no regrets, because it chose you the moment you stepped into this cell."

Her ears rang. Surely she didn't hear him correctly. "What do you mean?"

"When we escape from here, *kone*," he explained, voice dropping progressively deeper, "I will build you a beautiful den. You will cover it in your pretty paintings. Every day, we will eat together at our table, and every night, I will kiss your soft skin until you beg for me."

Beg? Beg for what? She didn't have the faintest idea, but she knew without a doubt that he was right. She already felt like she was on the brink of begging him to do something, to soothe the growing ache that made the tops of her thighs slick, that made her pulse pound and her nipples tighten.

"And when we leave here," he continued, "I will mark you as thoroughly as you will mark me, *kone*. You are not the only one who feels the need to bite."

It took her clouded mind a moment to catch up. A jolt traveled through her, rattling her very soul. "But you said—"

"That shifters bite their mates?" He rumbled again. Those powerful teeth closed over the thick muscle of her trapezius, biting down just enough to leave indents in her skin.

Josephine's vision exploded in a sea of sparks as pleasure, *need* unlike anything she'd felt before burst through her.

"We do," he finished, releasing his bite. "I *will*."

She shook in his arms, overwrought with every imaginable feeling, good and terrible. "But you *can't*. You'll be shipped off to the front as soon as Papa injects you, and then we will never see each other again!"

"It is decided," he growled. Those strong fingers squeezed her nape, part possession and part censure. "My animal chose and I have long since accepted it, Josephine. You are my mate. I will not be separated from you, come dragonfire or the end of days."

Her heart soared, and yet she could not surrender to the hope he gave her. Even before she was changed, she had lived her life in shackles. It was a struggle to imagine anything could change, or that freedom could be more than just an abstract concept.

She had no one on which to rely. She had no money. She had no abilities. She had no experience in the world, nor amongst other beings. It was not merely the locks on the doors or the great green waste that kept her prisoner, but her ignorance of how to be a person in the world at all.

Her last escape attempt had gone horribly wrong, and when it was over, Josephine remembered how her mother had looked at her, lips pursed with disgust and eyes bloodshot.

"And what would you have done out there on your own, I wonder?" she'd asked. *"Become a whore? Starve to death in the streets? You have no education, no connections, no Coven."*

"I have a Coven," Josephine had belligerently insisted, though she knew her mother's response would tear her to pieces.

"You have none. Certainly not mine. Only witches have Covens, and you're arrant. Worth less than nothing to the family. Your only possible use might be in becoming a bondmate, but who would tie their soul to one as pitiful as you? Who would marry you, breed with you?" She'd lifted her lip and turned away, hand waving in dismissal. *"No one. You should be grateful your father has designs on making you his creature. Glory knows I have no use for you."*

Outside of the city, where she might escape into a hive of people and buildings, her father no longer bothered with shackles when she ventured outside the house. Josephine was largely allowed to wander freely — save for the nights of the full moon. After all, where would she go? The wilderness was as much a deterrent to her escape as bars on a window.

She had not the first idea how to survive in the wild. Equally humiliating was her mother's cruel truth: that she had little more idea of how to survive in the civilized world either.

But it wasn't about her. Standing in his arms, Josephine realized that it didn't matter. Even if the shifter abandoned her after it was all done, she couldn't let her father have his way. It had to stop here. It had to stop with them.

If I do not find a way to free him, he will be given lyssa, she thought, agonized. *I can't allow that, no matter what he says.*

She broke out into a cold sweat when she thought of escaping on her own, but for him? That was different, she decided. A hitherto unknown well of courage, of animal ferocity made itself known.

They will not touch him. She sucked in a steadying breath. *I can do this.*

"I can tell you everything I know," she offered, speaking quickly, as if she needed to push the words out at top speed before she lost her nerve. "I know all of Papa's routines. I know where he stores things. If you tell me—"

"You'll not put yourself in danger for my sake, *kone,*" he growled. "I need to be freed. That is all you must do. Once I am out of this cell, I will handle your father and that other man."

"That is the only problem." She would have turned to glance at the door, but with the shifter's hand on her nape, all she could do was give him a helpless look. "I can walk freely when it's not a full moon. I can gather supplies. I can find the keys to your shackles. But I cannot open that door by myself."

"Why?"

"It's sigil-lined," she explained. "And I have no magic."

The shifter's brows drew together. "Yes, you do."

It was her turn to give him a quizzical look. "No, I don't. My father told me he was trying to open my m-paths when he first injected me with the venom, but that's not what happened. I'm as useless as I ever was."

He loomed closer. Running the tip of his crooked nose over the slope of her cheek, the shifter sucked in a deep inhale that rattled with a purr of pure pleasure on its release. His voice dropped to a deep baritone when he replied, "I have a keen nose, *kone.* I can scent the magic in you just as I can scent the need."

Her chest rose and fell so fast, she felt lightheaded. She cycled from disbelief to confusion in the span of a heartbeat. "Need?"

"Need." His prickly beard tickled her skin as he moved his head, angling it so that his lips hovered over hers. For several tantalizing seconds, they shared air that was so thick, it clung to the back of her tongue like honey.

"You need your mate," he whispered. "You need my touch. You need me to pet you and stroke you and soothe the ache between your soft thighs."

Oh. That need. Of course he could smell that with his shifter nose. Josephine felt as though the raw desire to *feel* him oozed from every pore. It blocked everything else — his insistence that she bore some spark of magic, that she bite him, that they must escape. It was all-consuming.

A single word escaped her on the heels of a whimper: *"Yes."*

"Ask me for my name." His voice was a serrated edge of pure desire. "Ask me, *kone,* and I'll kiss you the way you need."

Josephine had wanted many things in her life. She'd *never* wanted something as fiercely as she wanted the shifter's kiss.

"Tell me your name," she begged, heedless of the consequences. Josephine desperately rubbed her lips against his, as if to encourage him to take from her, to teach her. "I want to— I need to know your name. Please."

She felt his chest swell with a deep breath. There was nothing but satisfaction in his voice when he said, "My name is Otto Beornson, and I am yours until Grim takes me."

"Otto." The name left her on a dreamy sigh. *Simple and charming. A perfect fit.*

A great tearing sound erupted from his chest. Josephine barely had a moment to realize it was a savage animal growl, too loud for even his great body, before a hot mouth descended on her own.

She'd seen kisses before. Her parents occasionally exchanged a peck or two, and when they lived in cities, she'd seen a great many depraved acts in the alleyways below her windows.

Even so, she was entirely unprepared for the shock of *being* kissed.

Otto held her head between his hands and pressed his lips against hers again and again, as if he couldn't get enough, and then began to fixate on one lip at a time — sucking it into the hot well of his mouth, nibbling on it, pressing his teeth down until she gasped.

It was an unrelenting tide of sensation and warmth. Her stiffness melted away the longer he lavished her with attention. When at last she parted her lips for him, desperate for more of his taste, he made a sound of approval in the back of his throat and slowly dipped his tongue inside.

Josephine jolted, shocked by the intimacy of the act, the liquid glide of his tongue against hers, the taste of him, and the way it all made her sex throb with a terrible, distracting ache.

Instinct took over. The beast rose up in her mind. For once she didn't fight it. They were in perfect accord as they fought to get closer, to take more from him.

Josephine pressed her body against his until there was no space between them. Her fingertips curled into the flesh of his back. She met the stroke of his tongue with her own, clumsy and hesitant at first, then bolder, with a hunger that matched his.

There was the clink of chains before she was whirled around and pressed against the wall. Only yesterday, the thought of being pinned by his great bulk to the stone would have sent her into a fit of terror, but there was not even a whisper of fear in her now. It could not survive the heat of the desire that scorched a path through her.

Dropping his hands between them, Otto hiked up her skirt and chemise with frenzied movements. "Spread your legs for me," he commanded.

She didn't think. It was easy to follow instinct, and it only wished to please him.

Josephine spread her legs.

She wasn't entirely certain how it happened, but a moment later he had one of her thighs slung over a thick forearm, forcing her onto her tiptoes, as his right hand arrowed through the slit in her undergarments.

The roof of her mouth pounded with a terrible, urgent pain

when the rough pads of his fingers slid through dark curls to find her sex.

Josephine bit back a shout when a bolt of pleasure accompanied a slow, proprietary touch of her slick flesh. The roots of her fangs burned as they extended with a dull *snick*.

"What I wouldn't give to have you in a den now," Otto grated. "The urge to fuck you and mark you is like fire in me, *kone.*"

Would he do that here? Now? Josephine's mind was so hazy, so clouded with need, she couldn't summon any objections.

Josephine wanted to feel his touch on every inch of her skin. She wanted his taste to linger on her tongue. She wanted to know what it was like to feel his cock inside her hungry body.

She wanted to feel the ecstasy of his bite — deeper this time, hard enough to tear her flesh, marking her for all the world to see.

She didn't realize she was speaking until Otto cut her off with a desperate kiss. Speaking against her mouth, he panted, "Shh, shh. I have you. I will. I promise I will." His fingers moved restlessly, swirling and then dipping inside her, making her gasp at the strangeness, the sharp bite of untrained muscles stretching around a thick finger.

"Soon," he promised, pumping slowly in and out of her. Josephine clawed at his chest, his neck, his wavy blond hair. Every stroke of his finger felt foreign and delicious. It both soothed the ache and made it that much worse. She felt a pressure, as if he was pushing her closer to some unseen cliff. *Closer, closer, clos—*

The addition of another finger made her tense. The stretch was no longer quite so pleasurable. A whine built in the back of her throat as the pressure gave way to sharp discomfort.

Otto rumbled something in a language she didn't understand and slowed his strokes again. "Easy, easy. It will feel good again soon."

She was not entirely sure she believed him, but Josephine found herself relaxing anyway. The beast trusted him implicitly. *He'll make it better,* it whispered. *He'll take care of me.*

Burying her face in his hair, she held on tight as he opened her body for him, slowly reigniting the pleasure.

"I regret that it hurts you," he told her, beginning to increase his pace once more. The sound of his fingers sliding in and out of her was lewd. It was also terribly compelling. "But you must trust me, *kone*. I will make you come. I will *always* make you come."

She was not entirely sure what that meant, but she did not have the breath to ask. It was all she could do to listen to him and hold on.

Otto pressed the heel of his hand against her and ground down. Her back arched as pleasure bloomed from that simple touch. "There she is." He sounded both pained and proud. "Yes, claw me. Sink your little claws in deep and breathe for me, *kone*. Ah, gods, look at those fangs. Did they come out just for me?"

She did not have the presence of mind to ask why he might make that request, nor answer his question, but it became clear enough when he began to slowly work another finger inside her.

The breath wheezed out of her lungs as her muscles attempted to accommodate the sudden stretch. She'd thought herself full before, but it was nothing compared to this.

Otto breathed harshly in her ear as he gently but firmly stroked her from the inside, tangling pain and pleasure such that she could no longer separate the two. "I know it is uncomfortable, but it must be done. It would kill me to hurt you when I claim you. This will make it easier."

If this was the price for pleasure, Josephine decided she would pay it a thousand times. Besides, it wasn't so bad. Certainly she'd endured far worse than a burning stretch. After a few moments of careful, insistent stroking, the sting began to fade once more.

The pleasure returned in force. So too did the frenzy, the wild certainty that he needed to take her *just now* or else... Well she didn't know what might happen, but the beast couldn't bear whatever it was.

The beast took over. She became senseless, frantic, desperate for something she never knew she wanted and could never have hoped for.

Speaking against his ear, she breathed, "I love your hands on me. I love your touch. I want— I *want* you to claim me now. Please, Otto. *Please.* It aches so badly, I—"

He let loose a guttural groan, his hips rolling between her legs as his movements became faster, more forceful. The lewd sounds echoed off of the stone walls, accompanied by the clatter of his chains and their combined heavy breathing.

"Not yet," he gasped. "Not until we're free."

Josephine and the beast had never been more blended than in that moment, when they both went wild. "You *must,*" she heard herself growl over the rushing of blood in her ears. Her hips moved frantically, rolling hard into his hand, as she made her demands. "You need to! I need you to!"

"*Fuck!*" Otto plunged his fingers deep and curled them, hitting a spot inside her that made sparks fly behind her eyes and her mouth pop open. "Come for me now, *kone.* Come!"

Teeth closed over the side of her neck, just above the collar of her blouse, and bit down harshly. It was not enough to break the skin like the beast demanded, but the sensation still sent her careening over that cliff's edge with a hoarse moan.

Her inner muscles spasmed around his undulating fingers as wave after wave of tingling warmth rushed over her. At first she was stiff, every muscle locked, but as the waves began to recede, she became languid, her mind fuzzy with a glowing sort of pleasure.

She slumped against him as he gently set her on her feet. The rise and fall of his chest was rapid, and the blond hair covering his scarred pectoral was a little prickly against her cheek, but she loved it all the same.

Chains rattled behind her. Josephine felt like she was moving through molasses when she looked up and found Otto running his tongue over every inch of his glistening fingers, eyes closed and brows furrowed in bliss.

The roof of her mouth pulsed angrily, but the sharpest edge of her urgency had been dulled by drugging pleasure, allowing her to appreciate the expression of rapture on his rough features.

When he was done with his task, Otto looped his arms around her once more. Settling his cheek on the crown of her head, he croaked, "Now, *kone*, let us plot our escape before the last of my will does the same."

The beast snarled at being denied, but as her heart began to slow, she began to see the sense in his restraint. It would be a disaster if her father suspected anything. The gods only knew what wretched experiments he might concoct if he found out she felt the urge to bite him, or that Otto mate with her.

Besides, she wanted to believe in the future with the den and the table and the cubs. That future did not begin in the cell.

Pressing her nose against the hair-roughened skin below his chin, she shyly demanded, "First, tell me what *koh-ney* means."

His arms tightened. "Ah, my Josephine, it is a Danish word."

"For what?"

Gentle hands ran up and down her back. "It means *wife*."

CHAPTER TWENTY

AN EXCERPT FROM THE ARTICLE "EXPLORING LYSSA: The Story of Josephine Wyeth," written by Elise Sasini and featured in The San Francisco Light May 17th, 2048—

You have to win the animal, and you can only do that one on one.

I mull over Vanessa's words as we land in Seattle, the Coven Collective's cultural heart and capital, and then on the m-lev that seamlessly glides through the lush Pacific Northwestern landscape.

It's jarring to hear her refer to "the animal" so bluntly. Most Weres prefer not to speak of their dual nature openly, but the more I think about it, the less I'm surprised she did so. After all, Vanessa's father is a shifter. The idea of the animal is not an abstract one, nor a derogatory term meant to spawn fear of the Were nature. It simply *is*.

The subject of a Were's inner landscape is the source of almost as much controversy as the term itself.

Where, countless scientists and government officials have wondered, *do they fit?*

There has long been a connection between shifters and Weres. Studies have shown that Weres exhibit the same tendency toward dominant or submissive personality types — as well as the instinctive hierarchy of the pack structure — as shifters. Of course, there is the most obvious tether between them: the transformation of the Were from human to superhuman.

In fact, Vanessa's mother's own testimony that her father mutated the LYS-93 virus in shifter brain tissue was recently proven through gene sequencing. In a last ditch effort to keep the virus alive without a vampiric host present, Dr. Wyeth injected it into the tissue of an unknown shifter, where the virus "stole" DNA that massively altered its expression — most notably reducing its lethality.

So if every Were expresses the behavior and carries the DNA of a shifter, are they not technically shifters?

Some argue that they are. Others point out that biologically, Weres are much more similar to vampires. While they may carry shifter DNA, it is the vampire venom that develops the venom gland, the hollow, needle-shaped fangs, and extreme exertion after sundown, most notably during the full moon.

So, who's right?

As we climb into a rental car — a hefty truck the likes of which your city-born reporter has never seen in all her life — I clutch my backpack to my chest as I blurt out my question. "If you had to classify Weres, would you put them closer to vampires or shifters?"

Vanessa tears out of the parking lot, perfectly at ease behind the wheel of the behemoth vehicle. She's quiet for a while, thinking the question over as we plunge into a narrow strip of highway almost swallowed by hungry forest.

"Well..." she answers slowly. "I don't really think we're either. We're Weres. Lyssians. Werewolves. It's the virus that made us, not vampires or shifters. It took what it needed from both of them and then did a new thing in us. We identify with the virus, not the DNA it picked up on its way *to* us."

I hesitate. What I want to ask is an intensely personal question, and not normally something I'd dare say so soon after meeting an interview subject. However, I remind myself that we're in a rented truck hurtling toward her parent's home. Clearly Vanessa trusts me. I wouldn't be in the faux leather seat of a monster truck otherwise.

I plunge ahead. "Is it harder for you than some? Your father being a shifter, I mean."

Vanessa stares at the road. A little bit of her shine dulls. It's like watching a light dim, and I feel immediate remorse for asking. I open my mouth to tell her she doesn't need to answer, but she begins speaking before I can.

"It's hard. I think it will always be hard. Growing up, I struggled to understand why I felt the animal but could never shift. I know my brother did, too." Her long fingers, clad in delicate rings inlaid with colorful stones, tighten on the steering wheel. "But it's much worse for those people who are infected and then lose their ability to shift. It's a mercy to be born without it, honestly. I can say I'm a Were confidently. I know who I am. But those people who had to remake themselves after the loss?"

She shakes her head. "I can't imagine the pain."

CHAPTER TWENTY-ONE

An excerpt from the diaries of Josephine Wyeth, *generously provided by the Wyeth-Beornson family to the Fairmont Museum of Art:*
  February 6th, 1868-

Yesterday the benefactors came to take the boy away. He howled all night. A terrible sound. It hurts me even now. I swear I can still hear him crying.

I will miss him desperately. He was so young. No matter how I coaxed, he would not give me his age, and so I must believe he is quite young indeed. Perhaps 17. Maybe younger, though it pains me to think so.

He was so brave, even when he was terrified. He did not like how I was treated and often asked me if I was well, if he could do anything for me. I did my best to soothe him as he told me about his parents' farm, his baby sister, that he had hopes of someday becoming a lawyer after his time as a soldier was done. My heart broke with every word, but I couldn't bear to crush his hopes. Even when I was honest with him about what will happen, how little choice either of us have, he was belligerent in that hope.

A true wolf at heart as well as in form. No child should have to be that fierce so young. I will miss him. Gods, I will miss him.

[Curator's note: This entry has been re-transcribed by Josephine Wyeth-Beornson for the ease of reading. In its original state, the handwriting was almost entirely illegible due to the mental state of the author at the time of its writing.]
February 10th, 1868-

I have not left my bed for days. I am too heartsick. The morning my sweet boy was taken away, raging and terrified, I overheard my father and Harrod discussing his infection in the hall outside of the laboratory.

What I heard made me vomit there in the hall. I am sick with it. I am so ill with guilt and horror that I fear it will kill me. Papa has had to force food and water down my throat, but I can hardly keep it down. I don't want to. Everything is ash and bile in me.

I cannot stop thinking of my sweet boy, with his fierce courage and wolfish grin. I cannot keep food down, nor sleep. I am undone by grief so great it is breaking me apart into ever-smaller pieces.

Rasmus will never shift again.

This is what my father so casually discussed with Harrod — that the child I adored so has had his soul stolen with a single injection of my venom. It is apparently standard with shifters, though he still wishes to test this theory on more types to be sure.

Sweet Rasmus, you didn't deserve this horror. By all the gods, I am sorry. I am sorry. It would not be an even trade, but I would give myself for your wolf if I could. Gods, I would. I would. I would.

CHAPTER TWENTY-TWO

IT WAS A GOOD THING, JOSEPHINE THOUGHT, THAT they had twelve hours together. It took about that long to work out a rough plan of escape, and about as long for Otto to convince her to attempt the sigil on his cell door.

He was determined that she not put herself in more risk than absolutely necessary, and stressed that desire frequently as they worked out the best way to set him free. He said he did not want her to do anything more than find the keys to his chains, unlock his door, and throw them inside. Once that was done, he would handle the rest.

Josephine, having determined that nothing mattered to her more than getting him out of her father's clutches before he was injected with her venom, was markedly less concerned with her safety. After all, what would her father do if she were caught? Certainly nothing he could do to her would be worse than what he had already done.

Her concern was with Otto and him alone.

Get him out. Get him safe. Get his bite.

The thoughts circled around and around as she stumbled through the motions of a tense evening meal. Her mother had excused herself, claiming an uneasy stomach, leaving Josephine with her father and Harrod, who ignored her.

She was hyper-aware of them as she pushed her portion of boiled potatoes and salted pork around her plate. Did they suspect something? Did they know that Otto had pleasured her? That she'd begged him to bite her? It was a marvel they couldn't sense it.

To Josephine, it was as if he'd branded his handprints, his kisses, on her skin. She felt them burning her long after she forced herself to walk out of the cell and back into the house. What a beautiful feeling it was, too! Josephine had never felt more alive than she did after Otto whispered rough endearments into her skin, sealing them with lips, tongue, teeth, and breath.

Peering at her father and Harrod through her lashes, she only saw two men entirely engrossed in their discussion. Harrod's eyes strayed to her more often than she liked, but that was their new normal, so she tried to tamp down her paranoia as she picked up the thread of the conversation.

"...reckless," her father announced, slapping the tips of his fingers against the edge of the table. "We don't know how it will spread, and if they want to keep their soldiers under lock and key, they would do well to listen to an expert. If they want the *best*, they need me!"

"It's confirmed, then?" Harrod pressed, dabbing his napkin against the corner of his thin mouth.

"Unfortunately. They've begun to let them bite prisoners under completely uncontrolled conditions." Her father grimaced, his disgust palpable. "They aren't picking the stock. Anyone who can fight is good enough. Gods know what a mess that will make of things."

A deep internal chill settled over her as she grasped what her father was complaining about. Normally she held her tongue unless absolutely necessary, as her father was wont to take her art supplies when she pricked his temper, but in this instance she could not help herself. "They— they're making more werewolves at the front?"

Both men's gazes swung to her. She usually quavered under their combined stares, but she was so horrified by this news that Josephine found herself staring boldly into her father's lined face. She looked at him so rarely that it was always a shock to see how much he'd aged, his features worn down by stress, ill health, and his own relentless ambition.

"I've told you not to use that word," he scolded her, sniffing with distaste. "You are not a *wolf.* Your transformation is lupine, but these things are not the same. You are a *were.*"

Josephine couldn't care less about what she was called. "They're *biting* people? Infecting others? I thought only I could—"

Her father waved a hand dismissively as he reached for his wine glass. "Of course they can infect others. Lyssa is highly contagious. We use you because you are pure stock, entirely untainted by any illness that might skew results. You are fit and healthy, if not disappointingly weak. And it was *your* mutation that made the infection so powerful. Gods only know why." He paused to take a long sip. Cheeks flushing, he added, "Apparently we are not moving fast enough for my benefactor's liking, so they've begun allowing any disease-riddled trench rat to bite others."

Josephine dropped her eyes to her plate, overwhelmed by all the implications of this news.

Not only did this mean that lyssa was spreading beyond her father's victims but also that he might be losing his value. *She* might be losing value. If her father's benefactors lost their interest in him, or became capable of creating their own weres, then a great many things would change.

The only thing that had protected them all from the ravages of the war was the favor of the benefactor, bestowed on her father due to his value. If that evaluation dropped, the protection disappeared.

The memory of watching Washington go up in flames, of people running through the streets clothed in icy blue dragonfire, screaming until they sucked the fire inside, haunted her. Where would her father go if not in favor? Was there any place on the continent that was not ravaged by decades of the cursed war? What had begun as a territory dispute between the elvish sovereign and the Orclind had melted into a war so vicious, so all-consuming, that no one really knew what it was about anymore. From Josephine's pinhole perspective, it appeared as if all the world was on fire.

Where will we go? the beast fretted. *Where will we build our den if nowhere is safe? Otto must know someplace. He must. He promised a den. He promised cubs and a table and places for my paintings. Didn't he? He wouldn't lie.*

"We don't know that those bitten by others experience the same level of enhancement," Harrod chimed in, interrupting the swirl of her increasingly panicked thoughts.

Her father set his glass down on the table with more force than necessary. His eyes gleamed with the fervor she recognized too well. "From all reports, it appears they do. And now they wish to relocate us again, claiming we are too close to the front. They're demanding things, too. Always demanding more. No respect for the methods that have gotten them what they asked for! I suspect they will find an excuse to dispose of us all soon enough."

"Then perhaps it's time we revisited the discussion around continuing Miss Wyeth's experiments." Harrod said it so calmly, as if he were making note on the state of the war rather than the continuation of a decade of torture.

Josephine's fingers turned numb around the handle of her fork and knife. She was forced to set them down, lest she let them fall from her nerveless fingers to clatter against her plate.

"Which ones?" Her father made a dismissive sound with his tongue. "I've done everything I can."

"Not everything," Harrod argued. His long, tapered fingers

smoothed a fold in his napkin as he rested it on the edge of the table. Her skin crawled as she watched them move.

Speaking with the utmost self-assurance, he continued, "I believe it is time we experimented with the effects of a witchbond on Miss Wyeth. Perhaps exposure to high levels of magic will mutate the infection further."

Oh gods. Bile crept up the back of her throat. *Say no.*

"I'd forgotten we discussed that," her father replied, sounding churlish and perhaps a tiny bit slurred. Too much wine made him more temperamental, as she well knew. "Did I not say no already? I believe I did."

"You did, but that was before our situation changed." He didn't even spare a glance for Josephine as he made his case. "I am willing to test the effect of magic on her. It is the logical next step, and might help us craft an even more powerful version of lyssa: weres with the ability to use magic."

"You would tie yourself to my daughter?" Her father leaned back in his chair and crossed his arms. His expression was certainly churlish, but not nearly as displeased as she wanted him to be.

Harrod straightened his already tense shoulders. "For the sake of our work? Of course."

"A bond would muddle things," her father argued. "It creates intimacy. You might feel compelled to take her as a wife, which would make our work more difficult."

"I don't see why. If she was my wife, perhaps she'd be more biddable than she is at present."

A drop of cold sweat rolled down her spine as Josephine waited for her father's response. None came. Instead, he sat there, arms crossed, and appeared to be considering this point.

Slowly, as if he loathed giving up his ground but couldn't help himself, he said, "I have had designs on seeing lyssa's effect on children. Tell me, would you breed her?"

Harrod didn't hesitate. "Yes."

"Hm." After a moment of thought, her father shook his head

and pushed his chair back from the table. "I'll think on it and give you an answer tomorrow. Perhaps the day after. In the meantime, join me in the lab. I want you to look..."

The sound of rushing blood washed away the rest of whatever it was her father said. Both men abandoned their plates and left the room, speaking amiably as if they had not just discussed her future in intimate detail.

Harrod wants to bond with me. They've spoken of it before. Papa wants to experiment on children. Harrod wants me to have *his children.*

The horror was so immense, it threatened to crush her. She could scarcely draw a breath through the constricted muscles of her throat.

She couldn't be his bondmate. She did not want his magic slithering through her veins, keeping him alive as it filtered through her and back to him. Everything in her rebelled at the idea, let alone the suggestion that he might put a child in her belly, only to be used as an experiment as she was.

I'll die first.

Somewhere far away, she felt the deep tremors of great animal fury. It took her a moment to realize they came from *within* her.

I will not do it. I will not allow it. No more.

The feeling of constriction eased as the beast made itself known. Josephine stared at the table, her frantic breaths slowing, as she felt her fingertips burn and her canines lengthen. Even her vision grew sharper.

No, he would not have her.

Only one man could put his hands on her now, and he would *never* allow another to harm her. When she had the children she'd always longed for, they would be *his,* and they would grow up safe. Cherished. He'd made a promise to her. She would see that he kept it.

And if anyone dared stand in the way of that future, Josephine would tear them apart.

It was with a deadly sort of calm that she cleared the table and washed the dishes, as she normally did after the cook retired for the evening. Josephine took her time.

The anxiety that she might be caught at any moment had vanished. Her hands, still partially shifted to long, deadly claws, did not shake as she packed a sack full of non-perishable foods.

Her knees didn't knock as she walked calmly back through the house, past her father's lab, to hide it in her bedroom.

She didn't wonder what would happen after they escaped as she sorted through her meager belongings and carefully stowed them in a carpet bag. It went safely into her steam trunk beneath her bed.

Her courage did not fail her when she waited until Harrod and her father had gone to the sitting room for a night cap. Over the years on the homestead, they had gotten lax with locking her in at night. The likelihood was that they would not remember to do so until one of them went to bed.

Knowing they would not bother with Otto's chains until the second day of stage two, she slipped the twin keys to his collar and shackles off of their ring and into her skirt pocket.

When she laid in bed, listening to the sound of her father shuffling to her door, tipsy and muttering, to slide the bolt into place, she thought, *I'm coming, my mate.*

Chapter Twenty-Three

The next morning, Josephine was surprised to find herself still simmering with the quiet, calm rage. She half expected a return of the meek creature she was before, heralded by the cold realities of a new day, but it did not return.

Fury and determination carried her through the motions of preparing Otto's food, folding her blankets, and sipping from the cup that he would drink from — the first step of stage two.

Ridiculous, she thought. It was no wonder the benefactors were upset with her father when he wasted time on his *Wyeth Protocols,* knowing full-well they would never work.

Not that Josephine wanted them to, but now she saw her life with new eyes. She saw her father's arrogance, his single-minded determination to do things his way, no matter how foolish or cruel those things were. She saw Harrod's doglike devotion to her father, too, and was disgusted by them both.

Her new state of mind was a revelation. It was as if she had been seeing the world through a fog of terror, and now that she could see clearly, she did not feel small, nor weak.

When her mother turned her nose up at Josephine over a late breakfast, she felt nothing for the woman. No hate, no regret, no longing. All she saw was a miserable woman who did not know how to love anyone but herself. It would be as much a relief to be rid of her as it would be to throw out shoes that were slightly too tight.

When Harrod escorted her to the barn, her arms laden with her delivery, she didn't listen to a word he said. She stared straight ahead as he went on in his cold voice about how he was certain they would be bonded, despite her father's clear reluctance, and what he expected from her moving forward.

He demanded she be obedient. He would have her loyalty above all others, even her father. He would put a child in her as quickly as possible, for efficiency's sake, and she would do well to make that process as easy as possible, lest she spark his temper. He would require she tend to him often, and speak as little as possible.

He declared it as if the matter was decided. They would be bonded. He would tie his magic to her and he would consider marrying her if she pleased him well.

With every word, Josephine's rage expanded in her chest like a great Parisian balloon. If he continued, she wondered in a detached sort of way if she might simply float up into the sky, buoyed by the hot air of her fury.

You will not have me in your bed, she thought as they approached Otto's cell door. *Because very soon you will be dead.*

For all that he'd done to her. For all that he'd done to Rasmus and every subject who came before and after. Most of all, it would be because he'd threatened her mate and children.

Harrod would never leave Meadow Creek again. She would make sure of it.

She kept her jaw firmly clenched and her fingers tucked into fists beneath the blankets, hiding what would have terrified her only a few days ago — her fangs, fully extended, and her claws, which previously only ever showed themselves during the full moon.

If he continued to speak, she feared that the burning in her muscles would coalesce into a full transformation.

Her father had puzzled over her inability to change unless the moon was full. His other subjects transformed into their monstrous forms often. Even the slightest hint of aggression might see their bones extending, their faces stretching, the part of them that was human buried under the animal rage.

Never, even under carefully administered torture, had she shown the slightest transformation.

Until now.

The beast hadn't found its claws until her mate and her children, yet unborn, were threatened.

Nothing would happen to them. She would not allow it.

Otto said she had power. That submissives were some of the fiercest beings alive when provoked. *"A pack's submissives are the last line of defense,"* he'd explained in his patient, accented timbre. *"They are responsible for protecting the young. Tell me, kone, if submissives were truly as weak as you think, would we leave them to guard the cubs? Our elders? No. Once roused, a submissive is the most dangerous creature in the world."*

She doubted him before. No more.

Josephine watched Harrod carefully as he traced the sigil on the metal door. A flare of magic, hot and carrying the tang of blood, filled the air. That sigil was all that stood between her mate and freedom. There wasn't even a proper lock.

Was it possible that Otto was right about this, too? If she traced the sigil, would it work? She found it hard to believe. If one had magic running through their veins, she thought they ought to feel it. Certainly her father's tests had never revealed anything.

Then again, she had long suspected her father did not know nearly as much as he believed he did. Perhaps, like the protocols, her abilities were yet another part of his grand experiment he simply refused to see.

She would try. She had to. If she failed, they would simply have to find another way out.

Josephine stared straight ahead as Harrod pulled the bolt out of its place and then pushed the heavy metal door open. Her gaze landed on Otto without a moment's hesitation.

He sat against the wall, legs extended and crossed at the ankles. His hands, which had touched her so gently, with such passion just one day ago, lay neatly folded in his lap.

It took every ounce of willpower she possessed to stop herself from throwing down her burden to run to him. She felt as though she'd been starved and then presented with a feast held just out of reach. It was torture being so close yet unable to touch him.

As she watched, Otto's great, scarred body subtly flexed, as if he too fought the compulsion to go to her, chains be damned.

"In," Harrod commanded, gesturing sharply toward Otto with a toss of his head.

Josephine swallowed and forced herself to drop her eyes. It was essential that she not give him any reason to suspect her of their plans, and if she were to suddenly show how little she feared Otto, how desperately she wished to be *with* him, it could spell disaster.

So she walked stiffly into the cell, her boots tapping against the tile, and somehow managed to keep her eyes on his bare feet as she knelt to deposit everything he'd need before him.

"Food and blankets," she murmured unnecessarily, heart pounding with the need to close the distance between them. That was not all she brought, of course, but Otto would discover that soon enough.

A deep animal rumble filled the cell. "Thank you."

She stood up slowly, but found herself unable to take a step back. *Can't leave him. Don't want to. Won't.*

Despite her best efforts, she couldn't stop herself from looking up.

Their eyes met. It was like a current of pure heat moved through her, jolting every fine nerve in her body. The idea of leaving him was suddenly so repugnant, she felt the acid crawl of bile move up the back of her throat when she slid her foot backward a single inch.

Otto's brows drew together as the skin around his mouth tightened. He inclined his head ever-so-slightly toward the door. His gaze was understanding but hard, determined.

She could almost hear his rich, rolling accent in her mind saying, *Go, kone. We will be together soon.*

"Josephine." Harrod's voice was a blast of icy wind against her back. It was not his usual tone — cold, clipped, slightly stilted in an effort to hide his country accent. When he said her name, it was more of a bark, almost territorial in nature. Possessive.

More chilling than his tone was the fact that he used her name at all. No *Miss Wyeth*. It was Josephine. *His* Josephine.

She was not the only one who heard the message. Otto's gaze, luminous gold with the desire to shift, flicked to Harrod and stayed there. Slowly, her mate tilted his head to one side. Josephine's skin prickled as she watched an indefinable change overtake him.

Although he still wore the skin of a battle-scarred man, she knew with absolute certainty that it was the animal staring at Harrod.

And that animal wanted to crush his skull between its jaws.

Worried that her presence would provoke Otto into doing something rash, Josephine summoned the strength to take one step back. Immediately, a low, hair-raising growl rumbled from her mate's chest.

She desperately wished that there was something she could say to ease his mind. She wanted to tell him that she didn't fear Harrod, that they would escape soon, that at the very least they would see each other the following day.

The words stayed locked behind her teeth for fear of provoking more of Harrod's temper. She would not risk him taking out his anger on her mate, bound and vulnerable as he was. It would not be the first time he'd retaliated against a subject she was fond of for some slight, imagined or otherwise.

Once, she'd asked a question he'd deemed impertinent, a simple thing that apparently called into question his credentials as a scientist in front of her father. The next day, she discovered that Rasmus hadn't been given water since she saw him last — a nearly twenty-four hour span.

Now that Harrod wanted to marry her, have children with her, he was even more dangerous. The gods only knew what he might do to Otto if he discovered the intimacies they'd shared.

Josephine forced herself away, turning slowly to face her father's assistant, whose cold eyes moved slowly back and forth between herself and her mate.

As she neared the door, a long-fingered hand wrapped around her bicep. Josephine looked up, startled by the contact, to find Harrod squinting into the darkness of the cell. "Is that a scratch on his shoulder?"

She held her breath, vividly recalling how she dug her nails into Otto's back, neck, and shoulders as he thrust his fingers inside her. In her frenzy, it didn't occur to her to worry about leaving a mark. At the time, that was *all* she wanted to do.

Before she could think of an excuse as to why she might have had contact with the shifter before stage two, Otto's smooth, accented voice filled the cell. "A man who's fought on the front lines ought to have a scratch or two to show for it, don't you think?"

While Otto's tone was pleasant, the insult was clear even to her.

Eyes swinging up to gauge Harrod's expression, she was shocked to find his pale face reddening. Speaking stiffly, he sneered, "A smart man would know better than to be proud of a scratch he was too stupid to avoid, but then again, you're an animal, so perhaps I shouldn't be surprised."

Josephine's heart jammed itself into her throat as her eyes swung back to Otto just in time to catch the spread of a slow, terrifying smile. A shiver of awareness danced down her spine. It was the animal staring at Harrod, plain as day, with hunger in his eyes.

"Oh, I'm proud all right, but a man such as yourself will never know the pleasure of a good clawing."

"Continue speaking, shifter, and I'll have you muzzled." Harrod made a dismissive sound and pivoted on his heel. He took her with him as he stomped out of the cell, his face still ruddy and his eyes glittering with anger. It seemed that her mate had pricked a nerve. He might have done much more than that if Harrod understood the double entendre.

As it stood, she was surprised by his jerky movements, how he cast poisonous looks over his shoulder at the cell door. Doctor Harrod Pierce had always seemed rather unflappable, even in his anger. He didn't flinch when subjects raged at him and he endured her father's temper, his unreasonable demands, with neither sweat nor complaint.

The only times he seemed moved were recently, as he'd begun to turn his attention toward her, but even that had a cold, almost clinical edge to it.

She never would have guessed that the implication that Harrod was a coward for not fighting on the front lines would vex him so much. It shocked her to realize that perhaps the man who had been a figure of such terror in her life was *insecure*. Weak.

But of course he was, she realized. A man who was sure of his place would not grovel at her father's feet, nor jump to fulfill his every command. He would not find joy in exerting power over those below him. He would not take great pains to cover his accent, nor in presenting a precise image to the world. He would not exact petty revenge on the bound.

And he certainly wouldn't force the woman he desired into a union. He wouldn't *have* to.

Josephine looked at him with new eyes as he dragged her out of the barn, his lips pressed into a bloodless line and his grip tight. When he glanced back at her, she no longer felt the compulsion to look away. She met his gaze with the frank stare of one disgusted with a person's very existence.

The beast wasn't afraid of him. The woman wasn't either.

"What?" he snapped, stopping in the middle of the yard. Dry weeds and pebbles crunched under the heel of his fine, if dull, leather shoe when he swiveled around to loom over her.

This was the man who'd tortured her? Locked her in her room? Helped steal the lives of all those her father infected? Demanded she bed him and birth his babies?

He was a limp coward.

Josephine was not entirely sure what came over her then. She got the sense that her fear swept back, opening up a yawning chasm inside of her. What rushed into that empty space was a breathtaking rage and contempt so deep and dark it was practically its own element. Like a drop of ink bleeding into the delicate, interlaced fiber of paper, she was forever changed by it.

"Do not touch me," she commanded, ripping her arm out of his grasp with one sharp jerk. Her fingertips burned as her claws, long and razor-sharp, slid out once more. *"Never* touch me again, Harrod."

For the span of a heartbeat, he looked truly astonished by her show of spine. As she watched, that surprise was clouded by a storm of cold anger. The dreadful lines of his long face drew tight with unconcealed malice. Her heart raced. Cold sweat dewed between her breasts and along her spine.

Even so, she held firm.

"Submissives have power," Otto told her. She was not weak. She had endured more than Harrod could ever withstand. What would he do to her? Strike her? Hurt her?

Try it, the beast snarled.

Harrod took a step toward her, the tendons of his neck standing taut above the edge of his collar, and hissed, "You don't get to—"

Whatever threat waited on the tip of his tongue, Josephine would never find out. At that moment, a once familiar sound carried over the prairie: the clatter and steady beat of a carriage coming down the road.

They turned as one to stare at the dilapidated gate and the dusty, groove-ridden road beyond. The land around the homestead consisted mostly of low-lying hills and grasses, making it easy to see the dark, boxy shape of a horse and carriage making its way toward them.

A hurried glance at Harrod's face told her this was not a planned visit, nor their usual supply delivery. In a moment he'd gone from ruddy with anger to starkly pale. The ball of his throat bobbed against his stiff collar with an almost palpable nervousness.

She expected Harrod to run off to get her father, but he stood rooted to the spot beside her, his gaze locked on the nearing carriage, expression slack like he didn't know what to do. Seeing as *she* wasn't inclined to go get her father, Josephine watched it too, a knot of unease tightening in her belly.

It took only a moment for the sleek, modern carriage to crest the low hill that stood just before the entrance to the homestead. For a moment, the yard was a cacophony of sound and stirred dust. Josephine covered her nose and mouth with her hand as the cold wind blew grit into her face.

When she no longer felt the dust battering her skin, she blinked cautiously into the harsh midmorning sunlight to see a glamoured man — human, by his stature — hop out of the driver's seat to open a black lacquered door.

A guard emerged first, also glamoured to obscure his features but dressed in a dark burgundy uniform. He quickly stepped aside, spine straight and legs spread, to allow room for the other occupant to step down into the dusty, churned earth.

Going by the rigidity of the men she'd seen, the subdued opulence of the carriage, she expected an intimidating being to emerge from the shadows.

Instead, a small man dressed in a neat white linen suit placed one foot on the step before he leapt gracefully down. His features were finely wrought, his chin shaved, and his dark hair neatly parted in the center. He was rather unremarkable, save for the single gold chain around his neck. Beneath it lay a long bow tie of silk so red, it looked like fresh blood.

Adjusting one of his jacket cuffs, the small man turned in a slow semi-circle, taking in the barn, the stables they had no use for, and finally the home itself. When his eyes landed on them, a shudder worked its way down her spine.

Danger.

Even from a distance, she could see the empty, practiced smile he leveled their way. She could *feel* his magic pressing down on her, so hot it burned.

"Good afternoon," the man called out, striding toward them with that empty smile fixed in place. "Is Doctor Wyeth in?"

CHAPTER TWENTY-FOUR

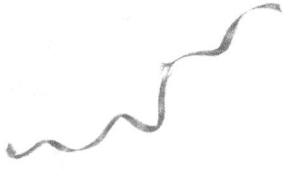

AN EXCERPT FROM THE ARTICLE "EXPLORING LYSSA: The Story of Josephine Wyeth," written by Elise Sasini and featured in The San Francisco Light, May 17th, 2048—

Despite over a century of study, lyssa's expression is still mostly a mystery. When I reached out to San Francisco Protectorate University's head of pathology to discuss it, her answers to my questions were tentative at best. The general tenor of her responses were *"Well, we just don't have the data for that yet"* and *"it's hard to say."*

Even seemingly simple questions like *"why do a Were's eyes change after infection?"* are impossible to answer definitively even now, in the age of gene alteration and advanced technology. I'm not the only one left to wonder why it destroys a shifter's ability to transform, nor to ask what triggers the mating urge in a Were. It is possible these questions may never be answered.

I sit quietly in the passenger's seat as Vanessa confidently steers the truck around blind corners and roads nearly overgrown with verdant vegetation. There are a million questions I want to ask her, but I am not in the truck to needle her about theories around immune system compatibility or the role of fate in the creation of her kin.

I'm here to meet her parents.

It's an exquisitely rare privilege I've been given, and I grow progressively more humbled as we plunge deeper and deeper into the lush mountains of the Collective's territory. It feels like we are diving into an unknown world, and I can't help but sense that every tree is a sentinel standing guard.

I roll the window down and breathe in the cold, wet air. I can feel a storm on the way. The energy of it tingles beneath my skin, amping me up further.

"Almost there," Vanessa says after about an hour of quiet. I look over and find her proud shoulders are more relaxed, her beautiful face at ease.

Of course I researched where we were going before I got on the plane, but I can't help but note, "We're pretty far in the woods."

Vanessa shoots me a sly smile. "What? You afraid I'm taking you out here to kill you or something?"

I laugh. "You could have done that at the hotel."

"True. These babies can rip through steel." Her smile turns just a little vicious when she lifts one hand off the wheel to wiggle her manicured fingers at me. Like all Weres, Vanessa's human-looking nails could transform into inch-long, razor-sharp claws at will. It should be hard to imagine glamorous Vanessa ready to rip someone limb from limb, but it's not. There is something knife-like about her. When she glitters, it is because the edge of her blade is polished.

Her rings catch the light when she lowers her hand back to the wheel, fingers strumming over the seams in the synthetic leather. She appears to be playing a tune.

"Have you?"

"Ripped steel?"

I nod.

Vanessa purses her lips. "Never tested it myself, but my brother once rescued an off-roader pinned beneath his ATV by tearing through the engine with his bare hands. So... yeah, it's possible."

"Wow. I can't imagine having that much strength. Especially — I mean, especially if it's new to you, right?"

"Oh yeah, it's a shock to new Weres," she agrees, slowing to pull off onto what at first appears to be a narrow, overgrown shoulder. I grip my seat reflexively as she steers the vehicle toward what I would consider a footpath, barely visible from the road. We plunge ahead. Branches and vines slap the sides, roof, and windshield of the truck as we go.

Apparently unbothered by the noise, she continues, "We're way stronger than most people think. Most Weres kinda— I mean, they go out of their way to keep it under wraps. We don't need people being *more* scared of us, right? Everyone expects elves and orcs to be scary strong, but us? No. Problem is that then you get folks who are turned and have no idea how strong they are, which creates different issues."

I can see a bit of sunlight up ahead, through a break in the trees. It's a relief to know that soon we'll be off the tiny trail, but my fingers don't unlock until we exit the forest and are dumped onto a dirt road running parallel to a breathtaking lake.

We take another turn around an outcropping of gray, glittering rock and then I see it: across the narrow lake, a gorgeous, sprawling log home climbs up the mountain on the other side. The wood is honey-colored and even from a distance appears hand-hewn. Seen through a veil of mist rising off of the snowmelt lake, it looks like a rustic palace cradled by wilderness.

Breathing a little easier, I ask, "Like your mom?"

"Mom's a bit different," she answers, tilting her head from one side to another. "There aren't a whole lot of turned, submissive Weres. People who get bitten tend to be on the dominant end of the spectrum. More aggressive in general. Being a submissive— Well, she didn't know her own strength because submissives prefer flight over aggression. Unless provoked, of course."

I'm still staring at the fairy tale cabin when I ask, "Do you think she can rip through steel, too?"

"Can't say." Vanessa chuckles. "Though, I know for sure that her claws can rip through people just fine."

CHAPTER TWENTY-FIVE

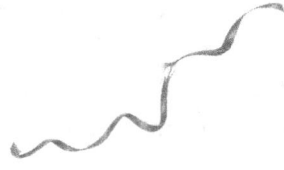

"SO THIS IS WHAT WE'VE PAID FOR."

Josephine sat perfectly still at the edge of her seat, her hands folded in her lap and her eyes down. The small man — compared to her father and Otto, at least — circled her slowly, his elegant, gold-ringed hands tucked behind his back as he examined her. She was not given his name. He was all false warmth when he introduced himself simply as, "Your father's patron."

Now his tone lacked even that hollow friendliness. The patron did not sound pleased at all.

Her father stood just off to the side, by the great stone mantel of the orcish fireplace. His face was shiny with sweat, his hair mussed, and his arms were crossed tightly over his chest. He was absolutely furious. Worse, he was also *terrified*.

Even her mother, who never appeared to know what was going on, watched the proceedings nervously from her seat on the velvet settee. She'd rushed to make herself presentable for their guest, but hadn't completely managed it. Dark tendrils of hair slid free of hastily stuck pins and hair net. The pale purple herringbone fabric of her dress was hopelessly pinched and rumpled in all the places it shouldn't be. Her eyes were bleary, bloodshot, and her cheeks pale.

Seeing as she usually napped until at least noon, Josephine strongly suspected she'd still been abed when the patron came down the lane.

In their life before lyssa, Evangeline was a refined and experienced hostess who often entertained witches of her circle. Josephine had vague memories of being forced into stiff gowns and told to sit silently as her mother's friends cooed over her as a child. Once they discovered she was arrant, Josephine was no longer cooed over. She was either expected to serve their guests or make herself scarce.

It was a terrible twist of fate to finally be the center of attention at the precise moment when she wished it least.

The only benefit to the change in her circumstances was that it was now Harrod who was dispatched to fetch the patron a drink — something she knew would prick his flimsy pride.

Her father's tight voice conveyed every ounce of his indignation when he said, "She is the source, not the final product, as you well know."

The patron didn't seem bothered by his waspish tone. "Indeed. I have seen the results of your work before, Doctor, and it is quite something. That's why we have continued to support you. I've never seen the infection in a woman, though, and find it intriguing how... delicate she appears compared to the others."

He circled her again. She held her breath as he settled his hands on her shoulders and addressed her father from over her head. His hands were unnaturally warm — nearly scorching her through the layers of her blouse and chemise. His scent was thick and cloying. It was herbal, smoky. Unusual and yet familiar at once, though she couldn't place it in her memory.

Those warm fingers gave her shoulders a small squeeze. "I am surprised to find Josephine is a lovely creature. You've done fine work with her and your other subjects, different as they appear to be."

This seemed to mollify her father some. In his haste to accept the praise, he didn't pick up on the *but* that hung in the air.

Chest puffing slightly, he opened his mouth to reply, but was stopped when the patron continued, tone cooling with rebuke, "However, first we were promised a new wave of witches for our ranks. Then we were promised an *army* of were-creatures. You have delivered on neither of those promises, Doctor."

Her father spoke through his teeth. "Science takes time."

Harrod emerged from the doorway beside the fireplace, a crystal glass of precious, war-rationed liquor in his hand. His expression was pinched when he hurried to cross the room, placing it on the side table by Josephine's chair.

"War moves fast," the patron replied, ignoring the offering. "And we have lost patience with your science, Doctor Wyeth. I've been sent to personally oversee your process and determine our next steps."

"Next steps? What next steps? Everything is moving as it should!" Her father sputtered, his outrage building. "You can't mean to take the project away from me now."

"Yes, I do."

A tremor moved through Josephine's frame. In response, one too-warm hand touched the side of her head. It was an almost fatherly gesture, as if he sought to comfort her, and yet she was absolutely certain that it was a threat. "We want an army, Doctor. We intend to get it."

It is strange, Josephine thought through the haze of cold dread, *that he speaks of an army as if he doesn't have one already.*

When they discussed her father's benefactors, Otto was certain it was the Orclind's government, the Iron Chain, supporting her father's research. He said there were rumors of monsters fighting amongst the orcish troops and that his own battalion had been assigned to investigate those rumors. It was the mission that landed him in her father's cell.

But the way the patron spoke didn't align with that theory. After all, the Orclind *had* an army. It was struggling to fight on two fronts and against two different armies, certainly, but it was still very much alive.

Perhaps he means a new army of weres. The thought was as disturbing as it was impossible.

Though she was different from the rest of her kind, Josephine understood that it was madness to try and form a cohesive, disciplined army out of werewolves. Not only did the patron not have their loyalty, but they struggled with rages, impulse control, and the ever-present threat of losing their minds during the full moon.

An army of them would not be a legion of fighting men. It would be a tide of pure devastation.

Her father uncrossed his arms to ball his fists at his sides. "I have explained in my letters why it is imperative that—"

The patron held up the hand that had cupped the side of her head. Josephine was discomfited to watch her father close his mouth with a sharp *clack*. Even her mother's bloodshot eyes widened with surprise at the sight.

Speaking in a low, fatherly cadence, the patron said, "Enough, Doctor. This is out of your hands now. We own this land. We own the food on your table. We own your subjects, your lab equipment, your bed." The tips of the man's fingers brushed the braid coiled around the crown of Josephine's head. "And we own your daughter."

He said nothing more for several moments, letting that truth settle over them all. Josephine's gaze darted around the room, taking in her mother's bemused, slightly slack expression, Harrod's pale face, and her father's reddened cheeks.

Never in all her life had she seen someone tell her father what to do. Everyone in his orbit existed at his whim. One did not challenge Doctor Wyeth.

This slight man, with a cloak of magic that hung like shimmering heat around him, did not challenge her father.

He *commanded* him.

It did not occur to Josephine until that moment that, in her limited experience of the world, she might have simply assumed that her father was a being of supreme authority. She had never imagined someone more powerful, more ruthless than him. Never would she have suspected that her father had fears, that there were men who even *he* would not cross.

To know that such a man existed, and that he was now claiming her as his property, was a terrifying realization.

Breaking the tense silence at last, the patron's voice took on a chipper note when he announced, "Now, here is how we will move forward: I am aware that you have a subject in custody at this very moment. I suspect by the lack of noise that he has yet to be bitten. We — excusing Madam Wyeth, of course — are going to adjourn to the barn, where I will oversee the administration of the bite."

Josephine jolted. *No.*

Her eyes roved wildly, desperate for some escape, some sign that her father would refuse. They were supposed to have one more night. They were supposed to have *time.* Had Otto even discovered the keys folded within the blankets? Certainly he had. She was supposed to sneak out in the night, before her door was bolted, and attempt the sigil on the door, supplies for their escape in hand. Free of his chains, they would make their escape.

That grand plan stood on the brink of ruin.

What would happen if they entered Otto's cell *now* to find him unchained?

Otto would fight. She knew that in her soul. He would fight until his last breath to free them both, but even the fiercest shifter might fall to so many witches in a confined space.

When Otto was subdued, all their planning would be for naught. Her father would inject him. His animal would die. Their chance at a future would evaporate before her eyes.

What could she do? *Nothing.*

The beast's rage wouldn't serve her now. Against Harrod? Her father? Perhaps she might have stood a chance, but not now, with two glamoured guards and the witch looming behind her? It would take more effort to subdue a kitten.

Her father didn't seem to realize just how powerless they all

were when he argued, "My experiments require a strict set of parameters and protocols—"

The guards moved subtly from where they stood against the
walls by the short staircase that led to the front door. It was the
smallest movement — the widening of a stance, straightening
shoulders, tensed fingers — but everyone in the room felt the air
change.

Still speaking pleasantly, the patron cut her father off. "Your
mistake is believing that your experiments are the important part,
Doctor. We do not care about your science. We do not care about
your parameters or protocols. We do not even care about *you.*"

The patron took one graceful step around the side of
Josephine's chair and held out his hand to her. Left with little
option, she slowly pressed her trembling fingers against the soft,
hot skin of his palm and rose from her seat. Her knees could
barely hold her weight.

"Now," he announced, shooting her a brilliant, cold grin as he
threaded her hand into the crook of his elbow, "let us make our
way to the barn. And then perhaps some lunch. Come along,
Miss Wyeth."

The trek across the yard was the longest of her life. Josephine felt every
step reverberate from the soles of her boots to the crown of her head.
She was deaf to everything except the rush of blood in her ears. There
was no sensation in the hand that rested in the crook of the patron's
elbow. Her mind was emptied of everything except a fear and grief the
likes of which she had never, in all her suffering, experienced.

Even the beast was quiet — struck dumb by incomprehensible fear for their mate.

It didn't matter that Otto consented to her bite. It didn't
matter that he demanded it, nor that he knew the consequences.
She felt in her heart that he still did not completely believe her

when she told him it would kill his animal. What sane man would consent if he *did*?

A person could not consent to what they did not fully comprehend. And even if he *did* know, she had fully intended on ignoring her unnatural urge to bite. She would *never* willingly steal Otto's soul, no matter what he demanded.

Josephine's gorge rose at the thought of what was to come. She wrestled with the urge to vomit up her breakfast as they made a grim procession across the yard.

The patron chatted gamely, completely unconcerned with the way her father's rage was beginning to turn his face purple, nor that she said not a word in response. He completely ignored Harrod, who hurried after them, helpless indignation grooving every long line of his face.

She barely heard the patron's comments on the state of the barn as one of his guards pulled open the cheerful red door. They paused as he ducked inside. A moment later he reemerged, nodded, and held the door for the party to enter.

Her vision narrowed into a pinprick. She moved on automation as the patron guided her forward. Her father must have pointed out which cell was Otto's because he led her right to it.

The urge to cry, scream, fight, run, or be sick all warred inside of her in the precious seconds it took for her father to step up and trace the sigil on dull metal door. Teeth gritted, he slid the bolt free and opened it.

The patron gently removed her hand from his elbow with a small, encouraging pat of her knuckles.

And there he was. *My mate.*

Josephine couldn't decide if she was relieved or horrified to find him still chained to the wall, his shackles linked. He hadn't even touched his breakfast.

He had, however, moved the blankets.

Josephine met his concerned gaze with a look of pure agony.

I'm sorry, she wished she could scream. *I'm sorry, my mate. I wasn't fast enough.*

If she'd acted the previous night, none of this would have happened. She'd had the keys. The chance. But he'd warned her not to move too quickly, that they had time to prepare, and that he would not tolerate her taking risks with her safety. They needed supplies, he said. They would be traveling through the wilderness to find his battalion. She was to be safe, to collect what they would need, and then release him. There was no rush.

She listened to him and now she bitterly regretted it.

If they somehow managed to escape, and if by some miracle he still wanted her after she killed his soul, then Josephine was quite certain she would never listen to him again.

The patron's impressed whistle bounced off of the stone walls. "Quite the specimen you've got, Doctor."

"Yes," her father answered impatiently. "A strong, healthy subject creates a much stronger were. This is why the process takes time."

"No, the process takes time because you are focused on *it* and not the *result.*" The patron made an annoyed chuffing sound and waved an elegant hand at the wall of unused cells. "Every one of those cells could be full, and yet you claim to only be able to accept one subject at a time? For what reason? Your daughter could bite several soldiers a day, every day."

"We do not have the staff—"

"Because you refused to accept ours," he cut in, a hair-raising thread of censure entering his pleasant voice. "You requested only your assistant, if I recall correctly."

"I don't trust outsiders."

The patron's eyes took on a strange quality then. A ring of pure white light formed around his pupils when he answered, "And we do not trust *you.* That is why I'm here."

It was a terrifying thing to see the true, raw power of a person one moment and then watch the mask come down again just as quickly. In what felt like a blink, the patron was once more jovial, his smile bright as he eyed Josephine speculatively, "How many men could she infect in a day?"

Josephine could almost hear her father's teeth grinding. "She only has so much venom. My estimate is three, if we were conservative with the dosage."

The patron's eyes glowed brighter. "Ah, another failing, then."

"What—"

"My dear Miss Wyeth," he said, turning to her with that unsettling fatherly look, "we are immensely grateful for your contribution to our efforts, but it appears you are not as efficient as we would like. Perhaps we will find better use for you when we return to the enclave. Tell me, Doctor, seeing as she is the only infected woman, have you attempted to breed her?"

Otto's chains clinked quietly in the shadows of the cell. A growl, so deep and low it was not truly discernible to the ear, thrummed in the air. Josephine squeezed her eyes shut, desperately attempting to stop the swell of nausea that threatened to drag her under.

It was Harrod who dared to answer. "Not— no, not yet. We have plans for her to be... We discussed the possibility of her bearing children."

"Ah, then perhaps we should investigate that possibility when we return. It would certainly be the long way 'round to making a were, but intriguing nonetheless." His eyes moved back to her father, dismissing Harrod with obvious contempt. As they did so, his kindly expression melted into one of cool displeasure. "You see, Doctor, we have been conducting experiments of our own. Miss Wyeth may only be able to infect three men a day, but our maximum has been fifteen."

Josephine swayed on her feet. *Fifteen a day? They don't need him.*

He didn't need to say it. The words hung in the air, nearly visible to the naked eye.

Her father said nothing. It looked as if he could not comprehend what the patron was telling him. Words tumbled from his lips, but they were plaintive, almost confused. "The... the lyssa Josephine carries is— the *purity* of the—"

The patron waved a hand, stopping her father's rambling. He turned back to her. "Now, my darling, let us get this over with so we might get some lunch and then begone from this dreadful place. A nip to the shoulder should do the trick."

Chapter Twenty-Six

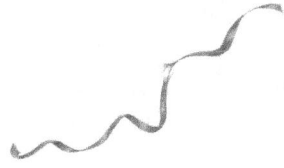

It was all happening too quickly for her to keep up with. She had only just grasped the fact that the patron and his people were infecting dozens of men a day when he gestured toward his guards with a flick of his fingers. Her heart seized when she watched them stride into the cell, intent on dragging Otto from where he sat on the floor.

Eyes glowing and voice pitched to an inhuman growl, Otto rose gracefully before they could set their hands on him. "No need to be rough, gentlemen," he rumbled. "I aim to cooperate, so long as no one threatens the woman."

"Lovely," the patron exclaimed, clapping his hands together. "My aim is never to harm a woman, you know. Goddesses tend to frown on that sort of thing."

He didn't believe in hurting women, and yet he intended to make her into a were broodmare? Josephine's clammy skin crawled.

As if sensing her disgust, her father's voice snapped like a whip behind her. "Do not fight this, Josephine. Not this time." It was clear to her that he believed his life now depended on her cooperation.

Refuse, the rational side of her demanded. *You always refuse. Make them take out the needle.*

She had never bitten another. Every time she fought, she denied her father the one thing she could. It was her final stand and one she became even more dedicated to after Rasmus. Never would she allow them to make *her* the one who changed them. They could beat her, prod her, sting her, rail at her. They could take away every comfort, every scrap of food or drop of water.

Still, they could not make her fangs extend. They couldn't *force* her to bite.

She'd fought it dozens of times over the years, but for the first time, her rebellion ran up against intense resistance.

Josephine couldn't draw in enough air as she stared into her mate's eyes. She could feel her racing pulse in the roof of her mouth. Her fangs extended with a deep, throbbing burn. All the while, Otto looked at her like she was the center of the universe, as if it was just the two of them there in the dusty shadows.

His mouth moved, forming words without saying them. *Come to me, kone.*

She wanted to fight. Everything in her raged at hurting him. It would kill her to steal his animal. It would do so much worse to discover he hated her after the fact.

But not doing so would force him to watch as her father plunged a needle into her flesh. There might be even more terrible consequences from the patron, whose capacity for cruelty was untested.

She would not be able to disguise the agony, and she had a gut feeling that seeing her tortured that way for his sake would destroy Otto as surely as the murder of his animal. It would hurt him immeasurably, and she had no doubt that he would never stand idly by as it happened. He'd defend her even if the cost was the exposure of their connection, their flimsy advantage. What would happen then?

There were no good answers. There was no escape.

Josephine's chin threatened to wobble as she forced her feet to move over the threshold and across the tile. Tears burned, hot and heavy, behind her eyes. *I'm sorry. I'm sorry. I'm so sorry.*

Otto's expression remained calm, encouraging. The warmth that glowed in his gaze threatened to undo her. *I know,* those eyes said. *It's all right, kone. Come to me.*

Tears began to fall. Not because of the guilt. Not because of her crushed hopes. She cried because she *wanted* to bite him. More than anything in the world, Josephine wanted to sink her fangs into the thick muscle between his neck and shoulder. She wanted to *claim* him.

I'm a monster.

What other word was there for a person who wanted so desperately to harm their mate? She was worthless. She did not deserve Otto's loving look, nor the low, rhythmic purr that filled the cell as she neared.

When it was all over, she would deserve his hatred.

In total, it must have only taken her a handful of seconds to cross the tile to stand before him. It felt like a lifetime.

His scent, rich and musky, filled her nose. That tether between them pulled taut, drawing her closer. Otto offered her a crooked smile.

It grew tense when the guards shuffled closer, reaching for his arms. Speaking with remarkable calm, he said, "I intend to cooperate fully, boys, but I'd appreciate it if you could give me and the lady some space."

"I apologize," the patron called from the doorway, his tone indulgent. "It's a habit. Shifters tend to fight when cornered, you see, and I'd rather not see you take a bite out of Miss Wyeth if I can help it."

"She's been nothing but good to me," Otto replied, eyes locked with hers. "I'd never hurt her. Not even now."

"You're much more amenable than most. Do you know what will happen to you?"

Otto's fingers twitched between them. His knuckles brushed the folds of her skirt. Josephine glanced down reflexively, her heart aching, and was bemused to see what looked like one of her ribbons threaded through the chain and knotted loosely around the loops that had once held the small iron lock securing his cuffs. Hidden against her skirt or tucked against his stomach, no one but her would notice.

His finger twitched again, upward this time. Josephine looked up and found him giving her an intense, pointed look. Speaking slowly, he answered the patron, "I do, but I'm an amiable type. It's in my nature, I suppose."

From behind her, the patron asked, as if inquiring about the health of a family member or the state of this year's crops, "And what nature is that, exactly? I'd love to know what kind of shifter grows as large as you."

A note of dry humor entered Otto's deep voice. "I don't see how that'll matter in a moment."

The patron snorted. "Very true! Might as well carry on then. You can tell me later."

Josephine couldn't stop the soft, pained sound that left her throat. Her fingers curled into fists by her sides as her mate gave her a warning look.

Slowly, he tilted his head to one side, exposing his left shoulder. "You'll have to move the collar," he instructed her, husky and warm.

The sound of his voice, the scent of him, the way he subtly swayed into her, set her aflame. Josephine tried to fight it. She raged against the compulsion that eroded her will, but it did her no good. Lust ran through her veins like warm honey, pooling in her belly, and the sweet ache in the roof of her mouth became unendurable.

Shuddering, crying, aware of every eye on them and yet *desperate* for him, Josephine lifted her hands to brace herself against the hot skin of his chest. His heart beat a thunderous rhythm beneath her curling claws.

Her blood rushed. Josephine the woman fell away, screaming all the while, as the beast took over.

Claim. Mark. Save him.

She arched onto her tiptoes and was only barely able to line her mouth up with the juncture of his neck and shoulder. A soft growl escaped her when his collar blocked her path. She pushed it up and out of her way, barely noticing how it seemed looser than it should have been, as her lip curled with a small snarl.

Otto was breathing fast when he dipped his head to rasp against her hair, "Remember, *kone*. Bite me deep."

She'd imagined what it would be like to bite him, shameful and horrifying as it was. Josephine had wondered how it would feel to thrust her razor-sharp fangs through that warm, salty skin. She'd grown wet and needy at the thought of him wearing a mark of her making. She'd even considered what his blood would taste like, how erotic it would be to know her venom ran through his veins, tying them together for all time.

Her imaginings paled in comparison to the real thing.

Her fangs slid smoothly through his skin. There was hardly any resistance at all, and the silken glide was its own strange, twisting pleasure. The taste of his skin burst on her tongue — tangy, salty, something unique that was just her mate. Josephine's claws curled into his chest, digging deep, as if her body feared he might try to pull away just as she fastened her grip on paradise.

And that was all before the *venom*.

Somewhere in the back of her mind, she knew she should be horrified by the way stars exploded in front of her eyes, how the sudden, shocking release of pressure in the roof of her mouth was a bliss so profound, she had no words to describe it.

Fire raced through her veins as wave after wave of pleasure rippled through her, following the rhythm of her heart. She could feel the venom draining from her in pulses, and with each one, Otto's breath stuttered, his hands twisting in the folds of her skirt. Sweat slicked his skin, making his taste all the more delicious.

From somewhere far away, she heard his whispered command, *"Harder."*

Aiming to please him, always to please him, Josephine bit

down until more than just her fangs were lodged in his flesh. Blood trickled out from the crescent-shaped wounds left by her upper and lower teeth.

Otto's chest rumbled beneath her hands as she felt the last of her venom leave her. Instinct compelled her to pull back, to ease the ache with her tongue and soft touches.

Mine, the beast sighed. *All mine.*

Strong hands closed around her arms, pulling her away. Josephine reacted blindly, her fury turning her into a wild thing as she kicked, clawed, hissed, and snarled. She didn't see the way Otto lunged for her, teeth bared, nor the way his eyes widened as she changed before him.

Josephine was not conscious of the fact that she had transformed into the beast. All she knew was that men were taking her from her mate. That he was in danger. That she would die before she let them be separated. That she would kill anyone who stood between them.

So she fought, claws swinging, lips pulled back from elongated fangs. A blow sent one man flying into the wall, and when another made to wrap his arm around her throat, choking her, she howled and kicked backwards, shattering bone.

Otto's roar of outrage was cut off as he fell to his knees on the tile, his body convulsing. Bloody spray erupted from his mouth to speckle the tile.

Josephine fought harder, more desperate to reach him than ever, but somehow they managed to drag her back over the threshold. She kicked and clawed and wailed, gouging anything and everything in reach.

Still, someone closed the door and bolted it shut. *Harrod.* She watched as he raced to draw the sigil on its surface, her vision a haze of red.

She screamed with guttural fury and lunged for him.

The patron's voice was pitched high with alarm when he commanded, "Restrain her. godsdamnit! Do *not* let her bite you and don't fucking damage her!"

Someone twisted a cruel hand in her hair, but she ignored it. Her attention was focused solely on the narrow-faced man who'd helped make her life pure misery, who thought to steal her future, who separated her from her mate when she needed him most.

She snapped her jaws a mere handful of inches from Harrod's stricken face, but was stopped from taking his nose by the hand in her hair. It wrenched her backward, snapping her neck into a painful angle and forcing her away from her prey.

Josephine landed hard on the packed earth floor and let loose a blood curdling howl. The guards pinned her to the ground. In this form her strength was much greater, but she was still a slight woman. She could not simply toss off two fully grown men when her limbs were pinned.

She fought, though. She would *never* stop fighting.

"You said she was docile!"

"She was," her father cried. His voice was pitched strangely, as if in pain. "She was! I don't know— she's never bitten anyone before. It could be that her instincts—"

"For Glory's sake, fucking *restrain* her!"

A fist slammed into the side of her head, but it only dazed her. Josephine knew from a decade of experiments that she could take much punishment in this form. They would not knock her out so easily.

Freeing one of her hands, she raked her claws down through the smoky glamour concealing the man's face. Blood sprayed over her as the flesh gave way.

The guard made an animal sound and reared backward, hands flying to his mangled face and throat, as Josephine turned on the other guard. He cursed as he grappled with her, but for once her size was an advantage. Josephine managed to wiggle out of his panicked grip long enough to pounce.

He fell to her claws, too, as she slashed them down across his chest and stomach. The beast wanted to finish the job, but it knew they didn't have time. Leaping from her gurgling, disemboweled victim, she regained her feet and focused on Harrod, who still stood in front of the door, petrified.

He raised his hands. An invisible force pushed her backward, the heels of her boots dragging through the dust, but even a telekinetic strike couldn't stop her.

The woman in her was not quite asleep. She was aware enough to remember all the times he helped her father slice her flesh, every moment of cold cruelty, the way he invaded her space, how he wished to make her his biddable wife.

He deserves more pain that I can possibly give him.

If the gods did truly exist, she hoped Grim, goddess of death, would press his face into the mud of her riverbank, choking him on slime and refuse until the end of days. Josephine would personally see him delivered to divine hands.

He must have seen death in her eyes, because he finally found the will to run. It was too late.

Josephine struck precisely, with every ounce of her strength. What had once been Doctor Harrod Pierce's head landed with a dull thump in the dust and rolled away. An arc of blood spewed, then sputtered pitifully as he crumbled. Harrod's body fell to the floor in an undignified heap just as the air behind her began to warm with unnatural swiftness.

"Now, Miss Wyeth," the patron called out, "Let us not—"

A beast's growl erupted from her throat. Crouching in front of the cell door, Josephine turned to look over her shoulder. The patron stood well away from her, hands up and glowing with that unnatural heat. He was inching toward the door of the barn, dragging the guard with the mangled face with him. Clearly terrified of being bitten, he'd decided to run.

Her father, meanwhile, lay in the dirt, his upper body propped up against one of the old, unrenovated stalls. His right leg was bent at an unnatural angle, pink bone and yellow fat bursting from his shin.

Her eyes shifted slowly between them as the beast weighed her options. They both deserved the reckoning of claw and fang, but who would come first?

The sound of chains clinking within the cell drew her back from the bloodlust that demanded she tear the heads off of those men, too.

Get my mate. Protect him. Keep him.

The words were a screaming wall of urgency in her mind. Ignoring Harrod's headless corpse, Josephine slapped her bloody palm against the door. She traced the sigil on the cold metal, leaving smears of his blood on the surface.

A heartbeat passed, then, with a familiar *pop* and metal tang, the door was unsealed.

She didn't have time to marvel at this development. She didn't have the presence of mind, either. Rising with a tearing, guttural sound, she grasped the bolt's handle and pulled.

She'd gotten it open a handful of inches before she was flattened against the floor by an explosion of magic so hot and bright, it blinded her.

At first she thought it was the patron, that he'd destroyed the barn and she'd simply yet to die, but less than a second later, she realized she recognized that great *boom* of energy from the fall of Washington, when even magically protected homes were wiped from the face of the earth.

It was the kickback of perimeter wards being broken.

Meadow Creek had been breached.

Urgency renewed, Josephine scrambled onto her feet and made to force the heavy door open. She didn't so much as get her fingers around the edge before something huge and heavy was thrown against it. She flew backward and landed with a wheeze against a stack of crates half-full of provisions.

Dust churned, choking her throat and nose. She opened watering eyes and, peering through the haze, was met with a beast of incomprehensible size and strength.

He burst through the doorway, knocking out the doorframe without hesitation. Through the haze, she watched him raise up onto his hind legs until his snout nearly touched the rafters and let out a roar so terrible, she could not imagine its like existed anywhere else in the world.

Black, blood-flecked lips peeled back from teeth the length of her hand as his forelegs crashed back down onto the packed earth. A magnificent head clothed in white fur, blocky in shape and tipped with a square black nose, swung in her direction. Wild eyes of gold fixed on her with a look of raw hunger.

It took him less than a stride to cross the barn. In what felt like a blink, he was standing over her — a monument to power, to animal magnificence.

Josephine froze. The beast in her breast held her there, perfectly still. Waiting for recognition.

And then those lips slowly uncurled from his great teeth. His head dropped. One paw, tipped with black claws the length of her middle finger, settled gently on her chest. He pinned her there with its weight alone. Even the tiniest bit of pressure might have crushed her ribcage to pulp, but he did no such thing.

A cold, wet nose snuffled at her hairline, down over her cheek, and beneath her chin. Josephine didn't dare breathe. For a moment he was perfectly still, his breath gusting in great bellows over her bloody skin, before a familiar sound boomed from his chest.

A purr.

She exhaled, her muscles loosening, and went completely limp beneath him. "My mate," she breathed, tears clogging her nose. "H-How is this... How is this *possible?*"

Of course, he had no answers for her in this form. A hot tongue bathed one side of her face, cleaning up the blood that dripped from a cut above her temple. Tears streamed through the dirt and blood. He licked those up, too.

Josephine basked in the touch, in the relief of staring up at an animal that was so incredibly deadly. She had no idea how it was possible, nor if it would last, but she would not take this time with him for granted.

She dared to raise her hand, touching the massive paw holding her down, and sighed at the softness and density of his fur. The drawings she'd seen in her father's natural history books didn't do even a speck of justice to the grandeur of the creature tending to her.

The moment was broken by the sound of a man's pained grunt. Otto's massive head lifted and snapped in the direction she knew her father lay, broken and bleeding. She watched his nostrils widen with a deep breath. His lips peeled back from his teeth once more. Bloody strings of saliva hung like spiderwebs between his jaws when he opened them wide.

A growl like rolling thunder filled the barn as the pops of gunfire and the shouts of men came through the partially opened door.

Otto gently lifted his paw from her chest and took one menacing step toward her father before he stopped and swung his head to look back at her.

Josephine saw the question in his eyes. In the split second between meeting his gaze and opening her mouth, she recalled every horror her father had put her through, all the lives he'd stolen, and Rasmus's screams as he realized what had been done to him. She remembered how he'd treated his shameful arrant daughter. She felt every injection, skipped meal, and prolonged period without sleep. She remembered how he'd asked Harrod about impregnating her over dinner, as if it meant nothing. She *remembered*.

It was Josephine, not the beast, who spoke. "Do it."

Otto let out a chuff of pure pleasure before he wheeled his great body around and, with a leap of his powerful legs, descended on her father.

Josephine turned her gaze away. He hadn't earned the dignity of a witnessed death.

He'd earned nothing but her contempt — and all the rage of a polar bear avenging his mate.

CHAPTER TWENTY-SEVEN

FROM THE WORLD HEALTH MEDICAL DIAGNOSIS Handbook—

LYSSA

Definition: *Lyssa (LYS-93) is a previously deadly virus spread through the saliva of infected beings, once exclusively vampires, now any being besides elves. The LYS-93 virus is most commonly transmitted through a bite but can also be transmitted via blood contamination.*

Before the Wyeth mutation (WY-1860), once a person began showing signs and symptoms of lyssa, the disease was considered one hundred percent fatal. Fatal cases are now less than one percent of infected. The modern LYS-93 virus (post-WY-1860) comes in two forms: dormant and active. Infected are considered dormant when not under the influence of the full moon or endangered. Infected are considered active when they show marked physical changes, such as extended canines, shifted claws (darkened and elongated), and extreme aggression.

Like vampirism (VAM-92), it is classified as a hereditary virus and has so far been passed to all recorded offspring with no exception.

Timeline of infection: *The first symptoms of lyssa usually begin within six hours of infection, but have been recorded as beginning as soon as two minutes after a bite.*

Symptoms may include: *fever, headache, nausea, bloody discharge from the lungs, agitation, confusion, excessive energy, inability to sleep, excessive salivation, and muscle spasms. An infected shifter will also lose the ability to change into their animal form.*

Magical ability: *The slight expansion of m-paths has been noted in infected beings previously unable to use magic. This is believed to facilitate the transformation of limbs, fangs, claws, etc, in the same way magic allows a shifter to transform into their animal. Some infected have reported the ability to use basic sigils and previously unknown abilities, but this is still being studied.*

Relation to the moon cycle: *Weres are commonly believed to be much more active during the full moon, leading to the myth that the moonlight itself creates a sort of "frenzy" in the infected.* **This is untrue.** *Research has shown that the excessive energy during the full moon corresponds to increased viral load, which reaches its peak roughly every 28 days.*

Exceptions: *If a patient knows for a fact that they have been bitten by someone carrying the lyssa virus and a matebond has been formed, they are unlikely to ever experience the active form of LYS-93, due to the antigen produced by the vector at the time of the bite. This antigen can only be produced once in a were's lifetime. In the case of a matebond and subsequent injection of the antigen, a shifter will never contract the active form of the virus and therefore retain the ability to shift.*

Chapter Twenty-Eight

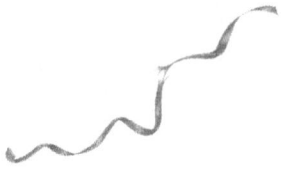

It wasn't that Otto hadn't believed his mate when she told him about lyssa. He believed that *she* believed it. Clearly something was going on, and since Josephine was a being he'd never seen before, he was forced to accept her explanation — and the danger she warned of — as the truth.

Still, he was a bear.

His kind tended to be hard-headed. Once they got something in their minds, they were loath to change it. They also tended to seek out the simplest answers to their questions. In this case, the simplest answer was *not* that his mate had a previously deadly disease that would kill his bear once he was infected, but that she was simply something new. They would figure out what that was together, after she was safe.

Otto had been working on their plans for escape for two days. He didn't want to take Josephine any closer to the front than he had to, but he also knew that he now possessed the intelligence his battalion had been sent to retrieve, making his return to Alliance lands imperative.

Lee Seymour, commander of the Northern Alliance forces and a friend, needed to know what was happening in the Orclind.

Someone, probably the Iron Chain, was making a new breed of soldiers to fight in the war and Josephine was the proof they needed.

Once they were reunited with his battalion and the information passed on, Otto would be expected to pull back from the military and be reassigned to the civilian guard. Mated men couldn't be expected to fight on the front line, after all. Instinct would never allow them to leave their mates and cubs unguarded. Luckily, that same impulse made them perfect for defending towns and cities.

Otto would request a reassignment to somewhere close to the northern border, to the smallest town they could find. He wanted Josephine somewhere quiet and as safe as could be expected in the war. A part of him wished to abscond with her to the Northern Territories, but he worried his mate wouldn't handle the rugged life well. Certainly, making the journey all the way back to Nuuk to stay with his parents wasn't an option, either.

His priority was keeping his mate safe. Unfortunately, there were few good options available to him. Certainly Meadow Creek, as he'd recalled the morning of the fourth day in the cell, was *not* safe.

His memory had come back to him in pieces. The morning of the first day of *stage two,* as his mate called it, Otto woke with a jolt against the cold tile floor. As usual, he woke agitated and confused, his instincts in a riot over the fact that his mate was not within reach, but as the fog cleared, his patchwork dreams came back to him.

Standing by a fire in their camp, listening to Rafael and Miles discussing the letters they'd received from their packs.

Sipping the boiled oat water they tried to pass off as a replacement for coffee as he stared bleakly into the flames, wondering what the fuck his life had come to.

Being summoned to the command tent, where Collin, Lee's second, was stooped over a map. "There's activity here," he'd said, pointing to a speck of nothing just on the other side of the Black Hills. "But we don't know what it is. Looks like a homestead. The hawks have come back saying there's routine shipments going in and out. We need to know what they're doing there."

The dream grew hazy then, filmy like the first frost on a lake, before he was suddenly beneath a hulking orc carrying a battle hammer, fighting to shift but pinned beneath the man's massive foot in the mud.

He woke up gasping, reaching for Josephine, and upon finding her missing, tore at his chains until reason slowly trickled in alongside the watery light of dawn through the tiny window over his head.

"There's activity here," he kept hearing Collin say, over and over, as he regained his bearings. *"But we don't know what it is. Looks like a homestead."*

And then, just as he forced himself up onto his bare feet to stumble toward the toilet, the memory snapped into focus.

Meadow Creek. The name was scrawled in messy handwriting just above that tiny speck on the map.

They weren't simply close to the front. They were his battalion's *target.*

Otto had spent every moment after that revelation frantically debating the best course of action. He knew that he'd been in the cell for a handful of days. In all likelihood, his men were already within spitting distance of the homestead, creeping across the border in their shifted forms to avoid detection.

This was good and bad.

On one hand, it was a relief to know that at any moment they would arrive to rescue him. On the other, he worried that they couldn't wait for that to happen. What if he was still locked up when they arrived? His men would never hurt a woman if she didn't attack first — particularly a submissive — but Otto had no idea what her madman father would do if backed into a corner.

Would he execute his daughter to save his secrets? Would Josephine get caught in the crossfire?

It wasn't a risk he could take.

So when she arrived, escorted by the lean-cheeked creature who looked at her like he wanted to get his spidery hands under her skirt, Otto decided they would go ahead with their plan to escape in the night. His keen ears had picked up his one-sided conversation with Josephine about what he expected from her, how he would have her in his bed soon enough. He heard it *all*. It took every last wisp of his restraint to keep from snapping his teeth at the witch.

The bear wanted to challenge him. The bear wanted to feel the crunch of his weak little bones between his jaws. The bear wanted to pull out the bloody ropes of his intestines through his fucking *mouth*.

But he couldn't. Not yet. Otto wanted nothing more than to wring Harrod's head from his scrawny neck, but avenging his mate came second to making sure she was safe.

Otto inspected the breakfast Josephine had delivered, noting with a smile that she'd apparently snuck him a far greater portion than normal. He decided that, should his men not take care of things, would simply have to return to handle Harrod and her father.

Finding the keys tucked into the blankets made him grin with unvarnished pride. *My brave mate,* he thought, burying his nose in the blankets that carried her earthy, luscious scent. *We'll be free soon.*

It took some doing, but he managed to unlock the shackles around his ankles and wrists, then the collar. The urge to shift was impossible to ignore. Never in his life had he gone more than a day without handing the reins over to the bear, and now that he was free, Otto took the risk. Leaving his shackles and linen pants in a heap, he let the animal out at last.

His magic, boiling hot in his veins with the mating fever, exploded.

The joy he felt was immense, animalistic. He wanted to roar

with it, but managed to keep the terrifying sound locked in his throat as he stretched out in the cramped confines of the cell.

In this form, he barely fit. An average-sized polar bear would have struggled, but shifters were almost twice the size of their animal counterparts. Even so, the freedom of the shift made the man inside nearly weep with joy.

Settling back on his haunches, he turned to look out the small window, nose twitching as he sought out his mate's scent. A deep, possessive rumbling erupted from his chest as he picked up the thread.

Not a moment later, the bear's keen eyes found her slim form crossing the courtyard with Harrod, her arm caught in his cruel grip.

His lips peeled back from his teeth. The man knew caution. He knew that they could not charge across the courtyard to bite the head off Harrod's shoulders for laying a hand on his mate.

But the bear didn't care about that. All he knew was the power of his limbs and the absolute certainty that Josephine was *his*.

Huffing with aggression, he watched as they stopped just before the circular house. Harrod made the mistake of taking one threatening step toward his mate as she ripped her arm out of his grasp.

Otto, mindless in his rage, threw himself against the stone wall. The barn shuddered under the force of his nineteen-hundred pound weight. Unfortunately, the wall was of fine orcish stonework. Each stone was carefully hewn to fit flush with its partners, making all but the thinnest amount of mortar necessary. Held together primarily by tension and its own weight, not even a blow from a fully grown male polar bear shifter in the grips of the mating fever would knock it down.

Not without considerable effort, at least.

Whipped into a frenzy of desperation, the bear tried again. His paws, big as barrel lids, beat and clawed the stone as he fought to get to his mate. *Need her,* the bear thought. *Protect her!*

The only thing that stopped him from breaking the window, fear of discovery long discarded, was the arrival of a carriage. There was a ripple of magic as the wards around the homestead bent to allow it through the old gate.

His hot, furious breaths fogged the window as he watched the sleek black carriage pull to a stop in front of the house. Both horses, great beasts nearly as tall as him, stomped their hooves and glanced restlessly at the barn as the occupants climbed out.

Much to both man and bear's frustration, the carriage blocked his view of his mate and the front of the house. By the time it moved, his mate was gone.

It took an enormous amount of willpower to keep himself from panicking. It took even more to force his shape back into the man.

Instincts told him that something was wrong, and that being caught out of his chains — even in the nearly unkillable form of the bear — was a bad idea. Certainly *he* could survive just about anything, but Josephine was delicate. Gods knew what might happen if she got caught in a fight.

Donning his trousers once more, Otto cursed as he attempted to reshackle himself. It wouldn't do to *lock* the cuffs or collar, of course, but he had to make it look like they were on in case anyone came sniffing around his cell. The illusion was easily accomplished with his ankles and collar, as they rested against the tops of his feet and the base of his throat, but his wrist cuffs proved trickier.

After some doing and plenty of muttered Danish curses, Otto reluctantly used Josephine's ribbon to tie the cuffs together. Should he need to change with a moment's notice, the ribbons would tear and the other restraints would pop off, freeing him.

That done, all he could do was wait.

What felt like hours later, his sensitive ears picked up the sounds of multiple people approaching the barn. An unfamiliar man held up most of the conversation, speaking to Josephine with a fake sort of deference that made Otto's teeth grind.

And then they were in front of his cell. Otto's stomach dropped.

Infecting others. Taking Josephine away. Breeding her. Infecting him.

Emotion whipped through him in great bursts: Rage. Bloodlust. Fear. Disgust.

He believed Josephine when she warned him about the infection, but the weight of the knowledge didn't truly hit him until that moment. It wasn't just her, who might have been fed misinformation by her abusive father over time, nor the doctor, who thought that he would lose his animal once bitten.

It was *all* of them. They'd tested it. By the sounds of it, they'd tested it *dozens and dozens* of times.

Otto's ears rang. His breath moved in and out of him in heavy, panicked gusts. The bear paced in the back of his mind, afraid and confused and frantic with worry for their mate, as the information sank in.

It wanted Josephine's bite with a deep, instinctive urgency, a yearning made all the more acute by forty years of deprivation and violence, but it didn't want it like this. It wanted her willing. It wanted her love.

Of course, the bear also didn't want to die.

How would it protect her if it no longer lived? It wanted to run with her, to know the joy of curling around her at night. It wanted to bury its nose in her hair and listen to her breathe as she slept, safe and content in their den. It wanted to teach their cubs how to swim and watch them play in the snow. The idea that he could not have her bite and also live to know those pleasures was utterly inconceivable.

The *man* couldn't fathom it either. Who would he be if he could no longer shift?

The very idea had made his skin crawl before. Now, faced with the very real possibility, his stomach threatened to purge itself on the tile floor.

He'd only just swallowed the rising bile when the door to his cell was opened.

There she is.

All at once, the tumult inside him died away. What was left was the familiar wonder he experienced every time he looked at his lovely wife, with her dark hair and striking eyes. He was attuned to her rapid breathing, the scent of her skin and fear.

Her eyes were huge and gleaming with tears. Never in all his life had he seen an expression of such profound pain as when Josephine gazed at him from the doorway.

He'd vowed to her that he would have her bite, no matter the consequences, and he'd meant it then.

That conviction paled in comparison to what he felt at that moment.

The bear settled into perfect stillness in the back of his mind. He wasn't a sophisticated creature, but he understood enough.

A shifter only chose a mate once, and the loyalty to them went beyond vows, beyond the desire to procreate and form a pack. It was a connection of the soul — immeasurable, utterly unique, and irreplaceable. The bear accepted that bond the moment she laid her hands on him that first time, and in so doing, it also accepted the fact that it would die to protect her.

If protecting his mate meant losing his life, then really, it wasn't such a terrible trade. She was worth it. She was worth a thousand of his lives.

So he didn't fight it, though he could have. At any moment, he could have burst from his shackles, shifted, and eviscerated the glamoured guards. But in the tiny space of the cell, outnumbered as they were, that would have put Josephine at tremendous risk.

Instead, Otto felt a blanket of calm descend on him as he silently encouraged his mate to come to him. If this was it, then he was determined to take her bite on his terms. He would make it about *them*. He would enjoy it, consequences be damned.

It took everything in him not to clasp her to him as she sank her hot little fangs into his throat. His erection strained against his thin pants, painful and throbbing, with the pinch of her teeth. Stars exploded in front of him when a flood of warmth bloomed from the tiny wound.

Fuck, he thought, battling the urge to bear her down onto the floor and bury himself between her thighs. The need to sink his own teeth into her throat was a screaming instinct that nearly drowned out everything else, even their audience.

Euphoria set in, muddling that pounding need. Tingles spread through him as his mate's little bite went pleasantly numb. He could still feel her as she licked the wound, pressing the softest, loving kisses there, but there was no pain. In fact, as the seconds ticked by, he began to feel a tiny bit *drunk.*

The thought that her bite was the best feeling in the world had barely drifted through his hazy mind before the warm tingles morphed into heat. In what felt like the span of a heartbeat, he was on fire.

His muscles seized. Otto could do nothing as Josephine was dragged away, howling with rage. He collapsed onto the floor as spasms wracked his body. His lungs burned as they, too, shriveled. He coughed reflexively, desperate for air, and a spray of bloody foam covered the tile in front of him.

Everything — every sinew, every nerve, every follicle — was agony.

Otto was only distantly aware of the cell door closing, of the screams and commotion outside. He could only focus on how he writhed on the floor, the way his eyes burned as if seared by a naked flame, and the roaring of the bear in his mind.

Fight! the bear bellowed. *Get up! Protect our mate!*

He couldn't get up. He couldn't even think. There was no room for anything more than pure endurance as the flames licked up from the inside out, consuming the man until he was naught but cinders on the cell floor.

And then, as if some force had dumped water on those flames, the heat died.

Otto curled into a ball on the cold, blood-speckled floor and retched until there was nothing left in him. His ears were blocked with his own labored breathing, the rush of blood, such that he couldn't hear anything that happened outside of his cell — until his mate's scream penetrated the fog.

Josephine was in trouble. She needed him. She was fighting on the other side of that door while he lay prone, as weak as a cub. Desperation was enough to see him up onto his hands and knees, but no further.

He willed himself to shift. Nothing happened.

Otto retched again, this time from grief as he registered the silence in his mind. Was it true, then? Was his bear dead? It did not *feel* as though a part of him had died, but then why was it so hard to shift? Where was—

The sounds of fighting reached him just as the scent of coppery blood did.

Fight! he thought. *You aren't dead! Fight, you stubborn fucking animal!*

Otto let loose a roar of fury as he clawed at the tile. He would not give in. He would *not* allow the bear to die — not now, after everything, after so many years of violence, after finding their mate and being so fucking close to a future they hadn't dared to hope for.

He wouldn't allow it. *We have a mate to protect! Don't you dare leave her to just me!*

At first there was nothing. No response. No familiar animalistic presence in his mind, him but separate. Otto refused to concede defeat even as he was wracked by more spasms, by rising and crashing waves of pain and the clammy sweat of fever.

Come back, he ordered, tears dripping down his sweaty cheeks and into his unkempt beard. *Come back to me!*

The door to his cell began to open. A razorblade of yellow light bisected the floor. Josephine's scent, tangled with fresh blood and putrid fear, slapped him across the face.

From somewhere deep in his mind, buried under shadow and ash left by the flame of lyssa, the bear roused.

Magic boiled in his veins. A sense of tearing, a great rending somewhere deep in his breast, accompanied the shift. Josephine's ribbon tore as he broke free of his shackles. The bear swayed on his feet, unsteady and gripped by pain, until his mate cried out on the other side of the door.

CHAPTER TWENTY-NINE

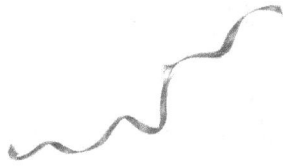

OTTO BURST FROM THE BARN, HIS MUZZLE STREAKED with blood and his mate limping behind him, to find the once sleepy homestead swarming with shifters. Acrid smoke hung in the air from the burning home across the yard. The turf roof smoldered, leaking smoke, while the beams and doors crackled with licking flames.

Some of his men were shifted while others stood on two legs, carrying rifles and dressed in faded uniforms. A few stood over a dazed, ash-streaked woman sitting in the dirt, while others darted in and out of the burning home carrying what books, trunks, supplies, and paperwork they could. There was no sign of the small man in the linen suit, nor the other guard.

He wanted to believe they were dead, but the only scent of fresh blood emanated from the barn, so he doubted it.

A howl of welcome went up as he emerged from the barn. Otto stood on his hind legs and roared back, half in greeting and half as a warning to stay away from the woman cowering against his back.

He could feel Josephine's little fingers twisting in his fur as a massive, gray-streaked wolf loped up to them and leapt from side to side, tail thrashing.

It was Rafael. Intelligent eyes of warm amber gleamed up at him as he barked and yipped with wolfish delight. Normally, Otto would have greeted his friend with a light swat of his heavy paw, but not this time. Lip lifting in a warning snarl, he dropped onto all fours and backed up, pushing Josephine into the side of the barn. If anyone wanted to see her, too bad. They'd have to get through a polar bear first.

Rafael cocked his head to one side, triangular ears moving, before he lifted his nose and scented the air. He blinked. Slowly, he sidestepped, eyes focused on the treasure Otto was clearly guarding.

Instincts in a riot and lyssa raging in his blood like fire, Otto couldn't tolerate the wolf's nearness to his unclaimed mate. Lifting himself up again, he dropped down onto his front paws with enough force to shake the earth between them and let loose a deep warning growl. *Back off!*

"Rafael, get your ass away from him *now*."

Otto swung his head to the side and found a welcome sight: Lee Seymour himself striding toward them, his rifle slung across his back and dark skin sheened with sweat. He was taller and a bit leaner than Otto, with a deep chest and long legs capable of running like no one Otto had ever seen before. An even-tempered elk shifter with a keen, tactical mind, Lee was the best commander the Alliance could boast.

Icy blue eyes took in Otto's territorial stance with perfect calm even as he grasped the wolf by the scruff and effortlessly tossed him to the side. Rafael yipped and sprang back with a growl. One hard look from Lee, however, sent the wolf loping off again, his tail a bit lower.

Lee propped his hands on his hips. "Shit, Otto. I'd say it's good to see you, but I don't think you'd return the sentiment. Would be nice to get a little gratitude for tracking your ass back here, you know. Care to shift and tell me what the fuck is going on?"

He knew he had to. Lee needed to know what had happened

here, what Josephine and all the other subjects of Doctor Wyeth's experiments were. But the more he tried to force down the aggression, the harder it became.

There were too many people near his mate. The stench of blood and ash in the air clogged his nose. He could still taste Doctor Wyeth in his mouth, could still hear his screams as Otto ripped him apart. He wanted to do it again. Bloodlust and aggression ran high in blood so hot, it felt like liquid fire.

Threats were everywhere. How could he shift? He couldn't protect his mate that way.

It had never been difficult to move between forms, but Otto suddenly found himself fighting the bear and the bear fighting him, neither willing to give up ground. Like in the cell, it was as if he had to reach deeper, try harder to connect with the bear. What was once effortless now took work. Focus.

Too bad focusing was almost impossible when all he wanted to do was snatch up his mate between his jaws and run off with her.

A growl built in his throat as the bear took stock of Lee and the men who had begun to gravitate toward them. Could they run? One swipe of his paw and—

"My mate." Josephine's shaky voice, no more than a hoarse whisper, snapped him back to reality. Her little hands shook as they petted his side, soothing him. "C-Can you turn back? Please?"

For you? Anything.

The thought had barely passed through his mind before his magic surged, hotter than it ever had. In a blink, he stood on two feet again, considerably shorter than he was a moment ago.

His muscles screamed and nausea threatened again, but Otto grit his teeth and pressed himself back against Josephine, shielding her from view.

It didn't do a bit of good.

Immediately, all eyes turned to his mate. It didn't matter that she pressed her cheek between his shoulder blades, nor that she made herself as small as possible. It only took a glimpse for the shifter instinct to know exactly what she was.

A ripple of sound moved through the assembled men. Expressions of astonishment and worry grooved every grimy face. As one, they all took a step back.

Except Lee, of course.

The commander stood his ground, though his eyes did widen with surprise when Josephine began to make a high-pitched, anxious purr — the surest sign of a terrified submissive. Otto's heart squeezed. Reaching back, he wrapped his arm around her and tried to better conceal her with his naked body.

"Who've you got there, Otto?" Lee asked, eyes drifting slowly down to the little bloody bite in the juncture between his neck and shoulder. The homestead was quiet except for the sounds of the fire, as if everyone was holding their breath as they awaited his answer.

Spots were exploding in front of his eyes, but Otto forced himself to stand up straight and answer, "My mate. Josephine."

"Shifter?"

He felt her stiffen and despite the awkward position, attempted to pull her even closer. "No. Something else."

"All right." Lee kept his eyes on Otto when he called out, "Miss, are you in need of assistance?"

Do you need me to separate you?

Otto bared his teeth at the elk shifter, furious at the idea that he would think to remove Josephine from him. He took one step forward, but could go no farther. His vision pitched dangerously to one side a second before his body followed suit.

"Otto!" Josephine's cry of alarm filtered in from a great distance. A moment before his vision failed, he caught sight of her leaning over him, her face streaked with blood and features pulled tight with terror. Her lips moved, but he couldn't hear a word she said.

Blackness swept him under as the flames consumed him, body and soul.

~

He was moving. That was all he knew when he woke some indeterminate amount of time later.

Otto's mind felt as though it were stuffed with cotton and his body had the achy clamminess of a fever recently broken. When he finally mustered the will to open his eyes, he found himself staring up at the cloth-covered ceiling of a carriage. Moonlight spilled in through small windows mostly obscured by swaying curtains of heavy brocade.

What on Burden's Earth...

He flexed his muscles, trying to wake sleeping limbs as he struggled to get his bearings, and discovered the soft weight of a slight body beside him.

The scent of botanicals and fresh, clean woman was a balm to the panic that had begun to close its fist around his throat. He *knew* that scent.

"*Kone,*" he rasped, turning his head to discover her sleeping form tucked against his side. One of her hands was fisted in the blanket draped over his naked chest. Even in sleep, her brows were pinched with worry, her rosebud lips pursed.

He was groggy, sore, and felt vaguely sick, but that did not stop the fever from heating his blood, nor his cock from giving a deep throb of interest when she rubbed her calf against it.

Cursing softly, he lifted one weak hand to cup the side of her head. *What happened?*

After her bite, everything was a smudge in his mind. He recalled terrible pain, the hot rush of the shift, and then... not much else. He only vaguely recalled blood in his mouth and then Lee's sharp voice from across the yard.

Lee? Yes, that was right. Lee had come with the battalion and... Everything else eluded him. A growl of frustration rattled his chest.

Josephine jolted awake under his hand. "Otto!"

Dropping his arm to tangle his fingers in the long, loose fall of her hair, he turned his head to peer down at her. "Good evening, *kone*."

Even in the dark, he could see the tears gathering in her lashes.

With a soft, mournful sound, Josephine threw herself on his chest and began to rain kisses on his cheeks, brow, jaw, and neck. "You're *awake*," she gasped between pecks. "Gods, you are finally awake!"

"Hush, hush now." He pressed her head down until her nose was tucked under his jaw, her lips aligned with her bite. Otto felt her hiccuping breaths as tears soaked his bare skin.

"I am well, *kone*," he assured her, though he wasn't at all certain that was true. He hadn't felt this weak since he was a cub! "Do not cry. Please, for your mate. The sight of tears wounds me, sweet Josephine."

"I'm sorry," she sobbed. "I'm sorry. I'm sorry for everything. If I could do it all again I would. I wish I had. I shouldn't have listened to you! I'm—"

"Josephine, calm."

The hard command startled her out of her fit. She stilled, breaths puffing against his throat, and slowly curled her fingers into the flesh and wiry hair of his chest. "I thought I might lose you," she whimpered.

Otto wrapped his arms around her slim back, noting the fact that she was dressed in nothing but a cotton nightgown, and pressed her more tightly against him. "Never."

"You've been feverish for three days. I was starting to worry you'd never wake up again."

"How could I die when I have not given you all I promised?" he asked, rubbing his lips against the soft, wispy hair that marked her hairline. "No, *kone,* I will not die until you and I are gray. We have many, many years yet."

She shuddered, nodding frantically, and pressed a reverent kiss to her bite. The simple touch only inflamed him more. *Nothing* was as pleasurable as attention to a mating bite. He felt that tiny kiss all the way to his fucking toes.

Trying to get a handle on the lust that threatened to make a fool out of his weakened body, Otto asked, "What has happened?"

Now stroking his chest, she answered, "After you collapsed, Lee said we needed to get over the border as soon as possible to get you help. The— the patron escaped with an m-gate, so we took his carriage. The men helped me make it comfortable for you and then we left with everything they could carry. Mother is with us too, but she's kept apart from everyone because she won't stop weeping. Mostly we've traveled at night. We passed over the border just this morning."

That was all good news and plenty to digest, but all he could think was, "Were they kind to you, *kone?* Have you been frightened?"

A submissive around an entire battalion of strange war-hardened, dominant shifters? A submissive whose mate was unconscious and might be dying? The more he thought of it, the more he felt like an idiot for asking. *Of course* she was frightened. Guilt lodged in his throat like a ball of thorns.

Some mate I've been.

Perhaps feeling his agitation, Josephine reached up to stroke his cheek and the rough hair of his beard with her gentle fingers. "They have been very kind," she assured him, sounding both shy and pleased. "They ask me at least ten times a day if I need anything, and they are very careful not to startle me. Lee said that anyone who scares me will get a week on latrine duty. It's been— I am grateful. I don't think I've ever been treated so respectfully."

The tension left him in one great exhale. *Thank the gods. I didn't want to have to kill anyone.*

"And you're well?" he pressed, hands running up and down her slim frame, searching for bandages, splints, stitches.

Josephine's breath hitched when his fingers skimmed the undersides of her breasts. "Yes. Only bumps and a few bruises."

"Thank the gods." He cupped her breast possessively, feeling its warm weight in his palm. The mating fever, forced to a simmer by his illness, roared to life.

Otto's heart beat faster when the faintest scent of her arousal, rich and sweet, reached him. *Need to touch her,* instinct demanded, desperate for her after so many days without. *Need her. Need her so bad it hurts.*

He was too weak to fuck her, and wouldn't do so in a moving carriage driven by a sharp-nosed and even sharper-eared shifter, but he couldn't stop himself from reaching down to hitch her leg higher up on his hip, pressing her cunt against his straining cock. Even with the layers of her nightgown and the blanket between them, it was bliss.

The rock and sway of the carriage made them both groan.

"My mate," he whispered, pressing kisses to her hairline and down her cheek. "I'm starving for you."

Josephine made the softest, neediest sound in the back of her throat. Still, she managed to protest, "You need to rest—"

"I need my mate," he growled, low enough that shifter ears wouldn't hear it over the clatter of hooves and creaky carriage. After all the fear, after days of drifting in the fever without her, he felt the desire to touch Josephine like knives running over every inch of his skin. "I need to feel you, *kone.*"

Blood rushed in his ears as he grabbed a fistful of her nightgown and wrenched it up around her waist. Josephine made that needy sound again. Pressing one kiss after another against the bite, she began to rock her hips against him in time with the sway of the carriage.

Otto slid his hand around the back of her thigh, over the silky curve of her backside, to find her cunt hot, wet, and ready for him.

He had to squeeze his eyes shut and grit his teeth to avoid spilling under the damn blanket. "I promise I'll take my time with you when we are settled," he whispered, fingers stroking through the slick heat between her trembling thighs.

A swift nip to the tender bitemark made his hips jerk. "If you won't rest, then touch me *now.*"

Otto didn't need to be told twice. Giving her ass a quick pinch, he growled, "Get under the blanket. And unbutton your nightgown. Show me your pretty breasts."

Josephine raised herself up until she was straddling him, pressing her center down against his cock with maddening pressure. Her elegant fingers worked the buttons of her nightgown free as her dark hair, long and shining, spilled over her shoulders. Moonlight limned her silhouette. All the while, her striking eyes watched him with the same furious hunger he felt gnawing at his gut.

"Never seen anything so beautiful as you," he rasped, unable to stop himself from reaching up to cup her perfect breasts. They were little more than a handful and tipped with small pink nipples already budded with desire. He rolled them carefully between his thumbs and forefingers, his eyes on her flushed cheeks, her parted lips.

Slowly, he used his grip on her nipples to pull her down again, until she was braced on her hands by his ears.

Gods only knew what contraption they had rigged to make a bed out of the carriage, but he was glad for it. The space allowed Josephine to kneel over him, putting her breasts at the perfect height to be kissed. And bitten.

He'd never tasted skin as sweet as hers, nor heard a moan as beautiful as the soft, breathy sound she made when he scraped his teeth over one berry-pink nipple. He could spend *years* kissing them and never get tired of it. He planned to.

When he dragged the blanket over her back, concealing her from any curious eyes that might catch a glimpse through the carriage windows, she shuffled down on her knees to align their bodies once more. Otto gripped her hips, her nightgown bunched under his hands, and slowly dragged her against his aching cock. Hot and wet — the drag of her over the underside of his cock was sweet torture.

Josephine's hips rolled. "Want you inside me," she breathed, pressing insistent kisses all across his chest and over his thundering heart. "Please, Otto."

"Not here," he ground out, with the help of some divine will hitherto untapped. He tossed his head back as the pressure built, maddeningly slow. "Not until I can give you my bite."

"Why can't you—"

He jerked her hips with more force, grinding them together until he heard her sharp gasp of pleasure. Hot arousal coated his cock. It would be so, so easy to simply notch himself at her entrance and thrust. He wouldn't even need to do much work. No doubt the motion of the carriage and his threadbare control would have him spilling in seconds.

That was not how a mate should be taken, though. It should not be hasty, selfish, or one-sided. It should be desperate, needy, and in all ways equal.

"Because," he ground out, to remind them both, "when I claim you, I want to take my time. And I don't want a fucking audience around to hear my mate when I make her scream."

In response, Josephine let out a tiny kitten's growl that somehow made him even more desperate. Her little fangs found one of his nipples and gave it a sharp, displeased bite. A fiery streak of pleasure ran down his spine, drawing his balls up tight against his body as he ground her down onto him.

"Fuck," he gasped, rocking his hips in an embarrassingly uneven rhythm. One hand shot up to grasp the back of her neck, holding her in place. "Do that again."

Those sharp little teeth scraped again, bolder this time. Otto began to pant and, knowing he was close, reached around her thigh to slide first one, then two fingers into her tight, rippling sheath.

"I want to feel you come," he whispered, pumping his fingers in time with his shallow thrusts.

Josephine's hips jerked erratically as she chased her orgasm, her muscles clenching around his fingers, until she bit down on the meat of his pectoral, muffling a shout. She squeezed his fingers tight. The feeling sent him over the edge.

Otto pressed his lips into her fragrant hair as he came, his release painting her cunt and his lower belly in long pearlescent ropes. They continued to grind together, chasing those last sparks of pleasure until they were no more.

Only momentarily satisfied, Otto gave into the pull of instinct and blindly began to smooth his release into her skin, her hot little cunt, and then across her lips. Without his bite, she was technically unclaimed, but anyone with a sharp nose would know instantly that she was *his*.

Josephine made soft sounds of pleasure and let him do as he pleased, her tongue snaking out to taste. "You're mine," he growled, licking at her glistening lips until her tongue came out again and all traces of his seed was gone. From her mouth at least.

Resting her body on his, completely trusting, Josephine nuzzled his bearded jaw and sighed, "I'm yours." A pause. "Well, unless you never bite me. Then I might kill you."

An exhausted grin cramped his cheeks. He curled his arms around her slim frame and squeezed them together so tightly, not even a knife's blade could have fit between them. The mating fever temporarily relieved, their connection reinforced by luscious touch, sleep closed in on him once more. "If I never bite you, it will be because I'm already dead. Now hush, *kone*. Let us sleep some more and face tomorrow together, yes?"

She huffed, but still managed to settle down. He felt her breathing begin to even out as the carriage rolled onward, soothing in its rhythm. His eyelids drooped. Within moments, they were both asleep.

CHAPTER THIRTY

An excerpt from the diaries of Josephine Wyeth,
generously provided by the Wyeth-Beornson family to the Fairmont
Museum of Art:
    November 15th, 1870-

My life begins.

CHAPTER THIRTY-ONE

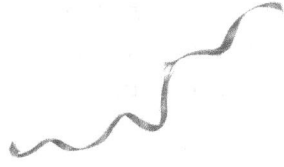

FROM THE INFORMATIONAL BROCHURE GIVEN TO guests at the Exploring Lyssa exhibit at the Fairmont Museum of Art:

THE FINAL CHAPTER/THE FIRST CHAPTER - DISPLAY 61

The November 15th diary entry, penned in the early morning the day of her chaotic escape, is the last Josephine ever wrote. The journal itself was badly damaged by smoke, as it sat on top of her clothing in the steamer trunk beneath her bed and was therefore the most exposed when 'the patron' set the house ablaze.

When asked why she didn't simply continue writing in a new diary after her escape from Meadow Creek, Josephine answered, "For many years that diary was my only friend. When we escaped, I suddenly found myself surrounded by people who wished to speak to me, to know my story, to be my friend. The diary became something of a symbol of loneliness. A talisman of a past life. I no longer needed it. And then when my children were old enough to begin asking questions, it became a new sort of talisman for them — one of understanding. It took on a new life."

[PICTURED: A lone, soot-stained page suspended in glass. The panel is several feet tall and the first thing to greet you as you step out of the darkness into a room of color, light, and soaring ceilings. The panel marks the end of the first half of the exhibit, a winding, darkened tunnel. It is the centerpiece in a sprawling space overflowing with paintings of people in motion, blond-haired children frolicking in grass, polar bears asleep in snow-drifts, and lively self-portraits of the artist at work in her studio, smiling into a mirror.]

CHAPTER THIRTY-TWO

IT WAS A LONG, EXHAUSTING JOURNEY FROM THE border to Minneapolis, but Josephine did her best to keep up with the battalion and make herself useful. It was that desperation to be useful that kept her from total collapse. It was better to dwell on the fear that they might suddenly find her too burdensome and leave her by the roadside than let herself drown in worry for her mate, terror at being surrounded by predators, and the complicated web of grief and fury that clung to her in the days after their escape.

Despite the mens' protest, Josephine ran herself ragged as she nursed her mate and assisted with what few camp chores she could. After two days, it felt like all she had left was adrenaline and anxiety. Paradoxically, her industriousness appeared to make the men pay more attention to her, which in turn increased her worry.

All the men were kind to her in their own, rough ways. Though it was clear their manners were rusty — and their general disregard for clothing shocking — Josephine found herself catered to like an honored guest.

Extra portions of food were allotted to her, much of it from the rescued stores of the homestead, one soldier or another asked her every hour if she needed something, and frequent breaks were called for fear of overexerting her. Many of the men skated around her, eyes wide and mumbled apologies on their lips, while others sought her out as she attempted to help cook meals, scrub laundry, and care for her sick mate.

Several of the men protested when she immediately put her head down and got to work, citing her minor injuries and captivity. They had no such compunction with her mother, though. Evangeline was hysterical more often than she was not, but upon learning of her part in Josephine's captivity, Lee had set her to mending every button hole, tear, and frayed hem of the battalion's uniforms. She existed at the fringe of the camp, always guarded in case she tried to flee.

Evangeline attempted to speak to her daughter often, usually pitched at a wail, but Josephine didn't pity her enough to indulge her. Seeing as they did not have jurisdiction over what happened in other territories, Lee said that Evangeline would be charged in the court of the Packlands for unlawful detainment of a shifter. It would be enough to see her rot in a cell for the rest of her days.

The beast would have preferred to let her mother starve to death in the dense, snow-dusted forest they cut through, but dying in a cell would have to do.

Still, the stark difference in how they treated her and Evangeline made her nervous. A part of her feared that all the special treatment would backfire. Would they grow sick of her sooner because they gave her more than her fair share? Lee, the large, dark-skinned man who apparently commanded the rowdy band of shifters, waved away her concerns when she whispered them over the evening meal.

"It's natural," he told her, nodding toward the two wolfish men, Rafael and Miles, who shadowed her every step. They were sitting not three feet away on an overturned log, their beaten metal plates in their laps and their eyes half-lidded as they stared into the fire. Both men had attempted to give her a portion of their meals.

"You don't know how nice it is to be around a submissive after so long without," Lee had continued as he swiped a corner of a chalky biscuit through what was left of his mash. "It reminds us that gentle things exist. That's good for the soul. I'd be immensely grateful if you let them coddle you for a bit longer."

Josephine had never been coddled in her life. She wasn't sure she knew how to be.

But as the days of hard travel began to bleed into one another, made all the longer by her worry over her feverish mate, she began to notice how the men gathered around her, drifting closer as if pulled by a current. Faces were cleaner. Hair was combed. Even the ones who rarely spoke to her looked more at ease.

In the cell, Otto told her that packs gave all the power to submissives. She hadn't really believed him. Now she thought she understood.

Just her presence, harried and afraid as she was, reminded the scarred men that they were people, not simply soldiers in a never-ending war. She became a symbol of the families they missed, the normalcy and peace of home. When they cared for her, they were really caring for the loved ones they missed.

By the time Otto's fever broke and he finally regained consciousness, she had begun to settle into her role. It wasn't easy being surrounded by so many strange, dominant men used to living rough, but they managed to find common ground.

For his part, Otto was alternately pleased and vexed to find her so well integrated into the battalion. It took him another day to regain enough strength to walk freely around the camp, and when he did, he noticed what she had: that the men flocked to her like flies to honey.

"They're pulling at your damn apron strings," he muttered one night as he helped her prepare dinner over the fire. His gaze, almost constantly lit with the shifter glow, flicked to Miles, who was casually leaning against the carriage, watching her with what Lee called *puppy eyes*.

It was with great relief that she concluded that her mate's

health was doing much better. For days she'd feared he wouldn't wake at all, that perhaps the lyssa had been too much for him, but his strength returned in leaps and bounds.

Almost as soon as he was free of bed rest, he'd shifted once more, dispelling both of their fears that his shift in the barn was a fluke.

She cried again when that massive, white-furred creature pressed her into the dirt to run his nose over every inch of her. Josephine didn't know what miracle allowed him to retain the ability to shift, but she fervently refused to question it. Every day she felt gratitude like a kick in her chest — a hard blow of feeling so intense, it knocked the wind out of her.

Otto hadn't lost his soul. He didn't hate her. Their future extended before them, bright and fragile. There was no long, constricting tunnel of terror anymore. It had been destroyed as surely as the homestead itself.

Even so, Otto *was* certainly infected. When not lit with the glow of an imminent shift, one of his eyes was dark brown and the other a pale green. He claimed that they were once plain brown. Josephine had of course tartly informed him that brown was a lovely, rich color of infinite variations. There was nothing *plain* about brown eyes, and indeed, she preferred the brown one to the green.

"Must be difficult," Rafael had teased, "having a mate so passionate about one's eye color, eh?"

Otto, slinging his arm around her waist to drag her against his puffed-up chest, replied, "If you think *that's* passionate, you should see how she is about the rest of me."

As the days passed, he claimed other symptoms as well — a quicker temper, restlessness at night, and increased strength.

When the back left wheel of the carriage became misaligned, he had no trouble lifting the entire thing to allow Collin, Lee's second, to hammer it back into place.

Though he put on a brave face, most likely to ease her worry, she knew he struggled in those hard days of travel. On edge from the constant threat of enemy soldiers even after they abandoned the carriage and began cutting through rougher country, he also struggled with what he called "the mating fever."

After stopping for dinner late one night, she noticed that he was particularly tense, his shoulders stiff and his eyes down as he peeled potatoes for their stew. Josephine smoothed her suddenly sweaty hands on her skirt. The glow of the fire and the attention of the slowly gathering men made her face hot. "Am I doing something wrong?"

Otto shot her a startled look. Seeing her nervousness, he cursed in his native tongue. Leaning over the stew pot hanging on a crude cast iron hook between them, he pressed a fierce kiss to her forehead. "No, you are perfect, *kone*. I am just bitter I must share you still. Bears don't do that well."

Truthfully, she wasn't certain she was cut out for pack life either. As much as she had come to shyly enjoy the company of the battalion, she also found the constant chatter, clashing personalities, and attention deeply unsettling.

Circling the fire, she tucked herself against Otto's side and pretended the stew needed stirring. Speaking very quietly, she said, "I would rather not share myself, either."

His deep, rhythmic purr rattled his chest. Speaking against her ear, he whispered, "Good. After this journey is done, you are all mine."

Josephine did her best to tamp down her bubbling impatience. *Soon,* she promised the beast. *Soon he'll be all mine.*

Chapter Thirty-Three

Zig-zagging around scorched battlefields and pockets of violence with limited success, they made their slow way to Minneapolis. It was the northernmost capital of the Packlands, which she'd begun to hear the men call *Alliance territory.* Her father had called the idea that the packs could ever truly form an alliance a fairy tale, but the more time she spent with the eclectic group of shifters, the more she believed it was possible.

Surely if hawks, wolves, bears, foxes, moose, and elk shifters could fight and live together in a single battalion, the packs could form a true, stable alliance. The only thing standing in their way, as far as she could tell, was the ego of the alphas involved.

That opinion crystallized when she and her mate were escorted to a meeting with not only the commanders of the Packlands — split into north, south, and east — but several of the territory's most powerful alphas. Lee, being the commander of the north as well as Otto's friend, spearheaded the meeting.

Though it was somewhat of a relief to be back in the familiar setting of a big city, Josephine dreaded the meeting. She'd already given Lee all the information she knew about her father's work and helped him sift through the charred remains of the notes and records his men were able to salvage from their burning home during the journey.

Still, he insisted that she and her mate meet with the alphas in the capital. This was necessary because most of them still could not accept that lyssa had been weaponized.

The only person less happy than her was Otto.

She got the sense that he was generally an even-tempered, easygoing man, and had heard many funny stories about him from his battalion, but it was obvious that he was suffering under increasing strain.

As the days crawled by, he became even more anxious about exposing her to others. Whenever someone got too near, he would step in front of her, teeth bared, and at night he spent restless hours standing guard over her, half-feral with the fear that she might be snatched from him while he slept.

Josephine might have found his behavior alarming if he didn't normally look abashed immediately afterward. It also helped that most of the men appeared to expect it. "It's difficult," he explained to her one night as they retired to the room Lee had provided them. "Not marking you has— it puts me on edge. The fact that you're a submissive makes the protective urge even worse. There is a reason shifters don't drag out courtship. We tend to lose our heads."

When she asked him why he didn't simply bite her, as she had bitten him, he gave her a desperate, heart-wrenching look. "Because, *kone,* I promised you a den first. A place where you feel safe. Don't you want that?"

More than his bite? No. The beast howled for it every time he touched her. It grew ever-more desperate as the days passed and he continued to refuse her even as he kissed her, taught her how to use her mouth on his cock, and then made her come on his tongue again and again. Several times she felt his teeth on her neck, and every instance saw him pulling back at the last second as he came on her skin with guttural growl.

In fact, she'd gotten quite mulish about it. It was an attitude her father never would have tolerated, but paradoxically, the more temper she displayed, the more at ease her mate seemed to become.

This was made all the more vexing by the fact that Otto appeared more dashing every day. Given access to bathing facilities, hearty meals, a shaving kit, clean clothing that fit his magnificent frame, and a hairbrush, he tested Josephine's patience constantly. In the light of day, his scars made him seem roguish, his mismatched eyes arresting, and his wavy blond hair akin to spun gold. The insufferable bear had even caught on to how much she liked the tickle of his beard and had decided to keep it trimmed close to his hard jaw and framing that boyish grin perfectly.

It was all monumentally unfair and she let him know it with increasing regularity.

"Ah, sweet *kone*," he breathed, grinning from ear to ear, "I love when you show me your claws."

He took it as a matter of pride that she trusted him enough to show her temper. Unfortunately, that same pride was tied up in delivering his promises.

After their nightly exertions, they spent hours whispering together, telling stories, getting to know one another without the weight of threats pressing down on them. She'd come to understand that her mate was a gentle, patient man of good humor — but he was also intensely proud and stubborn. In most things he happily indulged her, but there were rare subjects on which he had a will of iron.

His bite was one of those subjects.

As frustrating as it was, Josephine begrudgingly respected him more for it. It was not so great a flaw, she thought, to believe firmly in right and wrong, nor to stake your pride on promises kept.

Unfortunately, that didn't make their week in Minneapolis, nor their tense meeting with the commanders, any easier.

Otto held perfectly still as the alphas gathered around a table in Lee's dining room. Each one made her beast recoil. By the time all the men and women had their seats, she was gripping Otto's hand beneath the table so hard she feared she might break his bones.

Out of respect for her, most of the alphas did not stare at her for too long and were notably relaxed, their body language open, non-threatening. Not all of them cared enough to go to the effort, though. Some stared at her shamelessly, as if amazed to see a submissive across the table at all.

Even if they had all gone out of their way to make her comfortable, Josephine feared it was useless. There were too many scents, too much restless, aggressive energy. Too many eyes. Too much judgment.

It took everything in her not to turn into Otto's chest and hide away from them all.

Past the introductions, the meeting was a blur of discomfort, harsh breaths, and whispered explanations. Afterward, she couldn't remember much of what was said, but Otto assured her that she'd done beautifully. She explained who she was, what was done to her, what she and others like her were capable of.

Lee backed up her story with charred evidence from her father's lab and Otto did the same with his own experience. Every face in the room went starkly pale when he described his struggle to shift, and that he had no doubt in his mind that others may not be able to.

Her only clear memory of the meeting, unblurred by adrenaline, was when Otto admitted that the only reason he believed he was still able to was because of the matebond. Speaking with the utmost solemnity, he said, "The bear knew she needed him and refused to die. If not for her... No, I don't think he'd still be here."

There was some heated speculation from the assembled alphas as to whether or not a were might be able to regain their animal if a matebond was formed after infection, but Josephine had no answers for them. When the subject ran up against a clear lack of evidence one way or another, discussion turned to who was responsible.

Again, she had no answers. Lee backed up her description of the patron, who'd escaped via m-gate with his lone surviving guard after setting the house on fire, presumably to cover his tracks. Without a name that information was almost useless. The trail was further muddied by her father's death and the Wyeth family's frequent moves from city to city, territory to territory. A decision was made to question Evangeline, awaiting trial in a tiny cell far from Lee's home, but Josephine doubted they would get anything useful out of her.

Most of the alphas seemed to believe that the Orclind must be behind it, seeing as the homestead was firmly in Orclind territory, but others raised questions about why her father was stationed in Washington prior to that, and how they'd managed to slip across the Packlands to get to the homestead undetected.

Her part in the conversation clearly done, Josephine had allowed Otto to pull her into his lap, improper as that was, and did her best to block out the debate by tucking her nose under his chin. After they returned to their room, he stripped them both naked, dragged her into bed, and held her for hours as he murmured praise.

"So brave," he'd told her, deep voice rumbling with approval. "You faced a room full of alphas today and held your own. I'm so proud of you, my mate."

She continued to tremble even hours later. Recalling the packed room and the loud, terrifying world outside, Josephine found herself asking, "Can we leave soon?"

Tracing her spine with his rough knuckles, he replied, "I thought you would like the city. Are you so eager to leave?"

Josephine nodded. "I used to miss the city but I— I think there are too many people now. Too many eyes."

Besides, had she ever really known the city as she thought? Even before she'd been locked in the house, Josephine had never truly been allowed to wander freely. Her world had always been seen through the picture frame of a window.

Otto had taken her out to some of the less war-ravaged parts of the city, treating her to sweets and a few new dresses. She thought that she would love finally stepping out into the hustle and bustle, but Josephine quickly found herself overstimulated, frustrated, and anxious as people brushed by her, gawked at her eyes, spat things in the street, and so on.

"I will go wherever you lead me," she told her mate, "but... I would prefer it if we lived somewhere quieter than a city. Perhaps not as isolated as the homestead. A town, maybe?"

Otto let out a gusty sigh. "I am glad you feel that way. I agree."

"So we'll leave soon?"

"Yes," he answered, rubbing the underside of his bearded chin against the crown of her hair. "Lee is working on assigning me to a town a few days' travel from here. Away from the 'Riik's border. It will be small, but not like the homestead, where you were completely isolated from the world. How does this sound?"

Josephine swallowed thickly, overcome by the idea of living in a quaint small town with her mate. For the first time in her life, she would be free. She would be safe. No more experiments, no more Harrod, no more pins or scalpels. She could just... live.

Nowhere was truly safe from the war, but with Otto, she didn't fear that dark cloud on the horizon. She had discovered that living meant taking risks and seizing joy when it came to you. After everything, she intended to wring every drop of joy from the life she'd fought for, whether the war came for them or not.

Together, they'd make something strong enough to endure even the most violent storm.

"Sounds like paradise," she finally answered, voice thick with tears.

Otto tightened his arms around her. "It does, doesn't it?"

CHAPTER THIRTY-FOUR

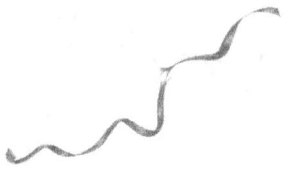

THEIR CABIN WAS BARELY BIG ENOUGH TO FIT THE both of them, needed its roof patched before the snow began to stick, and had a small family of mice living under the floorboards, but Josephine fell in love with it instantly.

Situated on the edge of Lake George and nestled amongst tall, stately pines, it was a fifteen-minute walk from a small farming town. In his animal form, Otto could cover that distance in less than half the time, allowing him to share perimeter rounds with the other dominant shifters with ease. It was far enough away to soothe her mind but also not completely removed from civilization. In other words, it was perfect.

Unfortunately, when they pulled up to the cabin laden with her charred trunk, supplies, and Otto's personal possessions, few as they were, her mate was visibly upset at the condition of the old hunting cabin.

Josephine assured him she was delighted by it — her own home! — but he could not stop huffing and puffing as he unloaded their things from the wagon and onto the old, rickety porch. He spoke quickly in his rich, accented voice, outlining all that he intended to do to make it a den fit for her.

Before he was a soldier, he'd mainly been a traveling carpenter, so it didn't necessarily surprise her when he immediately began inspecting windowsills, beams, and squeaky boards. While she set about sweeping and cleaning the interior, he'd pulled out his tools and began to circle the cabin with a feverish light in his eyes.

My bear needs to set his den to rights, she thought, peering at him through a small, bubbled window in the kitchen. He was stooped over, inspecting the little well nearly overgrown with moss and muttering to himself.

Shaking her head, she finished her cleaning, gently escorted the mice outside, and then descended on the cast iron stove with her brush and pail. By the time the sun began to set, snow drifted lazily down from plum-colored clouds and a fire roared in the hearth.

She had much to learn about being mistress of her own home, but years of being the equivalent of her parents' servant had given her a good base from which to build. Tidying, basic cooking, and mending were all skills she possessed. There were certainly worse places to start from.

Her tasks done for the day, Josephine sat in the center of the combined living and bedroom, her trunk propped open in front of her. Anticipation simmered in her belly as she waited for Otto to come inside. The full moon was creeping closer. She'd kept track of the days, but there was truly no need. She could feel the restless energy in her blood, the pacing of the beast eager to run free.

It would be her first full moon unsupervised. It would be her first transformation in front of Otto — or rather, the first he would remember. It would be their first *together.*

Thoughts of what would happen, what he would think of her afterward, if he would experience any changes himself had grown in volume and intensity with every passing day. Otto assured her that all would be well, especially now that they were blissfully alone, but she couldn't help the gnawing worry.

Of course, that worry was amplified by what she knew would happen tonight. What she would make *certain* happened, no matter what Otto thought. He'd given her a den. They were alone. They had all the time in the world.

Now, at last, on the night before the full moon, Josephine would have her bite.

Needing to occupy her restless hands, she decided to finally sort through her belongings. She hadn't had a chance to go through her things since their escape. In truth, she hadn't really wanted to, as everything she owned was tied to too many awful memories.

But she had also sorely missed drawing and painting. Now that she was in their new home — their *den* — she summoned enough bravery to inspect what had made it out of the fire while her mate's hammer tapped a rhythm on the roof.

Incredibly, nearly all of her possessions were intact. The worst damage was to her clothing, as the smoke had seeped through the cracks in the lid to stain them beyond salvaging. Her diary had shared a similar fate.

She made to set the diary aside but paused for a moment. Gazing down at the well-worn cover, she smoothed her fingers over every crease and fold, as well as the raw edges of the paper she had made and sewn in herself over the years. It was bittersweet to hold it in the light of their new hearth.

She'd begun keeping the diary only a few days before her father injected her with lyssa. It held every trauma, every memory of the people who'd come through her father's lab and later the barn. It was full of grief and pain.

For a taut moment, all Josephine wanted to do was toss it into the hearth. She wanted to watch the past burn just as the homestead burned. What greater symbol of her triumph than reducing her father's legacy to ash in her own hearth?

But then she remembered Rasmus. She remembered the man who pressed the pencil to her throat. She remembered the elf who fought so hard they were forced to call for help in removing him, and how he'd gone out of his way to avoid even scratching her. She remembered every face, every word. She remembered every ugly thing ever said to her in those cells, and every tiny connection made between herself and those poor subjects, good and terrible.

What if all those people were dead? What if they weren't? What if the diary in her hand was the only remaining evidence of their lives, of the crimes committed against them?

She could not destroy it — not only for them, but for herself. The diary was a record of pain, but it was one of resilience, too.

So Josephine gently set it aside, on the edge of the thin rug she'd laid down on the floor in front of the hearth, and thought, *I can't leave my past behind because I am my past. Better to keep it close and see it for the strength it has imbued in me than to attempt to destroy it in bitterness.*

Breathing a little easier, she turned her attention back to the trunk. It was a relief to find all her art supplies, carefully stowed away in pilfered cigar boxes, tins, and jars, were entirely untouched.

Josephine carefully laid out her stacks of drawings and rolled canvases on the floor before the hearth. There were hundreds of them, most of which were done on thin sheets of recycled newspaper she'd soaked, mashed, and dried herself. There were paintings of every size, of every subject done in paints of her own making, watercolor, or the very rare oil paint she'd been given for particularly good behavior.

Charcoals mingled with ink drawings and studies lay alongside master copies from books and newspapers. She had not kept much of her early work, finding it painful to look at such unskilled renderings and painstaking copies of woodcut newspaper prints, but a few pieces survived her culling. Peering at it all, she realized that she had inadvertently created something of an archive, beginning at her earliest attempts to those last, frenetic renderings of her mate done on her bedroom floor.

It was as much a chronicle of her life as the diary was.

Her whole world, real and imagined, lay in those piles and rolls now spread across the rough floor of their cabin.

"Now that is a sight."

Josephine jolted, surprised by her mate's rough voice. She turned and found Otto slowly closing the cabin's front door, his eyes heavy-lidded and his cheeks flushed from cold. A chill wind circulated through the tiny home for just a moment before the heat of the stove beat it back again.

Flushing, as she always did when Otto gave her a look like that, she explained, "I was waiting for you and thought I ought to go through my things." Worried that he might miss how homey she'd made the cabin while he worked outside, she moved to gather up the piles. "Don't worry, I'll put them back—"

Familiar body heat radiated behind her as Otto knelt, arms extending to stop her nervous hands. Callused fingers, cold from working outside, wrapped around her own. "Don't. You promised to show me, remember?"

Her throat convulsed with a nervous swallow. "I did."

Otto lifted one of her hands to press a kiss to her palm. "Then show me, *kone*. We will decide which ones to hang on the walls."

A deep bloom of warmth filled her chest. Her parents had never even considered hanging one of her paintings. They found her art to be as useless as she was. At first, Josephine had taken it up in a last ditch effort to impress them, but that hope was squashed when her mother sneered at a drawing she found in one of Josephine's pockets.

"Where'd you find this trash?" Evangeline had asked. *"You shouldn't pick things up off the street, Josephine."*

She was twelve.

It was a point of quiet pride that she'd kept at it anyway. Eventually, that pride had morphed into a solid wall of resistance. Her father could not take her art from her, no matter how he tried. In fact, she discovered that she could leverage his belief that he *could* take it away to her benefit. The act of creation fed her dying soul but her small exertion of power had kept the fire of defiance burning in her belly.

Still, she trembled with nerves as she leaned to one side, allowing Otto to peer over her shoulder as he got comfortable behind her. His fingers ghosted over several drawings before he reached for a rolled canvas. Carefully pulling at the twine that held it in place, he revealed an oil painting of a row of townhouses engulfed by writhing blue flame.

Otto breathed something in Danish before he set it aside and reached for another roll. So it went as he inspected still life paintings of half-eaten plums and crystal decanters, loose renderings of the world outside her window in ink and watercolor, and charcoal studies in their dozens.

He'd begun to make a considerable pile by his right knee. All manner of pieces were cobbled together there, even some of her roughest, most quickly sketched studies. Was he making a rubbish pile? Was it intentional at all?

Josephine sat stiffly, barely breathing, as he muttered to himself in a raspy voice. Were those compliments? Criticisms? It was impossible to tell. He'd promised to teach her Danish, but so far she only knew *lille mus, kone,* and a few curse words she stalwartly refused to use. None helped her in this situation.

Finally, when she worried that she might combust at any moment, Otto's fingers settled on the drawings she'd done of him.

"Oh!" Josephine felt her face go nearly violet with embarrassment. Her hands darted out to snatch them from his loose grasp. "Those are just—"

"Is this *me?*"

She wished that the old wooden floor of the cabin might open up and swallow her whole. "I... can't you tell?"

Her proud artist heart withered. *Gods, did I render his likeness so poorly?*

"It *is* me. Those are my scars!" he exclaimed, as if he hadn't heard her. Drawing the pages closer, he flipped through them several times, faster and faster, as if he couldn't decide which one he wanted to look at first. "When did you do these?"

"After the first day we touched," she shyly admitted. "The next day, when you asked me if I'd slept poorly— that was partly why. I stayed up until my lamp ran out of oil just... drawing you."

A hard exhalation puffed against the back of her neck. "You make me more handsome than I am, I think."

CHAPTER THIRTY-FIVE

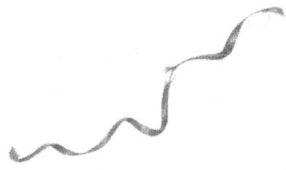

AT LAST BRAVE ENOUGH TO GAUGE HIS EXPRESSION, Josephine turned her upper body as much as she could. Otto looked stricken, his mismatched eyes gleaming in the warm orange glow of the stove. His golden brows were pinched together and his lips parted as he sucked in quick breaths.

Overcome by the emotion shining in his eyes, Josephine reached up to caress the long, curved scar that bisected one brow and the top of his cheek. "I was frustrated after I drew them because they fell so short of how magnificent you are. Those drawings don't capture even a sliver of my admiration for you." She passed her fingertips over his soft lips. "I suspect I will have to draw you a thousand times before I even come close."

The drawings drifted from Otto's fingers. Grasping her hips, he turned her so she knelt between his thighs. "I am humbled by you," he grated, cupping her cheeks with rough, trembling hands. "To have such talent, such kindness, such strength in this delicate frame—" He stopped abruptly, his voice cracking, before he began again. "To know that you trust me even when nothing in the world has taught you to do so— I am overcome by you, my Josephine. Every day. I fear that I will never be what you deserve, but I cannot release you. I will not."

Josephine's breath shortened. Tears were a hot pressure behind her eyes as her fingers stole under his wool coat and thin cotton shirt to find the raised, puckered scars of her bite.

"Were you able to, I would not allow it." She leaned forward to deliver a swift, punishing bite to his lower lip. A reverent kiss followed. Speaking against his mouth, she told him, "I have claimed you. You are *mine*, Otto Beornson."

A deep, tearing growl erupted from his chest.

In an instant, one strong arm was banded around her middle and his lips crushed to hers. Her world tipped as he laid her back, one hand sweeping paper and canvas aside, to spread her before the glowing warmth of the stove.

"You are *mine*," he rumbled, kissing and licking and biting between each word. "My mate in our den. Everything I need."

"*Yes.*" Josephine clutched him to her with fingers turned to claws. The beast in her breast crowed with need when she begged, "Bite me now, Otto. *Bite me.*"

He swore. Tearing himself out of her hold, Otto sat back on his haunches and began to yank at his clothing. The sounds of seams tearing made the rational part of her wince, knowing that she'd need to see to those later, but the rest of her cheered his haste.

The sight of him shucking his clothing would never get old.

He'd lost a bit of weight during his feverish days, but after weeks of steady meals and relative rest, his health had rebounded. Her mate was thick with muscle, his skin golden and luminous with health. Every morning, he allowed her to plait his thick blond hair for him. She loved grooming him, as he liked to say, but more than that, she found the sight of him removing the thin leather cord to allow the braid to unravel around his wide shoulders intensely arousing.

Watching him do so now, as he was gilded with firelight, made her claws curl into the rug beneath her.

Otto watched her squirm with a ravenous look in his eyes.

They flickered back and forth from mismatched to golden. His chest, scarred and sprinkled with pale hair, rose and fell rapidly.

"If you want to keep your dress and stays, *kone*, I suggest you remove them."

The beast didn't give one whit whether he tore her pretty gingham dress or not. Josephine, on the other hand, was rather attached to it, seeing as it was a gift from her mate.

His first gift was a replacement ribbon for the one he'd "stolen." She'd promptly given it back to him and made him promise to always keep it with him, just in case. He now kept it in his pocket when working or tied around his right wrist at night.

The dress, on the other hand, was the first non-hand-me-down she'd ever gotten as an adult woman.

"You touch this dress with your claws and I'll nip your nose," she promised, rising to unpin her undershirt, then work at the ties of her skirt. In truth, she would probably nip him anyway. Though she hadn't experienced even a twinge in her venom gland since she bit him, Josephine had grown rather fond of nipping whenever the opportunity arose — which was quite often.

Otto made a soft, hungry sound in the back of his throat. The buttons of his trousers popped one by one until he could reach in and grasp his flushed cock.

Josephine's fingers fumbled with the laces of her stays. Her eyes dropped to where his fist slowly squeezed. When a pearlescent drop beaded on the ruddy head, she found herself leaning forward, her task forgotten.

Otto gave himself one rough stroke. *"Clothes."*

"But—"

"I'll bite you through your underthings if I must," he warned her, extended canines flashing in the firelight.

Josephine shuddered, not at all opposed to that proposition, but somehow found the will to loosen her stays. Wiggling out as quickly as she could, she also disregarded the health and safety of her seams when she tore at her chemise and bloomers.

When her fingers landed on the ribbons holding up her stockings, however, Otto let loose a low growl. "Keep those on."

She looked up to find that in the time it took her to almost completely undress, he'd removed his trousers, boots, and socks. Her mate now knelt before her, surrounded by scattered piles of her artwork, nude as the day he was born. His cock hung heavy and livid between his spread thighs, a temptation she had no power to resist.

Josephine drank in the sight of his form with a desperate sort of hunger.

She no longer feared that he would look upon her body in disgust. For every silvery scar she possessed, Otto had triple that amount. That didn't stop him from being the single most handsome, virile man she'd ever laid eyes on. Why did she think *her* marks would be repugnant when she found *his* so fascinating?

Besides, he'd made good on his promise to kiss every one of them. He did so often. When she asked him why, he explained that he did not want her to remember the pain that caused them but the pleasure she felt when he kissed them.

"Lay back," he ordered, palms dropping to the rug on either side of her thighs.

Josephine eased back down. Her heart hammered, its beat echoing in her throat, chest, and between her thighs. He'd pleasured her plenty since their escape, but the sight of him prowling toward her on his hands and knees still made her cunt go slick and hot for him. The exhilaration hadn't changed even an ounce since that momentous day in the cell.

If anything, the knowledge of what was to come only made it more exciting.

When Otto hovered over her on hands and knees, Josephine allowed her legs to fall open, welcoming him in. The damp, silky head of his cock brushed the soft flesh of her belly as his gaze slowly roved over her face, down her neck, and further, taking in all she offered.

"Well?" she pressed, growing restless.

Otto flashed her a wicked, feverish grin. "I'm surveying my feast."

Josephine trembled, her anticipation building with every breath. She reached up to pet his chest, fingers smoothing over chest hair and dimpled scars, to run the pads over his flat nipples. "Do it faster."

His upper lip lifted, revealing fearsome fangs. They weren't like her own — thin, sharp, made for piercing. His were canines meant for tearing, crushing. In his shifted form, they were the length and width of her middle finger.

In another life, Josephine would have whimpered at the sight of them. Now, she returned his snarl with equal force.

Otto would never hurt her. The woman and the beast trusted him implicitly. They just wished he'd *hurry up.*

"My pretty submissive is awfully demanding." She'd never heard a man sound as smug as he did then. She rolled her eyes but couldn't suppress a smile.

Otto bent down to lay a trail of kisses and bites from her throat to her breasts. He loved her breasts and often spent a great deal of time with them, using his mouth and fingers to pluck, twist, and suck until she begged him to ease the ache between her thighs.

Though she complained, Josephine loved it just as much as he did. The feeling of his beard — trimmed now, but always prickly — and the sense that she was being worshipped never lost its appeal. Now, if he'd only use one of those talented hands elsewhere...

He circled one of her nipples with the tip of his tongue before he lifted his head, his gaze intently focused on the way it tightened. Josephine groaned when he did the same thing to its twin. The delicate touches tipped her into a frenzy, but Otto would not be moved no matter how she growled and whined for more.

Only when *he* deemed the task done did he move on. Otto scraped his teeth along the curve of her belly. He traced the dip of her bellybutton with his tongue. He kissed the tops of her thighs before untying her ribbons and rolling her stockings down with painful slowness.

By the time he settled his head between her thighs, she was sweat-slicked, her back arched, and her cunt aching so badly, she couldn't think past it.

The first lash of his tongue sent her head back with a cry of desperation. Her claws dug into his loose hair as he began to work her expertly. Otto sucked, licked, kissed, and nipped with the fervor of a man whose singular purpose was his mate's pleasure.

When he felt she was close, he gave her more. Otto had trained her body well. She had no trouble accepting the three thick fingers he thrust inside of her. The stretch was all pleasure even when it burned. Not so long ago she would have balked at even one, but after seeing his cock, she was grateful he'd taken the time to teach her body how to take him.

The stretch would always be shocking, but now she craved it. More often than not, Josephine's climaxes came from the feeling of his fingers curling inside her, pumping ruthlessly as he demanded her orgasm again and again.

The bowstring of tension snapped.

A short, hard orgasm burst through her, tightening her muscles around those thrusting fingers and arching her spine until her hips left the rug completely.

She'd barely begun to come down from the precipice when Otto lurched over her. Josephine opened her eyes just as he pinned her down with his weight. Their gazes locked as he hooked one of her thighs over his hip.

"Brace yourself, *kone*," he ground out, the words barely intelligible.

Josephine wrapped her arms around him to dig her claws into the taut muscle of his backside. "Give it to me, mate."

His head dropped. Their kiss was searing, deep, full of relief and fierce longing. His tongue slid against hers as one hand moved between their bodies. Something hot and blunt nudged her core. It felt enormous. A sliver of apprehension tightened the muscles along her spine before Josephine recalled that she'd had that same cock on her tongue, even down her throat. If she could manage that, surely she could withstand the bludgeoning of her cunt.

He pressed forward. Her body, open as it was, still found a way to resist him.

Josephine hissed against his swollen lips but did not back down from the challenge. Spreading the leg not wrapped around his hip even farther, she rolled into him.

"Easy," he barked, punishing her with a nip. Meeting his feverish gaze fearlessly, she bit him back.

It snapped whatever tethered him to his restraint.

Otto's hips pushed forward with enough force to drive her a few inches up the rug. Josephine gasped because she did not have the breath to howl. *Good gods,* she thought, eyes watering, *if this hurts so badly, how in the world do women have babies?*

There was a moment of complete stillness as he settled within her, their hips flush. As the pain began to recede, she swore she could feel his heartbeat, every fine tremor of his powerful body, every twitch. The discomfort was quickly smothered by a feeling of exquisite connection.

For those few moments, they shared every breath. Their lips moved slowly over one another's, simply *feeling,* luxuriating.

Slowly, Otto drew his hips back. There was a definite sting, but it paled in comparison to that first tearing thrust. Josephine breathed out and stared up into his tight features with the utmost trust. He would take care of her. He would make it feel good. He always did.

Gradually, he picked up his pace. Her nerves came alive again with every drag, every hard, possessive thrust. It was as if he lit a spark inside her with each determined roll of his hips.

All the while, he watched her.

Those golden shifter eyes, the ones she'd found so terrifying in the dark of the cell, gleamed like polished coins in the firelight. He watched her like he wished to devour her. A wild look that bordered on pain tightened his features when she began to rock her hips into his thrusts, her hands smoothing up the slope of his back.

She loved to watch him, too. The way his body moved was a work of art, each muscle flexing and relaxing with his rhythm. She found the way his brows drew together and how he sucked his lip between his teeth fascinating. And when he began to thrust in earnest, she watched a savage cast descend on his beloved features with the deepest satisfaction.

Her mate was fierce. He was powerful. He adored her. His body, his heart, and soon his soul would belong to her as well.

A sense of incredible power overtook her as their bodies slapped together. Wet sounds filled the tiny cabin, and Otto had to brace a hand under her neck and shoulders to keep her from being thrust up the rug and into the glowing hearth, but she loved every second of it.

In this moment, she was *everything* to him. He was everything to her. They were perfectly equal as they took and received pleasure.

Josephine cupped his cheeks and brought his head down to whisper against his mouth, "Every day, Otto. I want this *every day*."

He hissed out a curse, his rhythm stuttering. Then he redoubled his efforts, his hips snapping and retreating with a force that knocked the breath from her lungs. "Yes. *Yes.*"

He tangled his fist in her unbound hair. Turning her head to one side, he lowered his mouth to the juncture between her neck and shoulder.

Josephine held her breath, expecting a bite. It didn't come right away. Instead, his fingers left her hair in favor of sneaking between them. He rubbed her roughly, giving no quarter as he demanded, "Come for me, *kone.*"

She was sensitive from her previous orgasm, overwhelmed by his rapid, powerful strokes. When he gave her a swift pinch, she shattered with a silent scream, her neck bowing.

Sharp pain in her shoulder bled into a euphoria so

complete, she could not feel her fingers or toes. Josephine drifted as a wave of raw magic rolled through her. It was bubbling, animalistic, and greeted by her beast with a howl of pure delight.

Otto's rhythm became ragged. His growl of satisfaction vibrated her chest as he came, bathing her with his hot seed even as he locked his jaw, refusing to release her.

When he did, it was only to turn her over, his hands arranging her so her cheek was pressed against the rug. He entered her again, sliding easily this time. Josephine lost herself in the primal feeling of him inside her, his fingers leaving bruises on her hips and thighs. They growled, bit, clawed, and fucked until the fire burned out.

Even then, they didn't stop.

Otto was only satisfied when he'd bitten her thighs, breasts, and both sides of her throat as he painted her flesh with his lashing tongue and ropes of his seed. By the time the sun began to lighten the sky, they somehow managed to make it to the bed, their sweaty limbs twined.

Otto clutched her to his chest. She could feel his heart hammering under her cheek when he rumbled, "Did I hurt you?"

Josephine pressed a kiss to that powerful heart. "I will be sore for days and I'll love every second of it."

He chuffed. Those talented fingers danced over that first vicious bite, tracing the contours of what was sure to be a spectacular scar. "Are you happy? I know this isn't the den you dreamed of, but—"

"I am the happiest I've ever been in my life, sir. I'll thank you not to question it again."

She didn't need to look to know he was grinning from ear to ear. She could feel it.

"To think I called you *lille mus*," he teased. "Now you are a lioness snarling at her mate."

"Could I not be a bear?"

He made a *tsk* sound with his teeth and tongue as he rolled them over. Tucking her against his chest, he replied, "A small one, maybe. Perhaps a sun bear?"

Her pinch did nothing more than make him chuckle. Lifting his head just enough to peer at the floor, he added, "Though, you'll need to learn how to keep a den. Look at the mess you made of my piles."

"Your piles?" Josephine was too exhausted to move, but she could imagine what the floor looked like. She was also fairly certain they'd made love *on* some charcoal drawings. No doubt her back was smeared with it now.

Otto ran his knuckles over the curve of her backside. "My piles. I'll need to sort them all again."

"How so?"

"Into the ones that we'll hang now and the ones we'll hang later, of course."

Josephine stilled. The beginning of the evening was awfully hazy now, but she recalled that one of his piles had been quite a bit larger than the other.

Her heart jammed into her throat and made her voice embarrassingly squeaky when she asked, "Which pile was which?"

"The big one was for now," he answered, as if it should have been obvious. "The small one was for later."

Her breath hitched. "I... I don't think we have enough room to hang all of those."

Otto drew their quilt up and over them. Cupping the back of her head, he guided her to press her nose against the base of his throat. A low, rhythmic purr rattled between them, making her eyes droop.

She was already drifting off when he murmured, "You're right. Suppose I should get started on those extra rooms then, shouldn't I?"

Yes, she thought, lips curving into a sleepy smile. *You should.*

∽

True to his promise, Otto began work on expanding the cabin the following day. He was able to get a remarkable amount of work done in the few hours of winter light before the sun dipped below the jagged crown of trees to bathe the frost-touched lake.

When the moon rose, Josephine's worry about her monthly transformation withered away. She felt none of her usual dread. The beast was not frantic, desperate to escape.

When the transformation overcame her, Otto was with her every step of the way. He did not balk at her fangs, her claws, her elongated limbs.

He shifted *with* her.

The beast greeted the bear with pure, animalistic joy as they were both caught in the frenzy of the night. Despite the frigid temperature, they ran through the pines together to play and snarl and follow invisible trails in the snow.

The night was pure sweetness and lit by moonlight glittering in the frost. They indulged in a different, playful kind of courtship until the sun began to rise on a new day.

There would never again be claw marks on their floor and walls. There would never be shackles, cell doors, or bars on the window.

The beast and the bear, at last, were free.

EPILOGUE

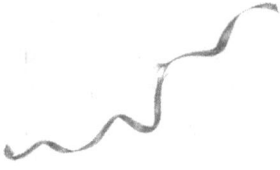

AN EXCERPT FROM THE ARTICLE "EXPLORING LYSSA: The Story of Josephine Wyeth," written by Elise Sasini and featured in The San Francisco Light, May 17th, 2048—

Josephine Wyeth is a woman not to be missed.

She is small, fine-boned like a bird. Her dark hair is streaked with gray and held out of her face in a messy bun speared with a paintbrush missing its bristles. Her eyes and mouth are framed with lines grooved by a life of laughter. When she greets us at the door, she wears slim-fitting black overalls embroidered with flowers over a cable knit sweater and thick wool socks.

Physically speaking, Josephine could not be more different from her daughter. But their aura, that indefinable *something* that makes every head turn, is precisely the same.

Her voice is soft, a little shy, as she ushers us into her log cabin palace. Vanessa has no sooner dropped her bag onto the entryway floor before she sweeps her mother up into a bone-crushing hug.

"Mama!" she exclaims, swinging her back and forth as her mother giggles. Her cheeks flush with delight and her striking eyes, dark brown and sky blue, twinkle like the precious stones in her daughter's rings.

"Hi, baby," she says. "Did you have a good trip?"

Vanessa assures her she did. Carefully lowering her much more petite mother back onto the floor, she turns to introduce us.

"It's an honor to meet you," I say, a little overwhelmed.

Josephine peers at me from under dark brows, watchful and wise, even as her lips quirk up at the corners. "Are you here to ask me a bunch of questions?"

I flush because that's precisely why I'm there, though it feels a bit impolite to say so. "Well... A bit, yeah. Mostly I'd just like to talk to you."

"I'm not so great at that part." Josephine wrinkles her nose and turns her gaze to her daughter, who has lifted her head to scent something in the air. I'm so nervous, I don't notice the faint smell of something sweet in the air until then. "My mate and children are the talkers, I'm afraid."

"Oh, hush, Mama. You're a wonderful speaker." Vanessa throws her arm around her mother's slim shoulders and drags her in for another hug. "And don't worry. Elise is very easy to talk to. She's fun. Now, do I smell banana bread?"

Josephine looks mildly affronted. The tiniest amount of tartness enters her soft voice. "Of course it's banana bread. I always make it for you, don't I?"

Vanessa shoots me an amused look over her mother's head. "Can we snag a slice? I'm *dying* for some good food."

We're led into a spacious kitchen as the two Weres catch up. I trail behind, taking in the exquisite craftsmanship of the home. Every hallway is a honeycomb of alcoves lit with warm, subtle light. Every single space holds a piece of Josephine's art. Some pieces are framed sketches on rough paper. Some are magazine advertisements from a hundred years ago carefully pressed between glass. Some are book covers, movie posters, still life paintings, scraps of paper covered in a mishmash of children's doodles and her own quick sketches.

Even the quick jaunt to the kitchen feels like a secret museum tour, an experience I am certain vanishingly few people have had or will ever have.

Josephine stands at the counter and slices off two thick slabs of banana bread for us. Vanessa hands me mine before she asks, "Where's Dad?"

"In the shop," her mother answers, nodding toward the window over the sink, which affords a view of a large workshop a few dozen feet from the house. "He's working on a new frame for me. I imagine he'll meander in for lunch soon enough."

I look around the kitchen with wide eyes. "Vanessa told me your mate is a carpenter. Did he build this house?"

Josephine graces me with a slight smile that warms me from the top of my head to the tips of my toes. "Yes. Our first den wasn't what he wanted it to be, so when we moved away from Alliance territory after the war, he went— well, you can see how far he went." She laughs. "For a while I worried that there wouldn't be a tree left in Bear Gulch once he was through."

"Mom was pregnant with my brother at the time," Vanessa interjects, reaching for another steaming slice of bread. "Shifters get a little nuts when cubs come along."

Josephine nods sagely. "They do. He worked like a man possessed."

Recalling the sheer scale of the home, I do a doubletake. "Was it all finished by the time the baby came along?"

"Oh, gods, no." Josephine waves a hand. Though creeping up in years, her fingers are still elegant — another trait she passed on to her daughter. "He had the kitchen, a bathroom, and one bedroom done by the time the baby came. By then we had to close it all up for the winter anyway. When spring came, he started up again. Hasn't stopped since."

"Dad promised to build her a new room every time they ran out of space for her paintings," Vanessa explains, sounding both sly and a little exasperated.

"Your dad keeps his promises."

"He does."

I know a little something about that. "My mate is the same way," I offer. Vanessa's eyes move slowly back and forth between us, clearly gauging her mother's comfort with the stranger in their midst. "If he says he's going to do it, he *does* it, no matter what."

Josephine's smile widens. "What's your mate's name?"

"Cal," I answer. I laugh when Vanessa sputters, demanding to know how her mother *doesn't* know who Cal is.

"Oh... I must have missed that." Josephine straightens and turns to leave the kitchen, one hand waving over her shoulder. "I've been busy, baby. Why don't you and your friend tell me the story while I work?"

And that is how I end up in the studio of one of the world's most mysterious and lauded artists, recounting the story of how I met my elemental mate and wrote a book about his life's story.

Josephine listens intently as she stands at an easel, her gaze intent on the beginnings of an oil painting. It appears to be a man's hands, weathered and scarred, holding an equally worn carving tool. She asks quiet questions occasionally, but mostly she simply listens, humming as she steps close, then several feet back from her canvas in a slow dance.

As I watch, her slight shoulders relax. Vanessa's eyes linger on her mother less and less. An hour later, after she has gone to look for her father and perhaps something to drink, I realize that I've been accepted, at least temporarily, into the Beornson home.

It is as I'm detailing my mate's harrowing past that Josephine pauses her work to look at me. Speaking quietly, she asks, "Is that why you wanted to write an article on me?"

"What do you mean?"

"Because your mate and I have similar pasts."

Oh, I think, having only just realized this myself. "No," I answer honestly, "I didn't even consider that. I wanted to write about the exhibit and you because I think your story is important. Everyone should know what happened to you."

She hums again, her eyes cutting back to the canvas. "That's not the important part, I think."

"It's not?"

"No. The only reason I agreed to the exhibit was because I wanted people to see the *end* of the story, not the start."

I'm silent as I try to work out exactly what that means. Josephine must see the confusion on my face because she continues, "Everything with my father was the beginning. It led me to *now*. It led me to Otto, and to our many yearslong mission to track down every one of my father's subjects, one by one. It led me to my career, starting with Otto encouraging me to sell my work to the town newspaper. It led me to my children. It led me to now. To you."

Josephine swirls her paintbrush in a paint-stained can of sweet-smelling chemicals. "I don't dwell on the past. I had to let go of it and the desire to place blame. We still don't know who my father's patron was, nor what government, if any, was involved. There are subjects who died before I could track them down. I'll always pity my mother, who died miserable in a cell only a year after her conviction. I'll always wish I could have warned people what was coming after the infection began to spread from trench to trench, then city to city. These things will always hurt me, but they aren't the focus of my story. They are footnotes."

She pulls the brush free and begins to wipe it on a rag so stained with paint and chemicals it looks like a work of art on its own. "I am proud to say that the majority of my life has been spent joyfully. That is the story I want told, Elise."

My throat feels a little tight. I have to clear it before I can speak again. "Do you think your daughter's exhibit accomplishes that?"

"Sight unseen? I know it does." There is not even an ounce of hesitation in her voice. "My Vanessa can do *anything*."

"Mama, are you bragging again?"

"Of course she is, *lille bjørn*," a deep baritone voice answers.

We turn to see Vanessa in the doorway, her arms crossed, standing beside a large man who can only be her father. He's quite a bit taller than his daughter. His face and arms, exposed by a well-loved baby blue t-shirt flecked with sawdust, are deeply tanned. A hook-shaped scar bisects one blond eyebrow to touch the top of his cheek, and deep laugh lines groove the corners of his mouth. His hair is tied back in a loose braid. I can't be sure, but I believe it and his beard have gone more white than blond.

One dark brown and one green eye watches me from across the studio. There is a taut moment, no longer than a heartbeat but almost unbearably long in the mind, before I appear to pass muster. Those laugh lines deepen with a huge, jovial grin.

"Your friend is so small!" he exclaims, striding across the studio to give me a welcoming wallop on the back that nearly sends me off my stool and out the window.

"Easy, my mate," Josephine gently scolds him. "She's a witch. They're fragile, remember?"

He holds my shoulder steady as I right myself on the stool. Looking down, I realize that I recognize the hand. It's the same one from Josephine's painting. "Apologies, *kone*. I forget not everyone is as powerful as you."

Josephine rolls her eyes before passing him what appears to be a jar of watery brown paint. "If I'm so powerful, why can't I get this lid off?"

"Because the gods know you would not keep me around otherwise," he answers, easily twisting the lid with hands the size of baseball mitts. He grins at her, as incorrigible as a five year old, and Josephine smiles back, her eyes shining.

"What were you speaking of?" Otto asks. Before Josephine can step back to her painting, he hooks one finger in the pocket of her overalls and reels her into his chest, where he cages her with his arms.

Josephine tilts her head back to look up at him. Watching the ease with which they melt into one another, my heart aches for my own mate back in San Francisco.

"We were talking about our story," she answers. "How good it's been."

Otto's grin softens. One callused hand comes up to stroke her cheek. "It has been good, hasn't it, *kone*?"

"The best." Josephine reaches up to smudge his cheek with vermillion paint. "The very best."

The exhibit "Exploring Lyssa" opens at the Fairmont Museum of Art on May 22nd. Tickets can be acquired online and in person in limited quantities.

Elise Sasini is a veteran reporter for *The San Francisco Light* and daughter of Bob Sasini, San Francisco's premier crime reporter of the last one hundred years. She is the author of two award-winning books, *A Golden Land: The Unvarnished History of San Francisco's Elvish Takeover* and *The Shrouded City,* which won the Pulitzer Prize for Non-Fiction in 2047.

[PICTURED: Josephine Wyeth and Otto Beornson stand before a glass panel, in which a single piece of paper is suspended. Around them, people move in blurs of motion, taking in the explosion of color and light of the second half of the exhibit. Their arms are wrapped around each other, their backs to the camera. A very faint reflection of their faces is visible in the glass. Josephine appears overwhelmed. Otto is grinning, his eyes clearly wet with tears. On the other side of the glass, their children stand, smiling back at them.]

THE END

A sneak peek of Burden's Bonds...

JULY 2045 - SAN FRANCISCO, THE ELVISH PROTECTORATE

"You're not supposed to be here."

Unsurprisingly, Delilah replied without an ounce of worry. "Certainly, but I am always exactly where I *need* to be."

Kazimier Rione shot his half-sister a baleful look as she settled onto the squeaky vinyl stool beside him. As usual, The Broken Tooth was smokey and loud. The bar top was just shy of outright sticky and the music piped in through the old speakers was something bluesy.

San Francisco's premier bar it was not — and that was exactly why he liked it.

He had no trouble fitting in with the other shifty patrons, who only wanted to score a drink, a companion for the night, or a lucrative deal in a dark corner. Perhaps all three.

His sister, on the other hand, looked about as natural on the duct taped stool as an ice sculpture would in a bus station bathroom.

Even with the smoky glamour obscuring her features from all but the most discerning eyes, her bearing made her stand out. But then again, Delilah Solbourne stood out *everywhere*. It would take more than the shifting tendrils of magically conjured smoke to hide her stature, her aura of casual dominance.

And that was before one considered her outfit.

Kaz felt a headache building behind his right eye. He'd been nothing but tense for two weeks. He did not need the added stress of his sister's unannounced and *unsanctioned* visit.

"What are you doing here?" he grunted, claws tightening around the cool glass of his beer bottle.

Delilah lifted her hand, motioning for the bartender's attention. "Lemon drop, please."

"This isn't the kind of place that serves *lemon drops*, Lilah."

"Oh please, she knows how to make a lemon drop. You think this is my first visit?" She wiggled her fingers at the were woman who owned the bar.

The owner glanced over from the other end of the bar, where she'd been talking in a low voice to another were, a man most criminals in San Francisco would know on sight. He was tall, thickly built, covered nearly head to toe in colorful tattoos, and had the signature were feature: two different colored eyes. He sipped from a glass of whiskey as the bartender waved to let Delilah know she'd heard her.

Kaz let his gaze linger on the weres for a moment longer than necessary. He knew the man well, though neither would consider the other a friend.

Rasmus Adams was the enforcer of the unofficial San Francisco were pack. He was in charge of maintaining discipline amongst the weres, a people prone to explosive tempers and even greater strength, and the head of all their illegal Underground smuggling operations.

He was also a mean son of a bitch. If Kaz were being honest — something he did his best to avoid — he would have to admit that it was half the reason he liked the man.

They locked eyes for the span of a heartbeat, neither willing to be the one to look away first, before Rasmus wisely lifted his glass up in a lazy salute. It was the smallest concession to the truth they both understood: that Kaz was a far more dangerous predator than he could ever be.

Satisfied that his position was still clear in the were's mind, Kaz turned his attention back to his beer — and his sister.

"You shouldn't be in the territory, let alone in the city," he warned her. "You're banished, remember? If Teddy found out you were here, he'd have you escorted out at the end of a bolt gun."

"I am well aware." She slid him a sly look. "Are you going to snitch on me, sweet boy?"

Kaz shook his head. *Fucking family.* "Why are you *here?*"

Delilah dropped her forearms onto the tacky bar top and craned her neck to peer at the feed screen to the right of the bar. An orcish woman and a gargoyle were duking it out in a ring bordered on all sides by a frenzied crowd.

Without looking away from the screen, she asked, "How was the wedding?"

Kaz forced another gulp of beer down his suddenly tight throat. "Fine."

"Did Teddy and our girl have a good time?"

He shot her a hard look. "Lilah, I might not be as pissed as Teddy right now, but don't mistake that for apathy. You have no fucking right to call her that after what you did."

"I did what was necessary." She turned her head to look at him, but he couldn't see her eyes through the glamour. Not that it would have helped. Delilah's black eyes — the *Solbourne* eyes — were always impossible to read. He'd wondered if it was a side effect of her ability to see so many possible futures or the damage their father had inflicted on her long before any of their siblings came along.

Probably both.

"I *always* do what is necessary," she continued, sighing the words out like she was the injured party, "but I understand that it is hard to see from your limited perspective."

"Limited perspective my *ass.* You put a bomb in Margot's

fucking house. I don't care that you knew it wouldn't kill her. It *could* have."

Kaz didn't care that women tended to call him stoic, unfeeling. He didn't even mind that his own family sometimes wondered if he had any warmth at all. What he *did* mind was when one of his people was threatened.

He wasn't good for much, but he'd dedicated his life to protecting what belonged to him — and Margot Goode, his brother Theodore's mate, was one of those people.

Another witch belongs to you, too.

The thought came out of nowhere. It was a deep growl in the back of his mind, a wave of instinct and prickling conscience.

She doesn't, he growled back, ruthlessly squashing the need that fizzed under his skin. *She never will.*

"Necessity is not always kind," Delilah replied. "In fact, it is often cruel. You'll understand."

"Doubt it."

She shrugged. They both watched as the owner walked over with a sugar-dipped martini glass in hand. Kaz rolled his eyes when Delilah accepted it with a flourish, telling her to put it on his tab.

They were quiet for several tense minutes after. He nursed his beer. She took delicate sips of her sugary concoction. The match on the feed screen ended with the gargoyle's narrow victory before it switched to a new one.

Delilah was halfway through her drink before she asked with no preamble, "How long do you intend to fight it?"

Kaz's fingers flexed around the neck of his beer bottle so hard, the glass developed hairline fractures. Speaking through clenched teeth, he said, "Don't."

"I'm only curious."

He turned his head to glare at her. Aggression bunched the muscles of his arms and shoulders beneath his thin t-shirt and beaten leather jacket. "Don't you fucking dare, Delilah. I don't want or need your help."

Even if Delilah's *help* hadn't nearly killed their brother's mate, Kaz wouldn't have wanted it. He'd made his choice. It was done.

His brother had indulged Margot's wish to be married on her Coven's land just two weeks prior. Kaz accompanied them as both security and a witness, though their family did not particularly care for the Goodes, nor for the ridiculous ceremony of *marriage*.

He shouldn't have gone. He should have let his brother go with a full unit of the Sovereign's Guard instead, but he'd felt compelled to. Not simply because he loved his brother and the woman who'd saved his life just by being *born*, but because...

Well, he hadn't been able to explain it even to himself.

All he knew was that he needed to go. He needed to be there when hundreds of witches and their allies arrived to celebrate Margot's marriage. He needed to watch the flames of the sacred fire burn, to smell the incense, to hand over the groom's offering and see over his sister-in-law's shoulder—

Her.

The matte black claws of his left hand dug into the edge of the bar. Only his tenuous control kept him from ripping a chunk of the wood off as he shoved the memory of warm brown skin, dark eyes, and a soft smile from his mind.

His sister sighed dramatically and set down her glass. She leaned back on her stool to stick one gloved hand into the deep inner pocket of her short black cape. He watched, jaw clenched, as she withdrew a bent legal envelope — the kind meant to hold a large amount of paper and held closed by a metal tab poked through a hole in the flap.

It wasn't altogether *bursting* with papers, but it still had heft to it. When she dropped the bent envelope on the bar, it landed with an ominous *thwap.*

"Never fear, sweet boy," she dryly replied, "this is all the help you'll get from me. Everything else will be your choice — whether you want to accept that or not."

"What is that?" he demanded.

He wasn't sure why he asked. He *knew.* The hair on the back of his neck stood up even when he refused to look at the envelope. Instinct went from a light fizz under his skin to a full on *buzz*, like a hive of insects had been roused inside him.

"Your favorite currency: information." Delilah picked up her martini glass and took another leisurely sip. Her claw-caps, platinum and set with diamonds, winked in the dim light of the bar.

Kaz couldn't help himself. His eyes were drawn to the packet like a magnet. No matter how hard he tried to look away, they kept coming back to it. In a hoarse voice, he asked, "On what?"

"You know the answer to that."

His heart, always calm, began to beat unevenly in his chest. A cold sweat broke out on his palms. "Why would you do this?"

"Because you'll want it."

Her throat worked as she tilted her head back to toss the dregs of her lemon drop down. Setting the empty glass back on the counter, she hopped off the old stool. Her cape fluttered around her shoulders as she adjusted the gauzy white blouse she wore underneath it.

Her tone was brusque, businesslike, when she continued, "You don't want it now. I can respect that. But you will need it later." He couldn't make out her expression through the glamour, but when she lifted her head again, her inspection of her clothing finished, he knew that her face was set in hard lines. "I am not here to stop you from making mistakes, Kaz, but I'll warn you now: you are going to regret not looking."

Fear, cold and hard, closed a fist around his beating heart. "Why are you telling me this? You *never* tell us—"

"Consider it a peace offering."

"A *peace offering?*" Anger burned through some of his fear. Kazimier planted one booted foot on the filthy floor, but stopped himself from standing up. If he challenged his sister in the bar, they'd draw all sorts of unwanted attention, and he really didn't want to have to find a new haunt.

Snarling through his teeth, he said, "You shouldn't be giving me a peace offering. You should be *apologizing* to our brother."

Delilah stuck her hands into the pockets of her slim-fitted slacks. "I won't apologize for doing what needs to be done. You'll accept it. Teddy will, too."

"Lilah, I—"

Quick as lightning, she was only inches away. If she hadn't been kin, one of the women who raised him and trained him, Kaz would have gone for her throat as soon as she moved. As it was, he sat ramrod straight, his lip curled over his prominent fangs, and allowed her to brush strands of his hair behind his pointed ear.

"Sweet boy," she whispered, leaning in to press a kiss to his cheek. "Tell your brother and his wife that I said hello."

Just as quick, she turned around and walked away.

Kaz watched her tall figure cut through the smoke to reach the flier-covered door. Even drunk, people hastened to get out of her way. They might not have been able to tell who she was, but there was no hiding that she was an elf.

And even if they didn't recognize that, only the dead wouldn't fear Delilah Solbourne.

A nudge with her silver-tipped boot pushed the door open into the warm night. He watched her slip out, the buzzing in his ears disguising the uneasy murmuring that followed her exit.

The door swung shut. His eyes darted away, back to the packet on the bar.

It sat there, innocent, bent nearly in half, and taunted him with what he could never have.

Without his permission, his hands strayed to the envelope. His mind rebelled. He knew he shouldn't look. Looking would only make the compulsion worse. It would only make the obsession he could feel budding in that dark part of his mind that much stronger, more resilient to extermination.

But he couldn't stop himself.

His fingers, large and calloused from years of fighting and handling weapons, shook as he fumbled with the little metal tab.

He held his breath as he lifted the flap. Tugging the papers out just an inch, his eyes snapped to the no-nonsense black text.

His heartbeat thundered in his ears. Cold gripped him again, the burning sort of fear that stole the breath from a person's lungs.

Kaz gnashed his teeth and shoved the papers back into the envelope.

But it was too late. The words were branded into the backs of his eyelids now. He could see them every time he blinked. When his heart beat, he swore he could *hear* them, each word keeping time with the unsteady *thump-thump, thump-thump.*

She was in him, her name seeping through his veins like a saccharine venom.

Atria Le Roy.

BURDEN'S BONDS RELEASES DECEMBER 12! PRE-ORDER TODAY!

He's chosen to be alone.

Kazimier Rione, half-orc spymaster of the Elvish Protectorate, doesn't want a mate. He's got too many rough edges and too much baggage for any woman. That's why he's done everything in his power to stay away from a certain lush little witch that makes every instinct bristle. A glimpse was all it took to seed a dark obsession, but it's one he knows he can never act on.

She was burned by fate.

Atria Le Roy learned her lesson a long time ago: the blessing of a mate is not for her. A witch groomed for a secretive priestess-hood from birth, she's spent years throwing herself into her potentially world-changing research and running from her complicated past. Now that research is about to come to fruition — if only she and her research partner can survive being hunted by the factions desperate to get their hands on it.

Keeping their distance is impossible.

When his witch is threatened, Kaz knows that rescuing her will mean giving in to the pull of fate, but doing nothing is not an option. He'll do anything to protect her, even if that means kidnapping her and going on the run himself. With every mile they cover and danger they face, the fire between them burns hotter. She wants to escape her past, the bounties on her head, and the overbearing, beautiful orc holding her captive. He wants to possess everything she is and be utterly possessed in return.

Surviving will mean giving in, leaving the past behind, and letting the fire burn...

ALSO BY ABIGAIL KELLY

Find all new releases, bonus chapters, and exclusive content on the Works by Abigail Patreon!

FRAGILE BEINGS: A NEW PROTECTORATE NOVELLA COLLECTION

In the first volume of The New Protectorate Stories...

Fate can't be contained.

#376: A fey Changeling is rescued from captivity by a reluctant demon on a quest to find his fate. Of course Dom expects trouble, but he is shocked to discover his fate is tied to an imprisoned fey woman. Charlotte's a kicking, spitting, hissing little Changeling — and she's his.

A dragon's kiss burns cold.

Astray: When Paloma Contreras, arrant scientist, accidentally dooms a rogue dragon to death, she'll do anything to save his life. If that means giving up the mountaintop she's called home her entire life, so be it. Too bad Artem Aždaja has no plans to steal her roost. He only wants one thing: *her.*

Desire fogs the mind.

Weathering: Elise Sasini, an intrepid reporter and weather witch, sets out to uncover the story of San Francisco's legendary sentient fog and gets a lot more than she bargained for. The mysterious elemental agrees to tell his story in exchange for a taste of the life — and the woman — he craves.

Three novellas. Three couples. One fractured world. Step into a magical near-future where love builds, breaks, and defies boundaries.

Available in Kindle Unlimited, ebook, and paperback!

Consort's Glory: The New Protectorate
Book One

Margot Goode, healer extraordinaire, knows that being noticed is the fastest way to getting herself murdered — or worse. But even with a secret like hers, she can't stay cloistered forever. On her own in San Francisco, she's on the hunt for the one person who can stop her magic from turning against her in a catastrophic meltdown.

Margot doesn't expect things will be easy, but even *she* is surprised when someone plants a bomb in her Healing House, nearly killing her and wiping out her anonymity in one fell swoop. Attacking a healer is an egregious breach of the laws that keep the races from war. Attacking Margot Goode, granddaughter of the terrifying Goode Matriarch and leader of the most influential coven in the country, is not just blasphemous — it demands retribution.

Theodore Solbourne, newest sovereign ruler of the largest Elvish territory in the West, has waited his entire life for the woman he will one day claim as his consort. With the power to keep her finally in his grasp, he's planned their meeting down to every last detail... only to have all the carefully crafted steps in their courtship blown away when she's nearly killed before he can even say *hello*.

With her life and his kingdom on the line, there's no time for subtlety. Earning the trust of the woman he's been mad about his entire life just became much harder: the speculation of war is sweeping through the city, a goddess's acolytes call for justice, and a traitor's shadow looms over his household. But nothing, not even Margot's single-minded determination to keep him out, will stop him from winning her heart.

Available in Kindle Unlimited, ebook, and paperback!

Courtship's Conquest: The New Protectorate Book Two

Their future hinges on a promise.

In the wake of her mother's death, Camille Solbourne is determined to follow through with her deathbed promise to arrange a union with a suitable partner and get out of the Solbourne family. A union is cold, more business than love, and negotiating them is a dangerous political dance. It's not what she wants, but sometimes happiness is found in compromise – and keeping one's promises.

Their choices haunt their past.

Nearly twenty years ago, Viktor Hamilton, alpha of San Francisco's lone coyote shifter pack, let his mate go. Becoming someone his pack could rely on for safety and guidance is the only thing that kept him sane in the long, lonely years that followed. When the opportunity to make a life-altering choice for the betterment of his people arises, he makes a promise to see it through.

What he doesn't expect is for the world to change around him in the blink of an eye. After a volatile run-in with Camille reignites the flame between them, he knows he can't leave the past alone. The only thing standing between them is their fraught past and Camille's furious determination to tie herself to another man. Pursuing Camille means gambling with the future of his pack, but Viktor won't let his mate go a second time – even if it means he has to put his life on the line to keep her.

Available in Kindle Unlimited, ebook, and paperback!

GLOSSARY

A full character directory and map can be found at Abigailkkelly.com

PLACES

United Territories and Allies: What we would consider the continental USA. A loose federation of sovereign states established after the Great War. The UTA capital is United Washington, in the Neutral Zone.

The Elvish Protectorate: Also known as the EVP. Stretches from Oregon to New Mexico. Capital city is San Francisco. Led by the elvish sovereign Theodore Thaddeus Solbourne.

The Coven Collective: Also known as the Collective. Encompasses Washington state. Capital city is Seattle. Led by a large coalition of witch covens, with Sophie Goode acting as their leader.

The Orclind: Encompasses much of the Midwest. Led by the Iron Chain, a close-knit government made up of orcish clans and family groups. Capital city is Boulder.

Shifter Alliance: Takes up a section of the midwest and all of the south. (Unfortunately includes Florida.) Run by a very, very loose alliance of shifter packs from three capital cities — Minneapolis, Oklahoma City, and Atlanta.

The Draakonriik: Also known as the 'Riik. The second smallest territory, it takes up all of the Great Lakes region and stretches to New York. Led by Taevas Aždaja, the *Isand* (ee-zand) of the dragon clans. Pronounced: *dra-kon-reek*

The Neutral Zone: Also known as the New Zone. Technically it is held by a coalition government consisting of representatives from the UTA, but in reality it is run by a syndicate of feuding vampire families. It is a small strip of land squeezed between the Draakonriik and the Shifter Alliance.

Gods

Light & Darkness: The primordial gods who created all the others. Also known as The Lovers and First Union. Both are generally represented as female.

Loft: God of the sky and creator of flying beings. Twin sibling to Tempest. They know no gender. Also known as the Boundless One.

Tempest: God of the ocean and creator of all water beings. Also known as the Hungry God and the god of love.

Burden: God of the Earth, creator of all beings who live within it — most notably the orcs. Husband of Glory.

Glory: Goddess of sunlight, magic, and creator of elves. Worshipped by witches for giving the gift of magic to humanity.

Blight: God of forested places and disease. He works in partnership with his daughter Grim and shares her dominion over demons and all reviled creatures.

Grim: Goddess of death. Known as the Merciful One and the Brilliant Lady. She is widely beloved.

Craft: God of change, newness, and messengers. Creator of humanity and viewed warily by non-worshippers as the Chaos Maker. They change their gender frequently, but generally is referred to using he/him pronouns.

TERMS

Alpha: a broad term used by many communities generally associated with a leader — either of a small family group, a pack, or even a territory.

Anchor: a vampire's mate. Anchors are carefully chosen and usually longterm-to-permanent arrangements, as they take considerable energy to make/become. A vampire must inject their venom into a host many times before their blood chemistry adjusts such that they become unsuitable for consumption by another vampire and their sleep cycle switches to a nocturnal pattern. At this point, they can can also produce/carry to term a vampiric child. Temporary anchors do exist, although they are relatively rare due to the intense withdrawal symptoms associated with ending the regular venom intake.

Arrant: someone born without m-paths, or the ability to channel and use magic.

Burnout: the colloquial name for the degenerative medical condition caused by excessive magic in humans. Over time magic can damage nerves and brain tissue, which will inevitably result in death if not treated with with development of a witchbond.

Change: an elvish term for a sudden shift into adulthood. This is marked by 5-14 days of "madness", usually triggered by some stressful event around the age of 16-18. The elvish body is flushed with hormones to the point where sudden growth, overwhelming hunger, and aggression take over. Viewed as an incredibly vulnerable time, only immediate kin are charged with the care of their loved ones — which includes isolating them, preventing harm to themselves/others, and feeding them. The change marks the second phase of an elf's life, when they are no longer coddled children but young adults who can accept challenges and family responsibilities. Formal adulthood is attained at 30.

Changeling: a term first used to refer to fey children fostered out to non-fey homes, now more widely used to mean any person raised by people who are not the same beings. *Ex:* A dragon couple raising a human child.

Chosen: the formal term for a dragon's mate. The act of finding a mate is called *Choosing,* and is considered sacred.

Consort: an elvish mate. A term used exclusively by elves to refer to someone they are biologically compelled to pair up with. This usually involves intense sexual attraction, but can vary from person to person.

Dragon: a person with a dual form. In their bipedal form, they have claw-tipped wings, horns, and a tail. In their quadrupedal form, they are roughly the size of a standard SUV and can fly at extremely high altitudes for weeks at a time. They come in a variety of extremely saturated colors that shift with the time of day (light to dark). They breathe cold blue fire and can see the

Earth's magnetic field. Identifying mating feature is marked change in behavior, including the overwhelming urge to nest.

Elemental: a being created by a spontaneous magical eruption. They often take on the attributes of whatever weather they happen to be born into, *i.e.* a lightning storm might produce a lightning elemental, or a blizzard might make a snow elemental.

Empath: a person with the ability to feel and manipulate the emotions of others.

Elf: someone born with jewel-toned skin, claws, pointed ears, and four fangs. Very secretive and considered apex predators who require a strict hierarchy to function. Average height of 6-7ft. Identifying mating feature is the retraction of claws.

Fever: shifter mating imperative triggered by the "animal's" choosing of a mate. Marked by a perpetual near-shift — elevated body temperature, increased aggression, build-up of magic, and the compulsion to mark. A shifter displays their readiness to find a mate by creating a den.

Fey: a person with nearly vestigial, insect-like wings, small fangs, and claws. Usually live in large groups. Identifying mating feature is bioluminescence.

Foresight: the ability to see multiple possible futures. The average number is between 2-4, with the likelihood mental instability increasing with each subsequent possible future.

Great War: a conflict between the territories of the North American continent that began in 1817 and ended in 1917 with the signing of the Peace Charter, which established the United Territories and Allies of modern times.

Halfling: the elvish term for an elf with mixed heritage.

Healer: a person who possesses the ability to see into and heal bodies through touch.

Isand: the title of the leader of the Draakonriik. Pronounced *ee-zah-nd*

M- : M- is frequently used as shorthand to denote when something is infused or otherwise combined with a magical element.

Marriage Sigil: a custom symbol branded into the foreheads of spouses (pairs or multiples). Each one is unique and infused with a small amount of magic as a reminder of the power love holds. They are typically sought out by worshippers of Glory — mainly witches and arrants. Elves, though worshippers, don't usually take a marriage sigil when they find their consorts or form a unions with other elves.

Mate: a catchall term for a significant other. Used by many cultures, it has varying degrees of weight. To shifters, orcs, and demons, the word mate is synonymous with family, monogamy, and dependence. It is much more loosely used within arrant society, as well as amongst elves, who generally prefer the term *consort*.

Met: acronym for *magically enhanced tech*. A branded home assistant that can do everything your Alexa can, as well as small, low-level magic to help around the house.

Metallurgic Inoculation: a vaccine given to all elves within hours of birth to make them immune to iron poisoning.

M-siphon: a containment device used to imprison a magical being and siphon off their magic. Highly illegal.

R-siphon: also known as *reverse siphon.* New technology that redistributes magic away from the siphon instead of into it.

M-lev: a play on *maglev,* meaning a high speed train that levitates using magnets. In this case, magnets *and* magic.

M-weather: magic weather. Very common, but can result in "clusters" or storms that wreak havoc if not properly contained. In rare circumstances, it can also produce a sapient being known as an *elemental.*

Orc: a person with green, gray, russet, or blue skin, two fangs, and claws. Widely renowned for their strength and beautiful voices. Identifying mating feature is "the kohl", or altered, dark pigmentation of the hands and feet developed after meeting their mate.

Pixie: a small, winged creature with compound eyes with about the same level of intelligence as a rat. In the wild they live in trees and in burrows, but have adapted to living in walls, pipes, mailboxes, etc.

Pull: elvish mating imperative. A sudden hormonal shift caused by exposure to a compatible partner's pheromones, marked by the retraction of claws and volatile mood shifts. The pull is only "satisfied" when hormone binding occurs — the term for long term exposure to a mate, resulting in permanent biological dependence on their pheromones. This process increases fertility and often results in the conception of multiples. Lack of exposure to a mate can cause severe physical reactions (lack of appetite, muscle pain, headaches, insomnia) as well as the deterioration of mental stability.

Shifter: a person who can shift into an animal form. They can partially shift (changing only parts of their bodies at will) and often take on characteristics of their other half. Famous for their strength and tenacity, as well as their dual-voiced "shifter purr" which many people find deeply attractive. Usually found in packs.

Sigil: a symbol used to channel magic. Western countries use the alchemical alphabet formally codified in the 1800's, though many, many variations are used all over the world.

Sovereign: the title of the ruler of the Elvish Protectorate. It is capitalized when used in place of a name.

Turbo Virgin (c): Theodore Thaddeus Solbourne, Sovereign of the Elvish Protectorate and Head of the Solbourne Family.

Union: an elvish marriage. Usually done for financial, political, or procreational benefit. The parties involved are not fated or biologically compelled to be with one another, and might have many lovers or even a consort outside of their union.

Vampire: a person who drinks blood to survive and cannot go out in sunlight. Vampirism can only be "caught" with the exchange of fresh blood, and as of 2045 is much more widely spread through procreation. Vampires can only breed with their *anchors*. Identifying mating feature is marked change in behavior, including overwhelming desire and need for total isolation.

Ward: a magical barrier with varying levels of protection. A ward can be something as simple as a proximity alert — "someone walked into my garden" — or as complex as full on defense — "someone crossed the threshold and has now burst into flames". The severity of the ward depends on the complexity of the sigils used to create them, and wards can have many layers, each one with a unique purpose. Personal wards can also be used, such as in clothing or embedded into jewelry, though they tend to be expensive and difficult to foolproof.

Were: a person infected with the were virus, a much mutated strain of the vampirism virus, resulting in altered physiology and magical ability. They can be identified by their heterochromia, or different colored eyes. They are the newest magical race and viewed warily by the general public for a variety of earned and unearned reasons. Identifying mating feature is marked change in behavior, including highly increased territorial instinct and the urge to nest. Pronounced *ware.*

Witch: Humans with the ability to use magic, which is passed down genetically. A person needs to be born with m-paths (a unique nervous system) to use it, however, humans were not initially adapted to use magic safely. Geneticists believe they acquired the ability through interbreeding with other beings. This interbreeding resulted in many unique qualities, such as the massive variety of abilities, power levels, and unique skills known to select families. However, it is also responsible for "burnout", which is the degenerative neurological condition a witch with mid-to-high level power will experience if they do not share their magical load with another being via witchbond. Witches are classified from least to most powerful — brightling, brilliant, and gloriana.

Witchbond: a magical bond formed between a witch and another being. Due to the nature of magic and humanity's much more recent adaptation to it, witches of *brilliant* and *gloriana* power must form a bond with another being usually beginning around 150-200 years old. This bond filters magic through the other being, neutralizing its damaging effects and reducing the chances of burnout to almost none. This bond also gives a power boost to the partner. A witchbond is permanent and can only be severed if one of the partners dies, at which point the surviving partner can form a new bond. Though commonly associated with a romantic partner, a witchbond is not inherently romantic and can be shared with a friend, sibling, or (ill-advised) an enemy.

PRONUNCIATION GUIDE FOR NAMES OF IMPORTANT CHARACTERS IN THIS BOOK

Josephine Wyeth: jo-suh-feen why-eth

Otto Beornson: ah-toh byuh-rn-son

Vanessa: van-es-ah

Elise Sasini: uh-lees sah-seen-ee

Joseph: jo-sef

Harrod Pierce: hair-od peer-is

Evangeline: ee-van-ja-leen

ABOUT THE AUTHOR

 Abigail Kelly is a writer and illustrator of alternate histories, love stories, and women with drive. Her work is heavily influenced by both her modest family roots and her passion for history. She is also a bookseller at an independent bookshop where she gets to badly influence impressionable young minds and put her favorite books in eager hands, as well as the host of the Kingdom of Thirst podcast, a show all about romance novels and why they matter.

Her favorite authors are Shirley Jackson, V. E. Schwab, Ursula K. Le Guin, Kresley Cole, Nalini Singh, and just about anyone who writes about the weird and wonderful. She lives in San Francisco with her dog, Babs, who remains stubbornly illiterate.

CONTENT WARNINGS

Content warnings: parental abuse (non-sexual), non-graphic medical experimentation, descriptions of the use of needles, blood, experiences of war, injury, disease, confinement, neglect, violence, and explicit sexual content.

www.ingramcontent.com/pod-product-compliance
Lightning Source LLC
Chambersburg PA
CBHW070847280626
47161CB00017B/2833

* 9 7 8 1 9 5 7 8 4 4 0 6 0 *